For Namgyeong

King Sejong the Great

A novel by Joe Menosky

Publishing Planning ARTFRAME STORY
Publishing fitbook
Publisher Seongwon Jeong
Editor Sanghoon Yeo, Cheonho Bae
Design Hyelyoung Youn, Junghwan Maeng
Illustration Areum Hong, Jeremy Jo
Marketing ARTFRAME STORY (Sunjung Park, Hyungjoon Park)
            SARAM ENTERTAINMENT (Soyoung Lee, Sonya Kim)

Printed in the Republic of Korea
First Published in Oct. 09. 2020 / Third Published in Oct. 15. 2020

ISBN 979-11-971633-1-9

B01, 24, Hangang-daero 54-gil, Yongsan-gu, Seoul
www.artframestory.com
Tel. 070-7856-0100   **Fax.** 0504-096-0078
E-Mail. fitbookcom@naver.com / artframestory@artframestory.com

A historical fantasy

더 그레이트

King Sejong the Great

Joe Menosky

King Sejong the Great

Prologue ··· 8

Chapter I Creation ··· 16

Chapter II Promulgation ··· 210

Post Script ··· 374

Epilogue ··· 376

"The Correct Sounds for
the Instruction of the People."
A novel based on historical events.

– Written by Joe Menosky

저는 지난 20년 동안 한국 영화와 한국 TV 드라마의 팬이었고, 한국계 미국인 프로듀서들과도 일을 많이 해 왔습니다. 그래서인지 한국의 역사나 문화가 생소하지 않았습니다. 하지만 5년 전에야 처음으로 서울을 방문해서 한국어를 배우게 되었습니다. 한글을 처음 알았을 때, 충격을 받았다는 표현이 부족할 정도로 정말 놀라웠습니다. 한글 자체가 가진 기록 체계의 정밀함과 기능적인 우월함도 대단했지만, 이 모든 것이 천재적인 왕에 의해 창제되었다는 스토리는 믿기 어려울 정도로 충격적이었습니다. 게다가 더 충격적이었던 것은 이런 이야기가 전 세계에 알려지지 않았다는 것이었습니다.

만약 유럽의 어떤 지도자가 백성들을 위해서 글자를 만들었다면 전 세계는 이미 그 사실을 알았을 겁니다. 그랬다면 전 세계의 소설과 영화 TV 시리즈 등에서 유럽의 지도자의 이야기가 소재가 되고 재해석되었을 겁니다. 저는 한국 외 다른 국가들에게서 세종과 필적할 만한 상대가 있었다면 과연 누가 될 수 있을까 상상해 봤습니다. 레오나르도 다빈치가 피렌체의 통치자인 경우

Prologue

I have been a follower of Korean film and television for twenty years, and have worked with Korean and Korean-American producers over that same amount of time, so I am not unfamiliar with Korean history and culture. But it was not until five years ago, when I visited Seoul for the first time and attempted to learn some language, that I first encountered Hangeul, the Korean alphabet. To say I was stunned is an understatement. Not only was I struck by the elegance and functionality of the writing system itself and the incredible tale of its creation by a genius king — I could not believe that this story was not universally known.

If a European ruler had invented an alphabet for his or her people, everybody in the world would have heard about it. That story would have been told and retold in novels, movies, and television series worldwide. I tried

일까? 아이작 뉴턴이 영국의 왕인 경우일까? 비교할만한 대상자 체를 찾기가 힘듭니다.

세종대왕에 대한 저의 마음은 마치 영웅을 숭배하는 것과 같 았기에, 한글의 이야기를 제 손으로 직접 쓰고 싶었습니다. 영어 로 쓴 세종대왕의 이야기가 한글을 아직 알지 못하는 영어권의 사람들이 세종대왕을 알게 되는 계기가 되었으면 합니다.

조선왕조실록에도 한글과 관련한 세세한 기록이 남아 있지 않아서인지 상상할 수 있는 여지가 많아 한국에서도 세종대왕 과 그의 업적에 관련된 소재를 활용한 역사 드라마나 멜로 드 라마, 미스터리 살인극, 심지어 로맨틱 코미디까지도 만들어지 고 있습니다.

저도 세종대왕의 한글 창제를 지금까지 다루지 않은 새로운 방식으로 만들고 싶었습니다.

앞에 언급했던 다양한 형태의 창작물에서 보지 못한 방식으 로 만들고자 했습니다. 세종대왕이 운영했던 조선의 '싱크 탱크 (집현전)'에서 탄생된 결과물이 아니라, 마치 예술가와 같았던 세 종대왕 한 사람에 의해 창조된 집념의 산물로 한글을 그리고 싶 었습니다.

한국은 역사적으로 인접한 중국과 일본 그리고 중국 대륙의 다양한 부족들을 상대해야 했기에 한글 이야기를 '국제적인 스릴 러'로 하거나 최소한 그렇게 해도 문제없으리라 생각했습니다. 그러는 과정에서 새로운 인물도 창조했고, 서너 명의 역사적 인 물들을 하나로 합치기도 했으며, 어떤 사건은 위치를 바꾸고, 시 대를 변경하거나 축소시키기도 했습니다. 바라건대, 정사의 기

to imagine what the closest equivalent to King Sejong outside of Korea would have been: Leonardo da Vinci as ruler of Florence? Isaac Newton as the King of England? There seemed to be nothing comparable.

Sejong's creation became something of a compulsion for me, and my estimation of the king something like hero worship. I wanted to retell the story of his alphabet myself, in English, for anybody who had not heard it, which pretty much meant anybody outside of Korea.

Those events, which appear officially in the Annals of the Joseon dynasty, also leave much unrecorded. And so Sejong and his accomplishments have been portrayed on multiple occasions in Korean fiction by way of different genres: historical drama, soap opera, murder mystery, even romantic comedy.

So, I wanted to treat the King's invention of Hangeul in a way I had not seen before: not as the outcome of a group effort, where Sejong is akin to the manager of a "think-tank," but as the product primarily of one mind. Sejong as an artist — and the alphabet as his obsession.

Japan, and the tribes to the north — I thought it appropriate or at least allowable to tell the story of Hangeul as an "international thriller." In so doing, I've created several new characters, combined two or more historical

11

록에 바탕을 둔 이야기가 익숙한 분께서도 제가 새로 창작한 역사 판타지라는 점을 받아들여 주시기 바라며, 받아들이기 어려우신 분께는 진심으로 사과드립니다.

figures into one individual, moved some events around, and at times altered or collapsed the timeline. Hopefully, readers who are intimate with the actual records will accept this historical fantasy with suspension of disbelief intact. If not, my sincere apologies.

ChapterI
Creation

GREEN LEAVES FALLING

As if through the Autumn air. But they are fresh and green and vibrant — in full life, not the familiar colors of Fall. No sign of a strong wind that has shaken them free — they fall naturally and easily. The bright sun behind the leaves refracts through the moisture beaded on their surfaces — the effect is both gentle and dazzling. Like fragments of something sacred — pieces of heaven, drifting, gifted, down to the world below⋯.

@@@@@@

King Sejong — late 40s, face generous, handsome and kind — opened his eyes. From nodding off, day-dreaming, deep contemplation or prayer — one couldn't say.

The King wore yellow and red royal robes, and was seated on the stone floor at a low writing table — hemmed in by the heavy walls of the command chamber hidden deep in the most impregnable part of this fortress. Armed with ink brush, ink well, and a pile of paper; flanked by oil lamps — he was drawing something. Shapes and figures.

The year — as numbered on the other side of the planet, in empires and kingdoms that based their calendar on a messiah unknown here — was 1443 A.D. The location was on the Korean peninsula, a day's march from the capital, Hanseong, in our time called Seoul. King Sejong was in the last years of his life. He had ruled with wisdom and even genius, allowing his people to thrive despite the great powers surrounding his kingdom: dominant China to the west, aggressive Japan to the east, restless Mongolian and Jurchen tribes to the north.

As the Asian superpower, the Ming dynasty of China expected tribute from the kingdoms within reach of its armies and its culture. Korea had agreed to its position as a vassal state under the Chinese Emperor's authority and protection — but was allowed relative independence in return. And the promise from China not to invade⋯.

Sejong had maintained that peaceful but precarious balance of power throughout his reign. If he quietly left the stage of history now, he would be remembered as a wise and just ruler; recalled fondly as an East Asian Leonardo da Vinci: a wide-ranging genius with a list of forward-thinking inventions in multiple areas of interest and necessity — astronomy, meteorology, warfare. But he had chosen otherwise. In opposition to his suzerain the Emperor of China; in conflict with the dominant Confucian morality of his kingdom and culture; in a race against his own physical decline — he had decided to pursue one, last 'invention'. Or he would not be known as he is today:

King Sejong the Great.

"Your Majesty⋯."

Sejong glanced up to see that two men had just entered the chamber — his Supreme General and his Chief Councilor — both in military uniforms of leather and fish-scale style light armor, battle-ready.

The three eunuchs who stood against the walls, making themselves invisible as possible until needed by the King, didn't dare to look up. But simply waited, as humble eunuchs were expected to do. Until proximity to power might give them larger ideas — but these three had no such notions. No one in the Kingdom was more devoted to this ruler.

"There is still no sign of the enemy," continued the Supreme General. Sejong considered for a moment, rousing fully from whatever contemplative state of mind he had been engaged — or indulging — in. "Perhaps," he responded, with the gentle smile that always seemed to accent his dealings with others — even in the midst of apparent battle, "They were given the wrong address."

The two newcomers exchanged a glance. Kindly as their ruler always seemed to be, it was never possible to know what he was actually thinking or feeling. As if that kindness was a screen — or a fortress wall — a way to protect his deepest thoughts. The King went back to his writing.

"Perhaps so, Your Majesty," the Councilor agreed — unable to hide the curious concern on his face, as he leaned forward to see what the King had been drawing — without making that curiosity obvious. He glanced at the General and the pair gave slight bows and backed out of the chamber.

The King dipped his brush in ink and added another mark to those which had alarmed his Chief Councilor: seemingly random and bizarre figures of shapes, lines, curves — apparently unconnected fragments of lettering and signs and symbols. Like the scribbling of a child — or a madman.

The two men who had just left the command chamber

emerged out onto the rampart, and stared at the landscape before them: the bare killing field in front of the southern gate of the fortress, the line of trees beyond it, and then, still further, barely visible in the moonlit night, the southern watchtower.

Manning that tower were two watchmen, also staring towards the south — as if extending the visual range of their superiors on the rampart. The never-welcome whoosh of wooden missile displacing the surrounding atmosphere made both of them instinctively glance up in the direction of origin: at the volley of arrows plunging from above, straight towards them….

Another pair of watchmen in another watchtower scanned the rocky landscape stretching out below the northern rampart of the fortress, taking note of any potential threat from the opposite direction as their comrades to the south. They heard a rustling and looked down to see two spears in the hands of two camouflage-wearing soldiers, being shoved towards their chests….

A commander on the northern rampart suddenly saw a reddish-yellow glimmer in the distance: a signal torch from the northern watchtower. He rushed along the parapet to convey this alarm to his superiors who continued that process of information transfer to the chamber of the King.

"And from the south, west and east?" Sejong asked calmly, not looking up from his writing.

"Nothing," answered the Supreme General.

"I would advise moving all batteries to the northern rampart," advised the Chief Councilor, "as that is where the enemy will mount their siege."

"It is said," interrupted the King, "'If you know the enemy and know yourself, you need not fear the result of any battle'." Sejong set down his ink brush. "I know both of us all too well." And stood up from the writing table. "The attack will come from the south." He stretched out his arms — the eunuchs immediately went into action, taking off the King's royal gown and replacing it with royal military garb — simultaneously functional but elevated, in the Joseon Dynasty style. As his two commanders glanced at each other in grave doubt.

Hidden among the rocks to the north of the fortress, an enemy observer took note of movement on the top of the fortress walls — some kind of wagons or machines were being wheeled into place. Upon spotting this crucial bit of intelligence, he immediately turned and vanished into the darkness, making his way across the rocky terrain, angling east, his path describing a large half circle into the line of trees, then continuing until he reached the enemy camp — hidden on the southern side of the fortress. Dozens of soldiers quietly maintained position, waiting.

Breathless, the observer delivered his report to the enemy General and enemy Advisor: "They have moved their batteries to the northern rampart."

The Advisor was pleased, quoting ancient Chinese military wisdom — as every actual and every would-be warrior in every part of this part of the world was wont to do: "'All warfare is deception'." He indicated the fortress in the distance. "His Majesty has nibbled on the bait. Now let him swallow the hook."

The enemy General turned to his commander to put their plan in motion. "Execute the feint to the north. Prepare for our main assault." The commander gave a small bow of assent and rushed off.

King Sejong now stood on the southern rampart of the fortress, dressed for battle. The sudden sound of alarm drums and shouting from the other side of the fortress broke the silence. The Chief Councilor, expertly keeping any indication of 'I told you so' out of his voice, observed simply: "The enemy attacks from the north."

Sejong considered for only a moment. Was he wrong? But his confidence didn't waver: "Launch only what we have in place." The Supreme General turned and nodded to a signal drummer standing within earshot. The drummer instantly pounded out a series of loud, coded booms.

That sound could also be heard in the distance by the enemy battalion that now rushed the northern gate of the Fortress — though their ranks were quite a bit thinner than might be expected for a full army. This was, in fact, the enemy's feint: a false, diversionary attack.

On the northern rampart of the fortress, artillerymen set alight the tangle of fuses dangling from a pair of wooden, mobile, multiple rocket launchers known as *hwacha*. The burning fuses sparked their way upwards to dozens of 'missiles' — wicked-looking fire arrows in wooden tubes. But there were only two of these deadly machines — the rest of the wall was loaded with wheeled carriages only. Fake launchers. The 'movement' on the rampart observed and reported by the enemy spy was a ruse. A feint to counter a feint. The arrows suddenly launched with a flaming WHOOSH towards the enemy soldiers below.

Holding their main position to the south, the enemy

command staff saw none of those details. Only those distant arrows heading towards their false attack.

The Advisor took it as confirmation.

"His Majesty is ours."

The General ordered his commanders into action.

"Launch the main assault. Mandarin Duck formation."

In a matter of moments, the full-force of the enemy army rushed out of the trees towards the southern gate of the fortress in tightly-packed formations designed to protect the battering ram being driven towards the gate and the ladder squadrons intent on scaling the walls.

On the rampart above, Sejong and his military staff watched the advancing army. The King had predicted correctly: the main assault would be from the south. Dozens of fire arrow launchers were lined up on either side of him. The King had kept the main batteries here to counter the predicted attack.

He gave the next set of orders quickly and directly, without gloating. "Set for high trajectory. And aim short. Fire when ready." The artillerymen went into action, lighting the fuses of the launchers. And as the fuses burned. "Set the White Tiger and Vermillion Sparrow battalions in motion." In response, drummers pounded out a loud sequence of BOOMS.

Reacting to the drumming they now heard in the distance, a battalion of the King's soldiers emerged out of the ground from where they had lain hidden — behind the current position of the enemy assault — and stared moving towards their right. A second group of the King's soldiers simultaneously arose from the earth, where they too had kept out of sight. And started moving quickly to their left.

Even from here, they could hear the distant WHOOSH WHOOSH WHOOSH as the fuses hit the gunpower fuel loads and thousands of deadly missiles were fired into the night sky.

Sejong watched from the rampart, as the missile-arrows described long, high parabolas soaring into the night sky. He watched one of them in particular; and in the King's mind's eye, the arc of that fiery trail turned into the curve of a line drawn with writing brush and ink across black paper. As if there was something deeply crucial about this simple figure….

The King's attention snapped back to reality — as the fire arrows descended like a cloud of locusts on their target….

The enemy commanders rushed forward with their

army into the exposed ground between trees and fortress and suddenly stopped in their tracks, stunned to see the fiery arrows falling from the night sky.

The army watched as the arrows smashed into the ground before them, burned for a moment with secondary payload fuses, then exploded with great violence. But the King had ordered his artillery to 'aim short'. Indeed, the arrows seem to have been aimed for a warning volley only: there was not even a single casualty.

The enemy Advisor sighed, "That constitutes a 'hit'."

His General immediately called out, "Sound the retreat." Soldiers banged raucous-sounding metal gongs in response — and the army pulled backwards⋯.

Only to be confronted by the King's hidden battalions — who had maneuvered behind the enemy army — blocking their retreat and catching them completely off-guard.

The battalions surged forward and struck with spears, swords, and arrows. But at close quarters, the truth of this battle became clear: the spears were blunted with heavy cloth covering the tips, the swords were all wooden, and the arrows duds. With little fuss, the enemy soldiers threw down their equally dulled weapons in defeat.

This was a war game. The two sides were, in fact, on the same side.

On the rampart, Sejong's command staff heard the sounds of victory drums from the field. The Chief Councilor was taken aback, "We have won."

No answer. Sejong hadn't heard his councilor or the drums. But was drawing with his index finger the same parabolic arc he saw described by the arrow in burning flight, using as writing substrate the ash-dust from the launchers that had collected on the stone parapet in front of them. The Chief Councilor took note of this odd and out of context royal activity — and glanced up at the Supreme General, who had seen it as well.

"Your Majesty," prompted the General.

"Yes?"

"We have won."

"Of course we have." The King had no doubt about his strategy. But again, there was no arrogance in his voice. There never was. "Let us reward those on both sides who showed valor and intelligence. And go easy on punishing mistakes. It has been a long day."

If the King saw the lingering doubt on the Chief Councilor's face — as the man wondered how it was that his monarch seems mentally both engaged and adrift — he did not let on.

As the 'armies' on both sides cleaned up and got packed to return to the capital, Sejong conferred with the 'enemy Advisor' — who we will call from now on by his name: Choe Malli, the highest ranking Academician at the Confucian Academy and Sejong's closest advisor and even friend. As much as a monarch can be said to have friends.

"How did you know?" asked Choe.

"For nearly two thousand years, Confucian propriety has required the monarch to face south. And his loyal subjects, north. Even in mock battle, I knew you could not violate those sacred directions."

Choe smiled. "Undone by my own fidelity."

"You have lost the battle but won the war," responded the King.

"Your Majesty?"

"You cannot even pretend to be anything less than my dearest advisor. I can only hope to be worthy of that faithfulness. For as long as I am on the throne."

Choe was deeply moved. To serve his ruler was his Confucian duty. But one cannot help but hope that faithful service is recognized. This sort of simple acknowledgment from the King was worth more in Choe's mind than any gift of rank, land or treasure might have been.

A mess supplier swinging a heavy basket shouted his way through the ranks, handing out rough rice cakes to the hungry soldiers. Sejong reached out for one — but acting without a thought, Choe instantly pushed the basket out of reach.

"Your Majesty, there is proper fare waiting for you at the palace."

"Of course." But the King's voice was just a little deflated. A Joseon Dynasty ruler was hemmed in by the stone walls of 'propriety' even with something as simple as a rice cake⋯.

⊛⊛⊛⊛⊛

A solitary lamb walked the passages and corridors of the Royal Palace of Joseon Korea. Deep night, the Palace was lovely in the moonlight. Buildings of brightly -colored wooden beams and panels, pagoda-like roofs of tile, walls of stone, walkways of brick. Surprisingly low to the ground: there were few upper floors here, and even those did not loft so very high — no soaring, cathedral-like vaulted reception halls dominated these spaces. All were surprisingly modest: no surfaces of beaten gold and jewels and jade glittered in the light from this night. Royal as these living and work accommodations might be for the hundreds of ruling family and staff who dwelled here, they were built to a human-scale. Not intended to overawe the masses, but to present a Confucian sense of modesty and correctness and even good government.

The solitary presence of this perfect lamb — for it was indeed pure and flawless — was strange and dream-like. Was this in fact, part of a dream?

The King's eyes opened. He was immediately awake. The chamber was still dark. But this was a big day. Another big day. In the life of a monarch whose life was never his own. Whose ritual calendar filled his seasons, had consumed the years of his life.

Still a few hours before dawn, the palace around him was already making preparations. The tailors and seamstresses of the Royal Wardrobe Department brushed any lingering dust motes from the silken surface of the King's ceremonial robes that hung down from the ceiling on a T-shaped wooden frame, the arms of the garment extending horizontally in opposite directions. The effect both practical and dramatic — as if these sleeves were the wings of a descendent of the Heaven.

In the Sacrificial Chamber, a man dressed in white

opened a small chest revealing a neat row of shining ritual knives. As an assistant carried the lamb we saw earlier into the room. "Where had he gone?" asked the man with the knives.

"For a last look around the Palace," was the answer, as the assistant placed the lamb on the floor, next to a pig and a cow. Also perfect specimens of their kind.

And like the lamb, also destined for the knife⋯.

In chambers, the King stood with arms stretched out, as his personal eunuchs and the wardrobe staff dressed him with the ceremonial vestments, now primed and ready for their wearer. The moment the robes descended over his head, the man with the knife a few chambers away brought the blade to the neck of the lamb, which watched without struggle. As if innocent and ignorant of what was happening — or in complete acceptance of its fate. The moment the knife pierced its flesh was the same moment the golden filigreed ritual headdress was lowered onto the head of the King. As if, synchronistically, symbolically, at this moment, in this world and the next, they were one and the same.

Queen Soheon — the King's official wife — dressed in her ceremonial vestments, strode through the Inner Palace — the environs exclusive to the women of royalty and their staff, kept from the staring eyes and other potential attentions of any man but the King or the eunuchs on his household staff. Soheon was followed by several of the King's secondary wives, each costumed according to rank, moving smoothly through hallways like a school of fish through clear water.

Across the still night-bound Palace grounds, situated in the 'working' areas of the complex, stood the elegant but functional hall of the Confucian Academy. Choe Malli, cleaned up from the last time we saw him on the field of mock-battle, was dressed in his ritual garment — simple and dignified robes, with rank-appropriate head-dress of fabric. At one end of the hall, past the rows of low writing tables and study alcoves, Choe lit a stick of incense and placed it before a painting of Confucius. The Chinese sage had been dead for nearly two millennia now, but his influence over Korean culture had never been stronger.

Confucianism was a moral and ethical philosophy without a God but with a heaven — a natural, creative and ordering principle rather than a place in the afterlife; No hard and fast commandments per se, but with an emphasis on the proper conduct and responsibilities of five primary human relationships: between Ruler and

Ruled, Parent and Child, Spouse and Spouse, Sibling and Sibling, Friend and Friend. With ritual as a cornerstone.

Today's Ancestral Rite, held four times a year, Choe knew as the most crucial on the Ritual Calendar. A public ceremony enacted by the entire government, based on ancient forms, a way to make the patterns of correctness inherent in Heaven and Earth manifest themselves in the Kingdom. To align everything with all that is correct. So Choe believed, with all his heart/mind. And so he had always lived: as Ruled to Ruler. Official to Monarch. Advisor, Councilor and even Conscience — to the King. As the smoke from the incense drifted upwards toward the painted face of the Sage, a wispy tendril brushed across Choe's eyes — but the tears of emotional fullness were already there.

The south gate of the Palace opened and the pre-dawn crowd of common folk that had gathered there stopped their chatting and gossiping and bickering to watch. Out strode and rode the ritual train — torch-bearers and uniformed guards, soldiers and ranking military commanders, government ministers and scholars, attendants and the royal family they were attending to — all in color and raiment seldom seen beyond those gates. Accompanied by drums, gongs and songs. The procession processed alone the main thoroughfare through town — a dirt road surrounded on both sides by shops and markets and dwellings all made of wood and thatch and rough fabrics — all functional, all crowded. Even in the darkness and chill, it was as if the entire population had risen to hold up their end of the Confucian bargain: ruler and ruled in mutual respect.

King Sejong, carried along on a decorated palanquin, kept his eyes facing forward and slightly lowered as dictated by ritual piety: but the hint of the smile in his eyes evidenced his joy at being outside the confines of the palace, among the people of his kingdom.

The sun was rising above the horizon just as the procession reached Jongmyo, the Royal Ancestral Shrine. Filing inside the gates, the participants arranged themselves in positions carefully determined by the Office of Rites after decades of research and stacks of ancient Confucian documents magnanimously provided by multiple generations of Emperors of China. A row of simple tables had been arrayed beneath the overhanging roof of the open structure: multiple altars representing the deceased progenitors of the Yi family rulers of which Sejong was the latest. The first rays of dawn reached the celebrants as the ritual proper was executed in a series of precisely choreographed movements: cuts of meat from the sacrificed animals were 'served' to the spirits, placed on each table, accompanied by multiple side dishes — as would have been enjoyed in life. The King poured a libation of rice wine from a three-legged bronze cup crafted for this very purpose, honoring the spirit tablet of the ancestral spirit all present believed had now alighted here, thus keeping up his end of the ritual: the founder of the Joseon dynasty, Sejong's grandfather. Choe Malli had been given the honor of pouring a libation to his own ancestor, who had been given the even greater honor of being included as a welcome spirit outside the royal line. He executed this small but precise gesture without hesitation — having practiced it at home in his kitchen at least a thousand times.

Dancers accented these movements with movements of their own. Accompanied by musicians producing sanctioned sounds from lyres, flutes, and most notably, a large percussion instrument of hanging chunks of stone, each cut and polished into a chime the vague shape of a Roman numeral '7' — an ancient lithophone known as the *pyeongyeong*.

The subtle climax of all this ceremony was the King

burning paper prayers over a candle — the thin, delicate material caught flame and vanished into vapor instantly, carrying those prayers to the Heaven. But the rite itself was not officially over for Sejong until the sun went down in the west and the procession rolled back through the southern gate and across the Palace grounds; until he exchanged enroute a small glance of mutual appreciation with Choe — and a silent agreement that the Rite would surely have pleased even the Sage himself; until the Royal vestment was hung back on its cross; until the King's head hit the pillow for the night, utterly exhausted.

It had taken tremendous physical effort for this dying man to execute his royal duties on this longest of days.

For dying he was. Even if no one knew that but the King himself⋯.

෯෯෯෯෯

Another day. Another ritual. This one both business-as-usual and — always potentially at least — a matter of life and death. A large diplomatic retinue representing Emperor of the Ming dynasty of China — traveling sixty days overland from Beijing to Hanseong — proceeded up the same thoroughfare that had carried the King and Company when they paid their respects to the ancestral ghosts. Only this time, the crowd that had gathered to watch watched with curiosity but no affection. Music played, but that music was foreign to their ears. Arms were displayed, but they reassured less than threatened···.

King Sejong and his entire Government waited at the Palace, gathered in the Main Assembly Hall that opened onto to the large courtyard designed for just such public occasions, costumed and arranged in accord with the Confucian Rite of Hosting Dignitaries. As China was suzerain over Joseon Korea — allowing the smaller kingdom control over its internal affairs as long as it paid both material and cultural tribute to the Empire — these dignitaries must be treated with the utmost regard. Respected as a Younger Brother should respect an Elder, a Son would treat a Father — the Ruled their Ruler···.

The tall, thick-bodied, heavy-mustachioed Ming Envoy was carried along on a red palanquin. Astride a horse riding immediately behind was his Vice Envoy — smaller and thinner, but more dangerous, like a tiny scorpion whose sting kills, while its larger cousin just puts one to bed for a week.

Entering the southern gate, they crossed the Palace

grounds at a stately rate, finally leaving their rides before the gates to the Assembly Hall. The Envoy and his party went the rest of the way on foot, with the Vice Envoy moving ahead, until he passed the positions of the King and his Company, reaching the Assembly Hall and the ornate stand designed to be higher than anyone now present, erected just before the now-empty throne.

With great import, the Vice Envoy placed upon it a rolled, wax-sealed official scroll. And spoke in Mandarin to all assembled: "Prepare to hear the words of your Lord, the Son of Heaven and Emperor of China, the voice of the Great Ming!"

Sejong and his ministers, still standing in subservient positions before the scroll, suddenly dropped to their knees and bowed down to it — as if the scroll was the Emperor himself.

The Envoy himself then moved to the scroll, and took it up. The thick wax that had sealed it sixty days previously in Beijing was imprinted with a complex sigil impressed by the hand of the Emperor himself(or at the very least, he was in the room when it happened). The Envoy dramatically broke the seal and unrolled the scroll. He read in Mandarin, in a strong voice for all to hear: "We greet the King of Joseon…."

When those words were written, sixty days previously, the boyishly handsome ruler, who was still in fact, a boy — Yingzong, the Emperor of the Ming dynasty — was seated on the floor in his private office at an ornate writing desk covered in gold. He was dressed toe-to-head in Imperial robes. Over-dressed, even. Peacock-like. The extreme wealth evidenced at the Imperial Palace in Beijing stood in great contrast to the more subdued style of the Korean Royal Palace and its occupants on modest display some 800 miles to the southeast.

A middle-aged eunuch named Wang Zhen fussed over the young Emperor's shoulder, his manner in equal parts toady and teacher, advisor and admirer. Not to mention, manipulator. Over the course of millennia and dynasties past, the human victims of eunuch-making — the prepubescent boys who managed to survived the removal by knife of their genitals, making them non-threatening enough to serve in the household of the Emperor(filled as it was with hundreds of females — the Imperial wives and consorts, attendants and maids, any one of which, depending on natural emotion and Imperial whim, might potentially bear the Emperor's next off-spring) — had fulfilled their duties as they were expected to. Only on occasion managing to garner for themselves as individuals or as a class enough power to be nothing short of the rulers of China behind the scenes. And as China had consistently been the largest empire on the planet, that made them, on occasion, the most powerful individuals in the world.

This, then, was one of those occasions. Wang Zhen had the apparently guileless and easy-going young man who sat upon the Dragon Throne sitting instead 'in the palm of his Buddha hand' as the saying went.

The eunuch dictated the letter over the Imperial lad's shoulder, "We greet the King of Joseon and all his subjects⋯." And the young man composed the words himself with brush and ink — an indication of how highly the Empire valued the Kingdom on the Korean peninsula, and how essential was the promise of mutual martial support to the survival of the Ming dynasty. "As we would a favorite son and all his children⋯."

The young Emperor paused his brush, repeating the words, "'As we would Our Favorite son' — Isn't that a bit patronizing?"

The eunuch smiled as if indulging a child. "As You, Emperor of Ten Thousand Years, are indeed the patron of the Korean kingdom, to be patronizing is not inappropriate." The Son of Heaven considered for a moment. Nod-ded in agreement, and kept writing⋯.

๛๛๛๛๛

In the Assembly Hall of the King of Joseon, the young Emperor's Envoy kept reading, "⋯and all his subjects, as we would Our favorite son and all his children⋯." These words were indeed patronizing in every sense of the word - and the Envoy did not attempt to keep the air of superiority from his tone of voice. If that tone bothered Sejong or any of the others, no observer would have known - they kept their faces even. The Envoy continued, "The education and safety of your Kingdom is always in Our thoughts. Accept then, to address the former, this modest gift from our library⋯."

The Vice Envoy on that cue nodded to his staff — who quickly moved a large, ornate wooden trunk into view, opening it to reveal beautifully bound volumes of books and scrolls. "⋯That you might continue to educate yourselves at your leisure."

Again, the patronizing tone. And now the other shoe — or rather, hard-toed boot — dropped, as it were. "And with respect to the latter, We request a tribute of ten thousand of your finest war horses⋯."

Ten thousand horses.

The casually delivered demand seemed to hang in the air like a hammer. To comply would wipe out the Korean potential for mounting a cavalry, for hauling arms and supplies — not just for waging war but for defense of the kingdom. It would require over two years of breeding or possibly trade with the aggressive tribes of Jurchen or the even Mongol Steppes to the far north to make up for that loss.

Standing quietly among the assembled, the Supreme General of Joseon blanched. He glanced towards the Chief Councilor and even the King — but far better at this game, their faces revealed nothing.

"⋯that We might counter any and all threats to Joseon's safety, no matter the cost to ourselves⋯."

The irony was not lost on anyone present — the 'cost' of their own security seemed to be falling entirely on the Korean kingdom. But again, Sejong's expression remained composed and unreadable. No response was appropriate at this time and place. The night to come, after the daylong festivities, and enough local rice wine to make faces red and lips free, would be the time for the real deal⋯.

And that night could not have come soon enough for the King. The evening banquet was held in one of his favorite locations on the Palace grounds: Gyeonghoeru, an open pavilion in painted wood and stone that seemed to float on an artificial lake just beyond the working and living quarters. The light from the setting sun scattered in multiple effects across the multitude of reflective surfaces and the effect was dazzling, like a rainbow descended to Earth.

As this banquet was by extension not only in honor of the Envoy of Ming but the Emperor he represented(and of course would be reported in detail to the young ruler in person), the best of the palace was put on display in terms of cultured amusement: dancers and musicians; Elaborate dishes and drinking. And conversation. If the constant one-upmanship of the exchange of words under the cover of diplomacy could ever be considered that.

In the last, scattering rays from the vanishing sun, Supreme General Lee Chun, despite his advancing age, performed in honor of the occasion a 'sword dance' — a partly choreographed partly improvisational martial arts demonstration with a pair of long swords. It looked both beautiful and deadly.

The King and his ranking ministers and scholars were

seated formally across from the Chinese Envoy, Vice Envoy and their staff. And all heads were turned to watch the General. But the atmosphere had indeed gotten loose from the food and drink and duration. As the General came to a big finish and bowed his respect, the Envoy now dropped Mandarin in favor of the local Korean language — which he sometimes mispronounced on purpose — as his patronizing demeanor had only become more and more demeaning.

"Excellent!" He clapped his hands in apparent appreciation. "No juggler in Beijing could do better."

The General had battled Japanese pirates and Jurchen archers and had never lost. But diplomacy was a war of a different sort. And he didn't like it. He reacted to this insulting declaration with a cold look in his eyes — but Sejong remained composed.

"No juggler in Joseon, either. Nor anyone else," declared the King.

The statement was literally true. The Envoy considered a comeback, but dropped all pretense for his real point. "And how did the General, the jugglers, or anyone else perform in Your Majesty's recent war-games? 'Take the Fortress' was it?"

Ming China obviously had informers here in Korea.

But the King did not show any surprise or hesitation. "All executed their duties at the highest levels of martial competence."

"China watches over Joseon. The Emperor is your fortress. And your army. What need is there to prepare for war?"

All the King's ministers and scholars and military officials were suddenly on edge at this. But Sejong had an answer. As he always did. "A state must be responsible for its national defense. And be ready to come to the aid of its patron. If the need should arise."

The Envoy considered this. "Of course. But the dtails — rumors perhaps? — were disquieting. Why did the 'enemy' in your games array itself in battle formations currently favored by the military advisors of Ming? As though you were being attacked by the Emperor himself?"

Suddenly, a fish could be heard breaking the surface of the stocked lake, leaping and then splashing back in the water. Sejong waited until the sound faded. "Any invader of intelligence must of necessity mimic the strategy of the Great Ming. Or how could they pose a threat?" As always with this King, his sincerity came with a hint of irony. Was he telling the entire truth? It was never possible to know his emotions and his thoughts — his heart/mind.

"How indeed." The Envoy cut to the chase,

"What about the horses?"

"They are yours." Sejong had not hesitated for even a moment.

The Envoy tried not to show his surprise at this immediate and full concession. Without the King even trying to bargain down what the Envoy well-knew was an unreasonable demand.

"All ten thousand?"

"Yours."

The General's face went red. The Chief Councilor looked stunned. But the Envoy from China was happy as can be. He took up his glass in a toast. This time, in Mandarin. "Hao! Hao!(Yes! Yes!)"

Running counter to the reactions of his colleagues, the Confucian scholar Choe's expression was one of deep admiration for the King's decision: he and Sejong exchanged a friendly glance as they all joined the toast, sealing the negotiation. All chimed in with perfectly accented Mandarin, "Hao! Hao!"

THE GREEN LEAVES

Fell, as before, straight downward, towards a ground unseen, from a sky that was also out of view, in air clear and still as a pane of glass⋯.

King Sejong's eyes opened. He awakened on his back as always, his face toward the heaven in sleep. And for a moment the afterimage of the dream of the falling green leaves remained across his field of vision. As it had done for as long as he remembered. As far back as when he had been the child known as Grand Prince Chungnyeong, the third son of Taejong, third King in the Joseon dynastic line. Taejong had wrested control of the kingdom from his own father who had taken it from the previous ruling family, the Goryeo. So he would hardly have had any qualms about pushing the preternaturally intelligent and self-possessed Chungnyeong over his first and second sons — leap-frogging the acceptable order of succession in favor of his favorite.

This strategy had succeeded beyond even the most prescient of Taejong's expectations: as ruler, Sejong had

47

held the kingdom together internally, kept the Japanese and the northern tribes at bay, maintained with balance the always precarious dynamic with China — and without the blood-letting methods of his father. Much of which might have been foreseen. But he also invented inventions, supported learning, exhibited genuine love for the common people and provided policies of relief to those whom other societies typically had cast aside: the poor, the elderly, the widow, the orphan.

And through it all, his personal eunuch, Dong Woo, had been there. Since they were boys. And he was here still. As he had helped the King into his battle-gear during the war games at the fortress, on this morning he brought gear for the domestic front: breakfast, tea, a change of clothing and a young helper to take away the chamber pot — all while humming a wordless tune. "A beautiful day, Your Majesty."

"Yes." Sejong had finally cleared the sleep from his head.

"And a successful reception for the embassy from Ming. Surely the Emperor will be pleased to hear."

Sejong's voice was light.

"One can never tell. With Emperors."

"Did you sleep well, Your Majesty?" asked the helper,

chamber pot in hand. Which he barely managed to hold onto as Dong Woo cuffed him on the back of his head. "Aigo! So familiar!"

The young eunuch winced.

"Out!" said his superior. And he fled to avoid getting smacked a second time. As Dong Woo opened the small chest of clothing, the King focused his attention on extracting some small pieces of roasted meat from a bowl mixed with rice and popped them into his mouth, forgoing the starch. "The boy is only following your example"

"I've taken care of your Majesty since we were boys!" replied Dong Woo as he held up the clothing. "Let him put in half as many years before so casually addressing the King"

"If only we had half as many years left." Sejong said it with a small smile, but there was a touch of the bittersweet in his voice. His joints ached from yesterday's all-day and all-night event. Which he hid as best he could. Lest any hint of discomfort let alone infirmity prompt a nagging lecture from the eunuch.

The garments that were held up for his approval were the absolute opposite of everything the King would be expected if not sanctioned by government policy to wear during his official duties and even private life. Nothing royal about the rough burlap and frayed sleeves. These were unmistakably the clothes worn by common folk — more specifically, that of a general tradesman.

All of which the King was expecting. Dong Woo took out a faded scarf as well. "It is the first week of Spring. And the sun is sunny today. But a sudden breeze can chill. Best be prepared."

The mystery of what the King was planning with this 'costume' had the well-worn feel of the old garments themselves⋯.

෧෩෨෩෨

Queen Soheon and a quartet of attendants were moving along the exposed walkways of the Inner Palace. The Queen was dressed elegantly and her attendants were a match — they looked like they radiated their own light; as if their feet barely touch the ground.

As one, they all spied Sejong — dressed in royal daily wear and heading quickly along one of the pathways out of the Inner Palace — as if on some personal mission — not yet spotting them. He was surrounded by a gaggle of eunuchs who seemed to make it a point of obscuring him from view.

The first of the Queen's attendants could not stop herself from exclaiming, "It's the King!" And the second, "How handsome he still looks!" And the third, "Still?" — as she raised a hand threatening to slap away that insolent remark.

But the Queen took no notice of the momentary spat — this was all a typical part of their group dynamic.

The first attendant quickly added, "Your Highness is blessed by the Heaven!"

But Soheon good-naturedly turned on her heel.

"Quickly, or the King will see us seeing him."

She altered course sharply away from Sejong, and her quartet followed in perfect synchronization. As the King continued away from them, ensconced in his pod of eunuchs⋯.

And as he went, he could not help but momentarily register the raucously discordant chirp of a small bird hidden from somewhere nearby. Something about it made him smile in passing. And he stopped himself from glancing in the direction of the source: a small walled garden, just outside the living chambers of the Inner Palace.

Within that garden, a royal consort named Lady Hwang — the very last of the King's several 'secondary wives' — in her 20s with plain, open features, was standing in the midst of a pair of ornamental trees, her expression concentrated. She stared at a small songbird hopping on the ground.

The young woman suddenly chirped — it was she who had made the sound recognized in passing by the King. And as before, this sound was wildly off-tune. The bird chirped back almost in annoyance.

A sudden breeze rustled the leaves of the ornamental trees. Lady Hwang pursed her lips and imitated it with a WHOOSH. The resemblance was only passing.

The distant cry of a crane flying overhead. Lady Hwang didn't even glance up to find it — but instantly attempted to mimic the sound. The attempt failed.

Then an uncertain, juvenile rooster perched up on the corner of a nearby rooftop let out a shaky crowing — as if this was his audition for the role. Lady Hwang duplicated the call — startling the already anxious bird with her rough parody of his life-work.

An unseen dog yapped from beyond the garden wall. Yet another dissonant attempt at imitation shot out of Lady Hwang's mouth.

She scowled. No matter how much she practiced, she never seemed to get better at this···. game? What was it exactly she was doing?

We will come to know soon enough — for now, the behavior seemed both eccentric and a little bit unnerving.

Sejong had finally exited the Inner Palace, leaving the royal women behind, and was crossing the grounds of the Outer Palace — the offices and supporting departments of the government — making his way towards the distant walls surrounding the grounds from the city beyond. His expression was one of confident routine, still surrounded by the eunuchs, seemingly certain no one had taken notice of his passage.

They rounded another corner together, and vanished from casual view. When they appeared again — the King was gone. But they all kept moving apace, as if nothing had happened.

Moments later, on the other side of a low wall, half-hidden behind a planted hedge, a lone eunuch helped the King quickly switch out his royal robes for the modest, nondescript garb picked out for him earlier.

An Old Guard passed by in the course of his duties — and couldn't help but notice the quick-change going on in the foliage — but he pointedly pretended not to. Then moved on with a slight smile on his face: of affection and admiration — and awe. Sejong was his King — and like most in the Palace, the Old Guard had taken that relationship to heart. Unlike most, it had defined his existence — and would choreograph his end. But we get ahead of ourselves⋯.

When the Old Guard continued on his way, Sejong suddenly appeared again from out of the brush, wearing his disguise. And the next time anybody might have perceived his passing, he had surreptitiously fallen in with a handful of daily-visiting provisioners moving along with carts emptied shortly before by the Royal kitchen staff. They too, took no notice. Or, like most everybody else — pretended not to.

From across the Palace grounds, Choe Malli of the Confucian Academy and Chief Councilor Hwang Hui — the two most powerful individuals in government who were not the King — did not pretend not to.

"The King has not fooled anybody with this game since he was a boy of twelve," said the Chief Councilor.

"Certainly, he is aware of that," replied Choe.

"Such shenanigans should no longer be tolerated."

But Choe knew this remark was only the opening salvo. "Chief Councilor, please say what you mean. If you are angry about His Majesty's decision yesterday."

"Capitulation. Ten thousand of our best mounts! The army just lost its cavalry! And Joseon any hope of defending itself! What if we are invaded? By Japan? By the northern tribes? By any kingdom in shouting distance of our shores?"

"Then China will come to our defense. With those same horses. And the largest army in the world."

"You put too much trust in the Emperor," said the Councilor. "And in those who manipulate him"

"The Ming Emperor is China. All that comes to us stamped and sealed with his approval is ours to obey. Not to question. Even if someone else wet his brush in the inkwell, moved the tip across the paper, and put the Dragon Seal in his hand."

"Even if it leads to national suicide?"

"Does one question one's father?" asked the Confucian in Choe. "Ming is superior, Joseon subordinate. For this…. relationship to work, devotion is required of us — as trustworthiness is required of China."

But the other man was stuck on the subject of the horses. As if all ten thousand of them were galloping circles in his head.

"His Majesty should have offered twenty-five hundred! And settled at five thousand!"

"Does a son bargain with his father? When the latter makes a request? The Sage would roll in his grave. Are we or are we not a Confucian society? Whose stability — indeed very existence — requires fidelity to proper relationships? Ruler to Subject; Father to Son; Husband to Wife; Elder to Younger; Friend to Friend? His Majesty understands the necessity of that wisdom in his very bones"

"His Majesty scribbles onto paper." This odd observation from the Councilor caught Choe off-guard.

"What?"

The Councilor recalled the figures he saw the King making at the open of our story. "In the command chamber. At the fortress. During the war-game. Instead of plotting strategy. His Majesty was making marks with ink."

Choe was puzzled. "Writing something?"

"In no language ever seen by my eyes."

Choe was dismissive. "His Majesty has made a study of languages — this is well known. And is part of the education of a Confucian ruler."

"These were the markings of a child. Or a madman."

"Chief Councilor," said Choe, voice cold,

"Consider your words carefully."

"And on the ramparts. When we launched the artillery against your forces⋯." The Councilor saw that moment again in memory: Sejong watching the long, fiery trajectory of a fire arrow, eyes glazing over. "His Majesty appeared amazed, watching the flight of the missiles. Like a very old man, who is wonderstruck by a rainbow or falling snow — as though seen for the first time. Or rather, as if he no longer knows what he is seeing."

Choe angrily cut him off.

"Sir. Again, I would suggest you watch your words."

"Choe Malli! You have made a career out of criticizing His Majesty! In Assembly Halls packed with ministers and scholars! In front of the King himself! Who are you to tell me now to silence my doubts?"

"My doubts are my duty. To our kingdom and its Confucian heritage. To our King and his betterment." He indicated with a sweep of his arm the Palace grounds around them. "To pound the Petitioner's drum at dawn. To force the entire government to tumble from bed to hear one's complaint. To bow so low and so hard as to split one's forehead off the flagstones and rise bleeding before King and company — indeed, before Heaven itself. All to make one's voice heard."

Choe had a look of near-rapture on his face. That was what he had lived for. And even now, near the end of his time, it still gave him cause to go on. "This is what it means to be the loyal opposition! Advisor to the King!

This is how good government works!" Choe shook his head, voice conciliatory. "Surely you have mistaken His Majesty's most trivial lapses for illness or worse? If lapses they were. And not behavior that only served to focus concentration on the task at hand? Do not forget whose strategy won that war-game. Does it matter what mental diversions His Majesty employed to get there?"

The affection — and even love — in Choe's gaze could not have been more evidence as he continued to watch the King heading toward the gate in his semi-comical disguise. "His Majesty is the closest thing to a perfect King that this world will ever see. And he is ours. Do not question Joseon's good fortune in that regard."

But the Councilor was not mollified. "I hope, Master Choe, that when Our Majesty's 'trivialities' leave this kingdom vulnerable to outrage and even destruction, that your commitment to 'good government' goes beyond a few drops of blood on the flagstones." These words of warning hung in the air as the King vanished into the gate towards the world outside.

The first time Sejong had been inspired to 'escape' the Palace — with the assistance of the same Eunuch Dong Woo — who had only recently been turned from boy to eunuch — with the same feigned ignorance of the Old Guard — who had been not so old at the time — he was a child Prince of twelve, and to all the world out of the running for his father's throne. The idea had come to him suddenly. From the window of a palanquin on a return trip from his mother's home town, he had seen children singing and rough-housing, stuffing their faces with any morsel they happened across, shouting, cursing, dancing, chasing after the Royal procession, and even — and this had been most shockingly revelatory — just plain ignoring him and his kin and their royal entourage. As if those children and their families had lives that needed absolutely nothing from the people inside the Palace. As if the Palace and all its occupants could vanish tomorrow — in a fire, from an invasion, under the thumb of some long-forgotten god — but the people would only blink. And go on. Whereas — and he had thought this thought from the time the palanquin entered the outer market to when it exited, turned left, then north, to see the western gate by which it would enter the Palace grounds — if the people suddenly vanished — by fire, invasion, god or of their own will — what point the Palace and all who lived there? For what reason would the Joseon Dynasty — his father, mother, brothers, sisters; his uncles and aunts and cousins to the 9th degree — what reason would there be for their continued existence?

That thought had been completed as the young Prince with apparently no chance of becoming King had entered the gate. And now that he was King, as the memory of a thought can be attached to the place and time at which it was first made, he remembered and thought the very same thing, as he went out the gate disguised as one of those same people, whose existence seemed to matter more than his own.

It was the thought that had driven almost every policy he had pursued after he came to power. Every invention, every intention. In his mind, the King existed for the People. And not the other way around.

Fortunately for Sejong, Confucian philosophy supported that idea. To some extent. If a Ruler did not fulfil his responsibilities towards his subjects, the latter were duty-bound to disobey and even overthrow that ruler.

But even Confucius had said nothing about a ruler

putting on common rags and heading into the market-
place for a stick of grilled meat.

CRONGEN

"Delicious," he said to the elderly woman vendor, as
he wafted the stick beneath his nose.

"You have not even taken one bite!" she chided him.

"The fragrance is enough." He took a deep breath.
Then made as if to hand the untasted food back to her.

"Now, I'm full."

"Aigo!" she playfully swatted at him.

He ducked the blow, then popped the meat into his
mouth, where it vanished. Did the old woman also know
that this was her King? Maybe she did⋯.

At first, he had done it to learn more about them.
Those who lived beyond the Palace walls. At first, and
for years afterwards, that was the dominant motivation. Or at least, so he had told himself. And had told his
father, that time he had been caught in the act. But the
truth was, he loved being out here. Where eyes were not
watching and judging his every move. He never took his
position for granted: that young Prince and now dying
King always knew he was a visitor from a place of pro-

found privilege. And could escape back behind the safety of those walls whenever he wished. Relative safety. For it was not entirely self-indulgent for a King to consider the Palace walls sometimes akin to the walls of a jail. Where one could be knifed by a fellow prisoner or executed by the jailer. Both possibilities were always very real⋯.

A sudden commotion jogged him out of his walking reverie. Half-a-dozen uniformed municipal security patrolmen moved with intent through the crowd, led by a crabby Constable who clearly thought he had better things to do than wade through the busy market in pursuit of⋯. Who exactly? Sejong spotted the boy before they did: clutching a small sack against his chest, pulling back far as possible to let them pass, suppressing a look of guilty panic so obvious as to appear like a comedic carnival character created for just that purpose.

But the patrol didn't notice. They vanished down a side-street and the boy instantly headed up an alley the opposite direction. Curious, Sejong followed him.

Down two streets and four alleyways, under a curtain and through a door, into a smoke-filled urban hovel, where a twisted face bobbed up and down, to and fro, to the beat of small drums and the clashing of tiny cymbals. The face was a mask of carved wood — staring eyes, gaping mouth, rosy cheeks — worn by a female shaman — a Mudang. As she gyrated in a small spiral across the dirt floor, reciting an off-kilter chant. As Sejong's eyes got used to the combination of deep shadow and low light — a few sunbeams that pierced the roof; flames from scattered candles — he took in the sights of this secret ritual.

The colorfully-robed Mudang swinging her ceremonial trident and knife, the table of offerings — animal carcasses, vegetables, alcoholic drink — the walls lined with garishly painted local 'gods' — like otherworldly family portraits. This was almost like an earthy, raw, commoner's version of the Confucian ancestral ritual of several days earlier. But in fact, it was the other way around. Shamanism was arguably the most ancient religious practice on the planet. A direct descendant of the tens of thousands of years old paintings found in caves throughout the world, wherever ancient humanity found itself. Even in this place and time — mid-1400s by the Western calendar — shamanistic rituals had mostly been replaced by major religions and civic rites. It still existed in Siberia — where a shaman would wear a reindeer headdress no different from those left on the cave walls. And it still existed on the Korean peninsula.

A persecuted existence. Sejong knew that he was watching something his own government had outlawed in his lifetime. Despite nearly zero being the number of government officials who would pass up a chance to ask a favor of a dead relative or a local deity with the intercessory assistance of a Mudang who would ostensibly make the contact.

The young boy that Sejong had followed here moved to the altar table and emptied the sack he had been carrying, adding a human-shaped root onto the offering pile — a missing ingredient he had clearly been sent to find.

The incense and herbs burned, the sunbeams flared and the candleflames flickered, Sejong's eyes watered in this hallucinatory atmosphere, and he stared at the garishly painted portraits hung behind the altar — of the Mudang's favorite gods.

His own face stared back at him.

The King had studied folk religion deeply enough to know this was an example of euhemerism: the process by which an historical or living person is mythologized into a local deity. Which itself was not so radically different from the ancestor worship of even the strictest Confucianists — whose founder had dismissed all consideration of ghosts and spirits and gods as being unworthy of consideration by the living, or more to the point irrelevant to living a proper life.

Nevertheless, to actually recognize himself in a potrait hung above a carcass-covered altar in front of which spiraled a woman in a trance — was still shocking.

Before any concern of being recognized might require some evasive action on his part, the very walls were smashed open and the municipal security patrol rushed inside, clubs swinging.

"By authority of the King!" shouted the Constable.

The Mudang and her clients screamed and shouted as the altar table and candles were knocked over, and everyone ducked and dove to escape beatings and arrests. The King included.

With a fine sense of irony himself, the paradox of Sejong scrambling to avoid clubs swung by security personnel who were enforcing the laws of the government he led was not lost on him even as a baton creased his forehead and a deputy whose recent bump in weekly paycheck he himself had authorized hurled him out into the bright sunlight.

A small stream turned a waterwheel which cranked a lever that pushed a bellows that sent air into a fire pit, super-heating the flames until they were hot enough to melt iron. Ingots of which, in fact, melted accordingly. The churning water and fiery sparks looked like an appropriately apocalyptic follow-up to the violent scene at the house of the Mudang.

The King had taken refuge in this place after the roust in town. The Swordsmith who lived and worked here was the same age as the King, with wild white hair and steely musculature. Their dynamic was familiar — like that between old friends or collaborators — as the man dabbed the blood from Sejong's forehead, still bleeding from the roust.

"I'm terrified," said the King quietly. With a vulnerability he could not reveal even to his wife.

"Of course, you are," replied the Swordsmith, as he finished treating the wound and turned back to the bellows, then made an adjustment to the water wheel as it turned. A lifetime of bending iron into shapes it would never otherwise find itself had given this solitary man a predilection for Taoist trains of thought.

"I can not⋯stop," continued Sejong.

"Yet somehow, cannot find the last step."

"The spinning inside your head — thoughts you do not control — the feeling of *han* that burns inside your chest. That is not your heart breaking for the people. Or rather, not only. It is the movement of Heaven."

Han. That specifically Korean emotion in the heart/mind. Like a fire being smothered: whether that burning was from a wrong that could never be righted, a desire that could not be sated, a hope that had no hope of coming into being.

Or in Sejong's case: a lifelong wish to do something for the people of this peninsula that would elevate their lives in a way nobody had ever before hoped or imagined or dreamed. That is what he had hoped, imagined, dreamed.

And now, was attempting.

"They are one and the same," he realized.

The Swordsmith pounded a piece of metal flat in answer. Shifted it onto a cold rod of iron, then pounded again — wrapping it around, conforming to the hard shape, forming the start of a long thin metal tube, like the barrel of a rifle.

"You have already stepped onto the wheel, the motion ends when the wheel is broken — or you are."

Sejong considered the waterwheel turning next to them. "But if that wheel is divine, by definition it cannot be broken."

"Then you know how this will end," came the reply.

"Heaven and Earth are without feeling; they treat all equally: as dogs made from straw."

He shoved a chunk of charcoal into the fire pit, replenishing the fuel, sending sparks into the air. Sejong watched them burn brightly enough to rival the afternoon sunlight — each of them itself like a little sun — and vanish in a heartbeat.

⊙⊙⊙⊙⊙

Later that night, a tradesman pushed a cart towards the Western Gate of the Palace grounds — along with a handful of other night suppliers of fresh foodstuffs and sundries needed for maintaining the royals and their staff the next morning. As he passed through, one of the security sentries — the Old Guard who had pointedly looked away from the King as he escaped the palace in disguise — took note of a small yellow ribbon tied to the tradesman's cart. He pointedly lowed his gaze — so as to avoid staring into the man's face — handed the man an entry pass, then turned his attention to the others trying to enter the palace grounds. As if he was deflecting any further possible attention to the lone tradesman.

"You — open that one," he pointed to a fish monger hauling a pair of baskets.

And the tradesman continued through the gate. Of course, that 'tradesman' was the King in disguise, reentering the Palace grounds as had been his habit for years. The small yellow tag was an unspoken but pre-arranged system with a handful of security staff who were in on the deception. The Old Guard had done it more times than anyone could count. Anyone but him. He had indeed kept count. Two-hundred-forty-seven times, in thirty-eight years. He remembered every single occasion. And sometimes, as he turned restlessly on his blanket, in the cold or the noise of his barrack-mates, he counted those times in his head, like counting sheep jumping over a wall, as a way to fall asleep.

Sejong pushed his cart into a covered supply depot, large enough to house a few horses and the crates hauled behind them, and was met by Dong Woo. Out of sight in the depot, the eunuch helped him change back into royally appropriate clothing, noticing the small bandage on his head — and the dried blood that had stained it from underneath.

"Oh, of course!" he said, not bothering to hide his annoyance. "I have warned you."

"For as long as I can remember," said the King lightly.

"As your warnings go unheeded, why persist?"

He had a point. The eunuch shook his head.

"His Majesty is far too old for drunken brawling."

"I could not agree more."

⊛⊛⊛⊛⊛

A short time later, in his own chambers, in his own nightclothes, his wife Queen Soheon redressed that same wound with care and concern.

"I was merely experiencing firsthand," explained the King, "the consequences of my government's ban on the people's expression of any religious practice that Confucius would have frowned upon. Two thousand years ago. In China."

The Queen finished her task. Kissed him gently on the head. As the King completed his thought. "To quote the Sage: 'Respect ghosts and spirits, but keep them at a distance'."

"Does that mean clubbing them in the head?" inquired

the Queen, with the same sense of irony exhibited by her husband.

"Apparently so."

The King considered her for a moment. They had a bond that dated back to their betrothal in childhood: closer than a brother and sister or a husband and wife. Something uniquely deep and binding. They had grown up together. Grown old together. Wept and laughed and been silly and smart together. They had hoped and had hopes crushed together. But still they hoped. Now, more than ever. One last time. Together.

"If Joseon can purge Buddha himself from everyone's sight, what chance has an Auntie swinging a large fork and wailing like a raccoon?" The King mimed the Mudang's waving hands.

The Queen suddenly remembered. "Ah! Speaking of which. A gift for us."

She reached inside the folds of her garment and found a small silk bag tied there. She took it out to show her husband, removing the contents inside: a small, very ancient, carved Buddha. In the lamplight, the burnished, partial gold leaf covering the old wood looked precious indeed. The King reacted to the beauty and uniqueness of it.

"Oh!" He took it in hand, inspecting it from several angles. "From the Abbot at Huibang Temple?"

The Queen nodded yes. There was never surprising the King. His thoughts were ever able to put two and two together before a lesser mind would even realize there even was a 'two' — let alone two of them.

"He said it came across the Old Silk Road to Dunhuang, passed through Beijing — where it was stolen and ransomed not once but twice v and finally to his Temple, arriving only last week."

"The Abbot pays us back," analyzed the King. "For keeping the ban on his faith limited to the capital. Or his temple would be in ashes···. and the Abbot himself a mountain hermit. Or hung from his own rafters."

He set the small statue down next to the lamp. Wife and husband then lit a stick of incense and placed it before the image.

When Sejong's grandfather and father had overthrown the Goryeo dynasty that preceded them, they had overthrown Buddhism as well. Replacing what had been the dominant religion of the state with Confucianism — of the 'Neo' variety that had been so popular in China over the past few centuries. With its emphasis on reason over mysticism and reality over world-as-illusion. A philosophy rather than a religion. And specifically identified with the Joseon dynasty 'brand'.

And yet.

When age came, bringing illness and intimations of mortality, thoughts of personal death, of the loss of closest family and friends, Buddhism — with elaborate descriptions of the afterlife and the concept of reincarnation — had reasserted itself. For individuals at least — and in hiding. For the law still decreed otherwise. And what the King and Queen were doing now by legal precedent of their own government could earn them fines and even beatings.

Without thinking, they took each other's hands. Then softly whispered a prayer — the vow of the Bodhisattva: "However many the sentient beings, I vow to release them from suffering; However unquenchable the cravings, I vow to extinguish them from my heart; However difficult the Way, I vow to follow it…."

A long moment of thoughtful silence followed. Then the Queen raised the same question she felt duty-bound to ask every evening.

"Who would his Majesty like to join him…tonight?"

And as he had for the past decade at least, Sejong just sighed and gave her a tired look.

"Lady Sangchim feels neglected," continued his wife helpfully, "Soyong has all but given up, and Lady Hwang — I must remind you - has never been given···. consideration. Beyond the···. games you play together. Is it not time to reward her efforts? She does not even know what you are doing"

"Her ignorance may be the only thing that keeps her alive," responded Sejong, "if I should fail···."

The Queen had done her best to goad her husband into spending the night with one of the secondary wives — his several consorts, added to the Inner Palace over the years — but his attention was focused elsewhere. On something that was a mystery to all in this world save the two spouses who were discussing whether or not the King would sleep with another woman tonight, and whom it should be.

"You will not fail," she said. "Heaven itself is with you. How can Heaven fail?"

He took her hands in both of his. His eyes suddenly glistened, hiding the terror he admitted next to the Swordsmith's furnace earlier today, grateful for her belief in him.

"Heaven is you," was his simple answer. "And I but the beneficiary of proximity."

She smiled and arose to go. But when she turned away from him — that terror returned to his eyes.

Moments later the Queen reached an adjoining corridor, where a handful of consorts had been waiting expectantly. They were all dressed for the potential occasion — makeup and night gowns to accentuate elegance and beauty but also propriety. As even in the bedroom, Confucius was looking over everyone's shoulder.

Queen Soheon nodded towards Lady Hwang — whom we last saw in a walled garden badly imitating the sounds of animals.

"Your Highness!" Lady Hwang answered the command, barely able to contain her excitement. She did a quick curtsy, then started to hurry off towards the King's chamber

"Slowly. Slowly." The Queen moved her hand as if to pull her back with invisible strings. A warning to maintain her dignity. Lady Hwang nodded. Slowed herself down. Then continued around the corner and out of their sight. The Queen turned to the other women with a pleasant look on her face. Then with the tiniest movement of her head to release them, they all turned as one and headed off towards their own chambers for the rest of the evening.

None were disappointed at doing so. At this point in all their lives together, spending the night with the King felt far more like an extra work shift than it might have felt thirty or twenty or even two years before. All his wives loved him — but mostly with the same awe-inflected distance as his subjects. Only Soheon had his heart/mind. And only Lady Hwang had his⋯. well, nobody was quite sure of what she had of his. Or why the King had defaulted to her company almost daily and nightly over the past couple of years. The ladies of the household all had eyes with which to see. They perceived this most recent addition to their number as not particularly comely or especially smart. It was also evident that King and consort were not attempting to add another child to the dozens of offspring already produced within these chambers in the attempt to secure the continuity of royal descendants — or indeed take any physical pleasure at all in each other's company. This left Lady Hwang exposed to Inner Palace gossipand curious speculation. Just what did the King see in her?

Nobody but the Queen knew the truth. It was not what the King saw. It was what he heard.

And now, in the King's chamber, he heard a mouthful.

- Songbird

- Wind

- Crane

She repeated the sounds she had been mimicking in the palace garden, standing before him not like a companion but more like a student giving a recital.

As before, the sounds were delivered with ear-grating infidelity. When she finally mimicked the Rooster and the Dog, Sejong could not stop himself from smiling — even as he stopped himself from wincing.

Then, he became thoughtful. "How is it, that all creatures seemingly produce sounds consisting of vowels and consonants?" He thought more about this. "Indeed, even that which has no body at all. Even the wind. Or the rain. Vowels and consonants."

The young woman was puzzled. "What is a vowel? And what is a consonant?"

Sejong hesitated. He just told the Queen, after all, that keeping Lady Hwang 'ignorant' of his mysterious endeavor was to keep her safe···.

"Tell me." She suddenly made the off-kilter songbird chirp — turning it angry, like a bird fighting with a rival.

Sejong complied. "A vowel is a sound produced by the unrestricted flow of air from the lungs to the throat, past the tongue and out the mouth."

Almost without thinking, Lady Hwang tried to demonstrate his point. "Ahh, uuu, ohh⋯."

Sejong nodded and continued the series, "Eee, ayyy."

And "consonants?" she interrupted.

"Everything else."

His 'secondary wife' scowled. She may have given up any hope of a husband's duty from him tonight but she was not in the mood for teasing. Sejong picked up on that immediately.

"The sound is obstructed. Partially blocked. By tongue, teeth, roof of mouth — who can say what else is going on in there?"

Lady Hwang considered for a moment. Then suddenly made a hard "K" sound. Sejong made a "Ch" back at her. Consonant for consonant. A playful dueling.

She moved closer to him. With a "Zzzz" buzzing sound. He responded with a "Bbb⋯." and mimed/pretended a wide-eyed fright at her sudden aggressiveness.

Lady Hwang got close enough to touch him, but they did not touch. She made a "Ppp" sound — her lips parting with the puff of air and the effect was erotic as she intended.

Sejong considered her for a long moment. Then was suddenly overcome with exhaustion. From this particular day — and from the weight of whatever his "Heaven-sent" mystery task might be. His eyes closed and he was instantly asleep.

Lady Hwang quietly leaned forward, lips close to his ear, as she completed their little exchange of sounds.

"Shhh⋯."

Then she watched him sleep. His chest rising and falling. Slowly. Even precariously. She slowed her own breathing until it was in sync with his. More in love with every breath⋯.

⁂

A long, high pile of rammed earth followed the shape of the wide river next to it, running from north to south as flowed the deep, slow-moving current, separating the territory of Ming China from the Korean peninsula to the east.

Two Korean travelers were on their way home. At least, they soon would be, if they managed to get through Customs at the Eastern Gate of China. The massive portal of brick and stone was set into the line of rammed earth like a jade pendant strung on a leather thong. As if to overcompensate for the rough composition of the wall proper on either side. This frontier border barricade paled in impressive intimidation in comparison with the other segments of the Great Wall that protected — more or less, typically less — China's interior from those on the exterior. But the Gate made up for it.

As the two men guided their lone cart and easy-going horse into the imposing passageway, they took stock of the artful construction, the multiple offensive and defensive offerings — portcullis on both ends, crossbow archers like nests of wasps, buckets lining the parapets that promised a sudden shower of boiling oil — all of which seemed a bit like overkill given how easy it would have been for an army to swarm over the dirt on both sides. But appearances were important in the maintenance of an Empire. And the traveling Koreans at least, seemed suitably impressed.

Or rather, canny enough travelers to appear so in the eyes of the gatekeepers. One of which examined the seal on their passage papers, speaking to them in Mandarin, the language of the Empire. "Returning to Korea?"

"We thank the great Ming for his hospitality," nodded Pyonghwa, the tallest of the pair, answering in a Mandarin a few notches less than he was capable of. No sense in adding an excellent command of the language to any list of reasons for suspicion.

"Oh," reacted the Gatekeeper dryly.

"And how was the Emperor?"

"I was speaking figuratively," replied the Korean with deference. "Regarding the hospitality of the Chinese people, as a whole. Under the benevolent rule of the Ming Emperor."

"Always the best of friends! Ming and Joseon!" added Maedu, the more cynical of the two, also in Mandarin. Then in Korean, "Let's get out of here."

The Gatekeeper ignored him, and continued to his assigned task, pulling a tarp away from their cart, revealing small stacks of flat dried seaweed. He broke a piece off, tasted it, then spat it out. Satisfied, or just bored with this job, he waved them on.

As Maedu goaded the horse and the Koreans and their cart headed out the gate, the Gatekeeper called after them derisively, "Say 'hello' to the King of Korea."

The travelers exited into the bright sunshine of a new day and onto the road towards the great river ahead of them, and the spectacularly lovely mountainous green terrain behind it. Their homeland.

Maedu shouted back over his shoulder, "We will say hello. And a lot more than that. Smug bastard."

As they headed towards Hanseong, the capital, and the King who had sent them on this journey and was thinking of them even now.

𝕮𝕮𝕮𝕮𝕮

If a flock of cranes had flown one thousand miles northwest in the other direction, high over Beijing, continuing over the defensive fortress of Datong, and leaving the Great Wall behind, it would have reached the grasslands of the Mongolian Steppe — which from their lofty vantage would have seemed like a sea upon the land. With the wind rippling across the infinite grasses as if across an ocean of water.

Descending from that elevation would have brought into view horses. Lots of them. Being ridden across those plains. Leaving tracks through the grass that in their own way were as clean and pure as the traceless flight of the cranes across the sky.

Hundreds of circular-shape tents appeared strewn across the landscape, organically, like tiny islands.

The roughly-dressed riders who galloped beyond and between these modest yurts, had, less than a hundred years earlier, been the rulers of the Chinese Empire.

To go back a few more years from the time of our story. Nearly three thousand or so, when China first appeared as a people and a political entity, there was, even then, and had never been since, a Center and a Periphery. The sovereign — a King or eventually an Emperor who ruled China — and those beyond his rule. Other, smaller kingdoms, of course, but mostly, and always, those bothersome horse-riding people and their tents. Apparently attached far more to their mounts than to the grasslands across which they navigated. But fond as well of anything they could take from China — by theft, negotiation, conquest.

The ebb and flow of this power dynamic ebbed and flowed for millennia, until it overflowed in the person of Genghis Khan, the chieftain who united the perpetually quarrelsome tribes of Mongols and took over the known world in the largest contiguous territorial landgrab in human history. Chinese resistance lasted until Genghis' grandson Kublai Khan moved into the Imperial Palace and declared himself Emperor of the newly-established Yuan dynasty. Which lasted about a hundred years — a momentary belch in the stomach of the dragon that is China.

Pushed out of the center by the Chinese internal rebellion that went on to become the Ming Dynasty, the Mongol ruling class left the Imperial life and its trappings behind: the fairy-like palaces of the Forbidden City, the precious commodities, the poetry and painting, the ancient philosophy and long-tested wisdom, the opera — and resumed their ancient lifestyle.

Horses. Grass. Yurts.

It goes without saying that like human languages — not one of which is any more advanced, superior or sophisticated than any other — no human culture is any less complex and internally rich than any other. And the semi-nomadic tribes of the Steppe were no different. Between and amidst those horses, grasses and yurts was a mythos no less deep than Chinese Taoism and a material culture no less capable of crafting a tiny horse and rider from bronze to rival in miniature the life-sized terracotta army of a buried Chinese Emperor.

But for the members of the Mongol ruling families, their ancient heritage was no longer enough.

To quote a lyric from the other side of the world, half a millennium into the future of this era, "How do you keep 'em down on the farm after they've seen Paree?"

Of course, no Mongol would be caught dead on a farm either. But that's beside the point. Their grandparents had conquered the known world and ruled from the Dragon Throne of the Imperial Palace of China. The very center of the center of the world.

To gallop across the grass was no longer enough.

"Khan," said the Chieftain known as Esen to his leader.

"My warriors grow restless. Don't you think it's time to conquer China? Again?"

They were inside the largest of the tents in this encampment, and Taisun Khan — the Western Khan — grand leader of this branch of Mongol tribesmen — was seated on a painted chair, slumped down, unhappy with what he was hearing from his foremost underling, the Taishi known as Esen. Esen was second-in-command, but the title of 'Taishi' connoted 'almost-Khan' — the qualifier because no matter how much he might have wrangled the bloodlines, there was just no way to convincingly trace his ancestry to Genghis Khan — the all-important qualification for supreme leadership of the Mongols, both West and East. So Esen would forever remain the power adjacent to whomever bore the title of Khan. Though that power was great indeed. And his superior had no choice but to respect and even fear it.

The male tribesmen scattered about the interior all had the recognizable shaved heads of their people, with an isolated, noticeable forelock. The women had strings and beads woven in their hair. All were engaged in drinking, eating, or at small tasks — but all listened at least with half-an-ear to the conversation between these two power centers.

The Khan grumbled, "To be bored with the Steppe, and the horse, is to be ready for death." It was a not — so veiled threat — even if it was bluster. "When our dynasty fell, we fell back into our old habits. West is west, East is east. We have nothing in common with the Eastern Mongols."

"We have a common enemy. The Ming."

Taisun Khan could not help but notice that everybody in the pavilion had stopped what they were doing and were listening intently. The Khan was content where he was in life. He knew his own limitations, knew what it took to mount a war. And knew he was incapable of doing it. Which meant that if there was to be a war, it would be Esen Taishi to rise to the occasion. The Khan knew must say something to shut down this discussion.

"Unite the tribes of the West and the tribes of the East," he said with false sincerity, knowing there was virtually no chance of accomplishing this. "And I will consider it."

There was a long silent moment in the pavilion. Then

everybody went back to whatever they were doing. In the belief as well, that the Khan had just asked for the impossible.

But the look in Esen's eyes said that this was all the permission he needed.

If that flock of cranes we followed earlier dutifully followed the change of seasons and flew back the other direction, towards the southwest, giving the painters and philosophers in the lands below something to paint and ponder — as such folk always did when cranes, with their alleged thousand-year lifespan and transcendent honking, the perennial stand-ins for Heaven, Immortality, and Goddesses and Gods too many to count — the feathery archetypes would have eventually left the Chinese mainland and the Korean peninsula, and winged it over Japan's Seto Inland Sea.

From that same lofty vantage point, among the innumerable mid-sized, small-sizes, and tiny islands below, could be seen three atolls several miles away from each other, arranged in a triangle, each rocky and forbidding, each crowned with a stone-walled fortress that looked impenetrable.

The waters around these islands perpetually churned. Everything about the setting had a suggestion of violence, both sudden and ruthlessly-planned.

This was the seascape of the Sea Lords of Japan. Island Ronin. Sea-going Samurai. Wokou. Or as they would have been called on the other side of the world: Pirates.

Three rival Murakami family sub-clans were based on those three imposing rocks: Noshima, Innoshima and Kurushima.

King Sejong had suppressed their raids against the Korean coast a couple of decades before the time of our story — and they had never forgotten⋯.

Above the crashing surf, a loud and raucous drumming came from one of the three islands — the accompaniment to a boating contest. Not a race, but a test of skill.

The waters immediately surrounding the small island were at mid-tide — currents and waves crashing violently against each other, shifting direction wildly and unpredictably. The nearly impossible to negotiate currents were part of the natural defenses of these islands.

Three small skiffs waited just outside the torturous waters churning between them and dry shore. Each was operated by one man with a long pole. Suddenly, the drumming stopped.

On that cue, the first oarsman shot off towards the dangerous waters and the island finish line. He barely lasted three seconds until the impetuous waters upended his boat and sent him flying into the water.

On shore, a couple of dozen roughly-dressed onlookers roared their approval of this dunking failure.

Seated among them — on the only chair — was Sea Lord Red. He looked like a wilder version of a Samurai chieftain or Shogun, characterized by the bright crimson accents to his clothing — and his armor when he went raiding. A servant waved a huge fan to generate a breeze against the Lord's stony face. It was a face that never smiled. Certainly not in public.

As the first sailor was being assisted out of the water by a couple of his fellows, the Sea Lord spoke one quiet word. "Again."

An Attendant repeated the command with a shout for the benefit of the Drummers behind them. "Again!"

The drumming renewed. As Sea Lord Red calmly raised his hand off to one side.

After several seconds of loud drumming that built the tension and excitement, he dropped that hand: silence.

In the distance, the second skiff responded, surging forwards towards the beach. Getting smashed back and forth by the currents, the oarsman jammed his pole into water below him, pushing off from the sand beneath — and barely managed to stay afloat, getting closer to the shore. The onlookers cheered and shouted him on.

Then two currents erupted upwards into waves twisting against each other — it seemed barely possible for water to behave like this — the oarsman's face went white with panic — as his small craft was snapped in half.

The man was plunged into the water. And didn't come up. Everyone waited in silence. Then the tide sent the man's body shooting up along the sand, depositing him at the Sea Lord's feet.

Everyone was dead silent. The jaw muscles of the Sea Lord tighten with suppressed emotion. It was as if some god of the waters was sending his challenge right back at him. But rather than intimidated, the man gave off a low rumble like a growl and kept the challenge going.

"Again."

The Attendant took up the command, "Again!" The drummer pounded; the Sea Lord raised his arm.

The pilot of the last remaining skiff stood with his long guiding pole ready — but he was not alone: a small, ten-year-old boy — his son — was seated in the bottom of the boat, his expression opaque.

We will call this man and boy: Shark and Pup.

The Sea Lord dropped his arm, the drumming stopped.

Shark jammed down with his pole and sent his skiff shooting away — not directly at the shore, but at an oblique angle. Already his style and skill seemed apart from the first two failures.

It was an incredible contest of human versus sea: with every crash of wave and twist of current and ripping tide, Shark managed to both go with the flow but resist just enough to negotiate the waters — while inching closer and closer to the shore.

At one point, the boat was spun around 360 degrees — then once more — in the opposite direction.

Onlookers shouted and cheered and were aghast at each moment. The Sea Lord keeps his iron demeanor, but his eyes were wide and riveted.

Pup stayed utterly silent, never speaking — and his father never spoke to him or indeed paid him any attention at all. The boy, however, did not just hold on for dear life — he seemed to be shifting his own weight in subtle ways, helping his father as he piloted. But the child stayed so expressionless that this impression might have been an observer's imagination····.

Finally, as they seemed in reach of the finish line of the shore, Shark saw a sudden crest erupting, about to sideswipe them — there was no way it would not capsize the boat.

Without a word, Shark dropped into the base of the boat pulling the boy down with him — and tossed his pole overboard.

The onlookers cried out as the wave hit — and the tiny craft was churned under the water.

There was a long, tense moment. As the god of the waters seemed to have swallowed them whole. Then the skiff rolled back into view, righting itself with the passing wave.

Shark stood, pulling his son up with him. Completely soaked in water but now in the clear. As the boat slowly washed ashore in victory. The onlookers cheered wildly, the drummers pounded and pounded.

The discarded oar washed up with the next wave — and Shark reached down to retrieve it without breaking stride.

Father and son walked up to Sea Lord Red who had remained silently seated the entire ordeal, expressionless, stopping before the 'throne'. Shark gave a bow of his head.

The boy's face was blank as ever. He seemed not to know enough to bow. Not completely aware of his surroundings. The child was clearly without hearing, but an observer might have also thought him mentally impaired, so disengaged he seemed to be. Shark gently put his hand on the back of Pup's head and guided him into a head bow — and the boy did not resist.

The Sea Lord stared at both of them for a moment. Then gave a slight nod of approval.

As the most faithful and adept of the Lord's retainers — this was all the reward Shark could have wanted.

෬෬෬෬෬

A third of the way down the Korean peninsula, at a resting stop at the Sokka Pagoda at the Myohyang Mountain, the travelers Pyonghwa and Maedu rested. At the base of a cylindrical Buddhist tower that was some thirty feet high, seven in diameter, narrowing towards the top in a step-wise fashion, festooned permanently with over a hundred tiny bronze bells all the way up. It would have appeared to a modern eye a bit like a tall, thin, granite 'Christmas tree' hung with chimes.

Maedu considered the small bells — still and quiet. He scowled, as was his default facial position, "How many times have we rested under this thing?"

"Five trips to China," calculated his companion.

"We stop on the going and on the return. Simple arithmetic."

"Twelve times!"

"Or ten."

"And not once, a breeze!" Maedu intensified the scowl.

"We've never even heard the bells."

Pyonghwa considered for a moment.

"That is my recollection as well."

Maedu took a closer look.

"There must be a hundred of them."

"One hundred and four."

"Why would you know that?"

"It is a thing that is known."

"And not a sound!" shouted Maedu.

"Maybe the Heaven doesn't smile on our missions? Have you considered that?"

"The King does. That is all the smile I care about."

Maedu looks annoyed. "You and everybody else. Maybe that smile is overrated."

Pyonghwa remained unperturbed — as was his nature. His voice was ever calm and always pleasant.

"And maybe you should be tortured in ten thousand hells for that statement. Then reincarnated as a toad."

"Confucianists do not believe in hells and reincarnation. Or anything else."

"'Believing'" in nothing, we can make a rhetorical point with anything," answered Pyonghwa. "In this case, that point is: how dare you speak against our sovereign?" Despite the confrontational words, his voice remained nothing but kindly.

But Maedu just shrugged him off. "His Majesty is made of tears and dirt. Like anybody else. The bureaucracy criticizes his every move. Why can't I? When I am victim to every wild goose chase he commands?"

It was clear from their conversation that these were no mere hard-scrambling traders hoping to eke out some kind of livelihood from carrying sundry sundries back and forth between Joseon and Ming. They were, in fact, language interpreters in the personal circle of King Sejong, sent by him on seemingly capricious missions whose significance was known only to the King.

Maedu indicated the pagoda they were leaned up against. "Ten times or ten thousand by the time he's done with us!" He suddenly stood up. "I'm hungry."

He moved to the small cart. The horse, head down and grazing, didn't take notice as the interpreter rummaged around the supplies they were carrying.

Pyonghwa continued the conversation. "Perhaps His Majesty commands these 'goose chases' of us because His Majesty values our efforts ten thousand times more than what the bureaucracy can offer?"

Maedu paused for a moment. It was a valid idea. Even if he was not in the mood to consider it. "I'm still hungry."

He pulled out a sheet of dried seaweed to make a 'roll' of sorts with some cooked rice and fermented vegetables. As he did so, his movements revealed a pile of manuscript pages neatly hidden among the sheets of dried seaweed.

Smuggled from China.

"Border patrol never checks under the seaweed," he mused. The purloined pages were covered in exotic foreign writing — nothing like the Chinese characters in use in Ming and Joseon. The symbols snaked in and around a diagram of a cannon.

And a formula for gunpowder.

Was this information — apparently stolen from somewhere in China — part of King Sejong's mysterious project?

Maedu completed construction of the meal an handed some to his compatriot. He took a couple of big bites and again considered the silent bells on the pagoda, addressing them directly, as if they were listening. "Make some noise! This is your last chance to give a good impression of yourselves."

"An unsupported assumption on your part," said Pyonghwa. "The King will surely send us out again. And again."

Sejong, with his seemingly insatiable intellectual interests, had not infrequently sent officially sanctioned and budgeted scholarly journeys to China, the storehouse of ancient knowledge. But the multiple and typically mysterious missions of the two interpreters, for reasons known only to the King, he kept off the books — and unrecorded in the historical annals. Which never set well with Maedu.

"Enough is enough," he said.

"Will you say that to his magnanimous face?"

"Absolutely! We are not his trained monkeys! Jumping through another hoop"

"Trained monkeys typically play musical instruments and dance in imitation of humanity," offered Pyonghwa.

"Dogs and horses jump through hoops."

"Well, I will be the first monkey to do it! Try to stop me."

His companion shook his head. "How did you ever pass our Certification Examinations?"

"Studied my monkey's ass off. Like everybody else." Maedu stared up at the nearest bell. Blew on it hard. Nothing. He scowled yet again. Deeply as his face could manage. In a display of annoyance to his comrade across the grass, to any flock of cranes that might be overhead, to the Buddha himself if he happened to be glancing this way.

A rocket launcher sent its burning missile arching under the bright sun. The same artillery piece that had been in operation during the war-game siege at the fortress. The daylight revealed more details of the technology: each *hwacha* battery was a two-person operated, two-wheeled cart that carried an upright board of thick wood drilled with dozens of cylindrical holes, each holding an arrow. Fully loaded, with the multiple fuses all lit and burning down, the apparatus fairly bristled with death-dealing potential.

With a crackle and a WHOOSH, the arrows fired in a blaze of sparks and literal fire — looking not much different taking off than the American 4th of July or Asian Lunar New Year rockets of today that are its technological kin.

The secret firing range was half-a-morning's ride outside of the capital. Sejong and his two Generals — one who had been on his team during the war games, and one who had played the enemy — were here as well, along with his Security Chief and a small staff of adjutants and support staff. All watched the cloud of arrows ascend higher and higher and higher; then plummet, smashing into distant targets — exploding a moment later. It was always a dramatic display of raw power and technological achievement. But this was only the 'before' picture.

Sejong nodded to the artillerymen, who brought out dozens of thin metal tubes — the exact objects the King had watched being pounded out by the Taoist Swordsmith in his forge.

They rapidly inserted the tubes into the firing holes of the launcher — into which they fit like inner sleeves, each looking like the barrel of a gun when installed.

Supreme General Yi Chun looked doubtful.

"The iron will increase the weight of the carriage."

"That is correct," agreed Sejong.

"But the trade-off will be worth it."

He indicated the firing tubes as the arrows were now being re-loaded. "Wood binds with wood — seeking the company of its own kind," he reasoned, extrapolating from the 'scientific' concepts of the era regarding friction and hardness. "Metal overcomes wood — as a small ax can fell the tallest tree. Wood, therefore, will rush to escape from any hint of metal."

The loading was complete — and the King completed his thought. "Faster and further, then, the wooden arrow: in panicked flight from the metal firing tube."

He nodded to the artillerymen, who quickly lit the fuses at the base of each arrow.

"If I am correct," he said lightly,

"The range should be doubled."

WHOOSH! The missiles again shot away in a sparking fury. The small group watched the arrows soar over the targets that the first volley struck — finally smashing into a second set of targets set up twice as far away. Then, as always, there was a tense beat — followed by fiery blasts as each arrow's individual packet of gunpowder exploded.

Everybody was suitably impressed.

The Security Chief smiled, "When is Your Majesty not correct?" It was less the remark of a toady — Sejong did not encourage toadyism — and more a rhetorical question spoken almost as a jest. Because indeed: When was Sejong not correct? About anything? In the three decades he had reigned?

Any military officer, any scholar, any government minister in Joseon who could have glimpsed the diagram-covered manuscripts hidden between layers of dried seaweed by the two traveling Korean interpreters might well have concluded that this range-extending munitions development was the King's 'mystery project' If indeed, mystery project it was — rather than a series of random pursuits resulting from creeping dementia.

In fact, despite the practical and highly strategic value of this technological advancement — this confidential test half-a-morning from the palace was all a diversion. A 'secret project' to hide something more secret still.

Suddenly, one of the security officers cleared his voice to get everyone's attention. When they turned to him, the officer indicated in the distance an itinerant peddler, his multi-functional wooden backpack stacked with folk medicines and his own supplies. The old man seemed scared to death — he knew he was in the wrong place at the wrong time. That he shouldn't have seen this. The man turned and fled behind a rise.

The Supreme General was more intrigued than alarmed. "A spy?"

"Or a seller of remedies," offered Sejong.

The Security Chief frowned, "We will know soon enough."

"Ask him if he has something to help me sleep," said the King.

The Security Chief nodded at his Officer, who rushed with another man after the peddler/potential spy.

"Something for the pain in my limbs," continued Sejong with irony, as the two security men vanished over the rise in pursuit. "And something for my eyes," he finished.

The Military Advisor standing next to the King spoke up. "Surely, no such medicine is needed. Your Majesty is in the prime of life. And sees all the way to the mind of Heaven itself."

Sejong turned to consider the distant targets once again.

The objects were a hopeless blur to him. The King was almost certainly going blind.

The King's eyes — to any who might have observed

them closely enough, here, in the bright sunlight — appeared clear and shining. No one knew the trouble behind them. He turned to his Military Adviser, nodding with irony, "I will not say that you are wrong." That phrase was frequently his rhetorical, half-joking answer to all who praised his accomplishments, his condition, his state of being.

But this time, he was lying.

꒰꒱꒰꒱꒰꒱

On the Steppe, Esen Taishi — Chieftain of this local Mongol band under the auspices of the Khan of the West — maneuvered his favorite horse in a tight circle opposite his favorite wife who was doing the same. They 'waltzed' in this way — wheeling their animals first in one direction then the other — to a tune played on string and flute by two men who stood nearby, for the benefit of the small crowd of fellow tribe members and their own enjoyment.

Scattered tents, tribal women, men, children made up this large camp — and horses. Always horses. More numerous than human beings.

The dance came to a raucous conclusion, both husband and favorite wife leapt down from their horses to finish with a flourish. All cheered. As everybody went back to their activities, the Chieftain joined his closest companions — a dozen fellow warriors — gathered nearby.

"I have crafted a new toy," he announced, as if to continue the entertainment — or ease their idleness — as he took up a bow and a quiver of arrows. His companions reacted with interest. Anything to relieve the boredom. But one of them, whom we will call the Mongol Agent — paid particularly close attention. Deadly serious attention. Knowing full well that Esen never did anything without a very specific motivation that often resulted in...a results. Of the coldly calculated kind.

The Chieftain pulled a special-looking arrow from his quiver, showing off the peculiar color and arrangement of the feather fletching and curious cuts to the metal head.

"My 'singing arrow'," he said, suddenly notching and letting it fly. The arrow sped towards one of several practice targets nearby, emitting a loud humming and whistling sound as it went, before striking the target with a satisfying thunk.

The warriors were bemused. They considered in

silence for a moment.

"Why warn our enemies?" asked one of them.

Esen made a chirrup sound with his mouth and his favorite horse moved to his side in answer. He patted it lovingly on the neck.

"No warning. But a game. For us." He indicated the various targets in front of them. "Arm yourselves."

The dozen men took up their bows and arrows.

"At the sound of my arrow, you are to aim and release at whatever I have struck."

The warriors still didn't see why he was asking this of them — but they were accustomed to his quirky personality and requests. The Chieftain suddenly shot another 'singing arrow' at a target — it hummed loudly and struck the mark.

The other warriors with blinding speed did the same. But the Mongol Agent was quickest to comply — and the most accurate in his shot.

"A game," repeated Esen, suddenly smacking his favorite horse on the flank. It started away from him at a startled trot. He then gave a whistle and on that command the animal stopped and wheeled to face its master.

Then the Chieftain raised his bow and loosed another 'singing' arrow: It whistled loudly through the air — and struck the horse right in the chest.

A shocking moment. Then suddenly, the Mongol Agent followed suit — and so did the rest of the companions — shooting their own arrows into the hapless animal.

As it fell, it became clear that two of the men had not released their arrows — they were too surprised and too disturbed by the order. They stood with bows held loosely in their hands, arrows unnotched.

The Chieftain instantly moved to them, drawing a curved sword as he went, and killed each of them with one stroke continuing across both throats.

As the men hit the ground dying, the remaining warriors stared at their leader, stunned and confused by what just happened. But he dispelled that reaction with a shrug.

"A simple game."

Only the Mongol Agent kept his emotions to himself — his face unreadable.

⊱⊰⊱⊰⊱

It was always a thrill for the young scholars of the Hall of Worthies when the King paid them a visit. No matter how many times a week it might have happened; no matter how many hours of the day he might have stayed. Or night. Or even those times when Sejong spent day and night — and woke up with his head lying on the floor next to a reading desk. Lamp long burned out and supplanted by the rays of the dawn.

Sejong's father had established this 15th century Korean equivalent of a think-tank, but it was an institution in name only until Sejong assumed the throne and turned it into a working prospect. They had accomplished much together. From practical inventions to legal justifications to ritual clarification, the scholars had taken up whatever problem he had presented and inevitably delivered the results that he wanted. Surprising even themselves by the success Sejong managed to coax out of them.

But now? In the last decade or so, the King had brought younger and more esoterically-inclined intellectuals into the fold: Multi-lingual experts on ancient texts of mysterious origins, specialists in manuscripts covered with characters, symbols, and lettering from all peoples of the known world — and some that were barely known, thought mythical, even unheard of.

The King's men were flattered at first by the attention, by being taken serious in their capacities, by how much he seemed to rely on them, how greatly they seemed to carry his hopes.

But what exactly was he hoping for?

As the years went on, his assignments and requests seemed more and more whimsical. Motivated not by a genuine goal but passing fascinations.

Then the King began to include students and graduates of the Interpreters' School — polyglots who spoke not just their native Korean, but flawless Chinese and Mongolian, with Jurchen and Japanese and more far-flung languages that the most adept of them learned with the same ease a normal person learns to eat an unusual new fruit. More significantly, these were not members of the aristocracy as were those admitted to the Hall after great academic efforts and superlative scores on the General and Royal Examinations. The foreign language folks were Jungin — 'middle people' — whose work as mid-level government functionaries or skilled specialists ranging from accountants and astronomers to military officers and musicians raised them above the level of lower strata of commoners. But in the eyes of the Yangban — the aristocrats who occupied the Hall of Worthies — sharing with these upstarts the scholar's physical space and far more crucially, their time with their Sovereign, was tantamount to an insult.

And so these young scholars of the Hall of Worthies grew cynical, in spite of their otherwise fanatical devotion to the King. Were they being asked to chase after the daydreams of an increasingly eccentric ruler who was surrounding himself with increasingly eccentric and decidedly unworthy individuals?

As Sejong pored over the stack of manuscripts that the interpreters Pyonghwa and Maedu had smuggled out of China, the expression on Maedu's face seemed to indi-cate that those doubts were met from the other side as well: he was never comfortable among those who truly belonged here — as he did not.

The scholars gathered round in the large chamber that served as library and study room for the Hall.

"But this is wonderful," said the King. Interpreter Pyonghwa

accepted the royal gratitude with barely contained pride — even Maedu's perpetually cranky mood seemed to lift momentarily.

As Sejong leafed through the various pages, revealing a wide range of materials and sources: Pages torn from books, raw manuscripts, rubbings of grave markers, impressions of jade seals — the scholars pressed closer for a look.

"Why does it smell like dried seaweed?" wondered the Hungry Scholar nicknamed Hyollo — a young man incapable of study unless it was accompanied by a meal.

Maedu scowled, knowing the other's predilections. "Please don't eat the manuscripts."

A couple of the other young scholars seemed impressed but bewildered.

"Munitions, medicine, records of rainfall, positions of the planets," observed the Choe Hang — known to his colleagues as 'Number One' for having finished in first place at his Royal Examination. "Your Majesty has set his aim···wide." But there was doubt in his voice.

"As wide-ranging as His Majesty's accomplishments, over the years," said Scholar Shin Sukju cheerily, ignoring the doubt.

"Indeed," said Sejong. "And now, it is time to fill in some of the gaps in our knowledge. For posterity."

The scholars all reacted to this apparent reference to his mortality.

The youngest among them, Yi Gae — called the Bookbug because he rarely lifted his face up from one — objected. "Many more years surely lie ahead of Your Majesty? Posterity can wait."

They all laughed — a bit anxiously. But Linguist Pak Paengnyeon — a young man who had thrown himself into the study of language and phonology as soon it had become clear that Sejong was heading that direction in his own interests — ignored all other speculations for his new specialty. "I count seven different scripts here. That of Tibet, the Uigur, Mongol, that of the monk." Phags-pa, two types of Ancient Seal stamps, and something I do not even recognize." He indicated some bits of Latin rubbed off a grave marker.

Sejong kept his response sunny. "The knowledge we seek is ever recorded in multiple ways."

But King's eyes made contact with that of young Pak, and seemed to add silent import as he finished his thought. "The methods do not require special attention. Or even comment."

The Linguist took this as a subtle warning to not pursue the topic any further. He silently nodded his understanding.

But the King was already on to the next step, announcing to everyone present, "Please make copies for me? Of everything here."

The scholars nodded and assented to the command:

"Yes, Your Majesty."

"Of course, Your Majesty."

"Right away, Your Majesty."

Sejong turned to exit the Hall, motioning casually to Pyonghwa and Maedu. "Gentlemen···. I must thank you again for your efforts···."

They immediately moved to follow him.

And as the three continued into the covered pathway just outside, it seemed clear that Sejong's entreaty to gratitude was just a way to get them alone and out of the earshot of their colleagues.

He immediately got to the point. "A certain scholar, exiled from Beijing to Liaodong, is rumored to have a Mongol rhyming dictionary. Complete and exquisitely executed."

Maedu's face fell — he could see where this was going. He just stared — not at the King, but at his partner — who said nothing.

Finally, Maedu spoke up. "The Mongols have been chased out of China back into the arms of their horses. What is the use of a Mongol dictionary of rhymes? Begging Your Majesty's pardon."

"My pardon seems to have been an afterthought."

Sejong kept his voice even.

Pyonghwa came to the rescue. "Your Majesty, we have

been long on the road. My traveling companion knows not his place."

"My place is on the road, clearly," interjected Maedu.

Sejong pretended to take him at his word.

"Excellent. I knew I could count on you. Again."

As they rounded a corner along the pathway, Sejong continued to fill them in. "Our scholar is said to be eccentric. But agreeable if said eccentricities are accommodated."

He stopped walking; the two weary travelers followed suit. He took their hands in his. "When can you leave?"

It was a rhetorical question.

ಲಾಲಾಲಾ

Another day on the Steppe. Another day, in Esen Tai-shi's mind, condemned to the prison of knowing that his tribe's territory at exactly this moment was as far as his eye could see. But no further.

The Chieftain calmly turned a single-stemmed rose flower over in his hands, inexplicably seeming to study it; as his warrior companions ate and drank a mid-day meal. A short distance away, four of Esen's wives shared laughter and buttered tea amongst themselves.

"A simple game," said the Chieftain quietly. At those words, the Mongol Agent was suddenly at high alert. The other warriors took another moment to register the implication of the Chieftain's words. And the easy-going meal was suddenly fraught with unease. They stopped eating.

"Golden Rose," Esen called out to his favorite wife. She turned at her name and smiled. "Dance with me."

She stood up and he tossed the rose in his hand through the air — she ran to catch it.

A terrible humming pierced the atmosphere — and one of the Chieftain's 'singing' arrows buried itself in her chest. A fraction of a second later, a second arrow did the same in the exact spot.

Esen still had his bow in hand and so did the Agent — who had been ready for this and had instantly shot the second arrow.

Before the startled young woman even registered what had happened — before the pain could overcome the shock and call out to her brain — multiple arrows struck her, loosed by the rest of the warriors. Some of whom cried out in emotion as they let go the strings.

Then the Chieftain's 'favorite' toppled to the ground, dead. He turned to find one of his men shaking with terror, bow and unloosed arrow still in hand — he could not bring himself to shoot her. A flash of the Chieftain's sword, and the man fell dead.

"Traitor." Esen threw the sword to the ground and walked away.

This time, the Mongol Agent's face was indeed readable: he seemed to be thinking ahead, wondering where this increasingly disturbing 'game' might be headed.

◈◈◈◈◈

The Queen had called Lady Hwang to her bedchamber in the dead of night. Being called for by royalty was always one thing or the other. One was praise and elevation of status, the other chastisement and at the far end being encouraged to take poison before bed. A consort at all times must be ready for either. But in the dead of night, which was more likely? Lady Hwang's natural optimism carried her into the chamber, despite the potential for a disagreeable outcome.

"You must allow the king to do what he wishes tonight," the Queen told her, "…With your body."

Lady Hwang was taken aback by this — but did not object. "Yes, Your Highness!"

"Even if it seems···strange."

"Yes, Your Highness!"

"Do not be afraid."

"I won't be, Your Highness!"

The Queen considered the over-eager young woman — who seemed barely able to contain her frustrated physical desires. Rather than treat her as a rival — as all secondary wives are potential rivals in the game of succession — the Queen seemed to have a different agenda.

She clasped Lady Hwang's hands and smiled with encouragement and something much like affection.

"I believe you."

Lady Hwang had first entered the Inner Palace as part of a promise the King had made to the cousin of the uncle of a powerful official who had frequently made Sejong's life easier over the decades — especially with respect to excusing in public Assembly the inordinate amount of time the monarch had spent on intellectual pursuits that bent the spirit if not the letter of Confucian-sanctioned areas of knowledge. The young woman had no distinguishing qualities — not beauty, nor intellect; she tripped on her feet and could not carry a tune — but something about her had apparently caught the King's desires, for he spent an inordinate amount of time over the past couple of years sequestered with Lady Hwang in his chambers, calling for her at all hours of the night and day. The other consorts and their staff speculated about this to no end. Wondering if the woman had some carnal abilities that no one but the King was privy to — or even if she had some kind of sorcerous hold on him.

But the truth of it was, the otherwise undistinguished young woman was nothing but this: Utterly agreeable. To whatever seemingly random, trivial, even possibly ludicrous request that Sejong asked of her. And for reasons known only to the King — and the Queen — that quality was exactly what he most needed of⋯somebody. That somebody happened to be her.

A couple of hours later, Lady Hwang was seated on the King's bed, as he held a tiny oil lamp with reflector attached to bounce light into her mouth — which he inspected closely as she opened her jaws wide.

"Ahhhhh."

Sejong took a look then asked for another sound.

"Eeeee."

Lady Hwang complied. "Eeeeee."

"Wider please."

The consort tried to force her mouth open further. The King put his face close as he could — staring inside.

"Once more: Eeeee."

"Eeeee."

Then she started coughing — too much saliva had collected in her throat from this exercise.

"Forgive me," said the King. But he looked frustrated. He turned away from her, thinking.

"Lady Hwang's fault Your Majesty!" exclaimed the young woman. "Please try again!"

"No. We are finished for the evening."

His most recent and certainly last secondary wife was upset by this. "Once more! I can do it! Whatever it is! That we are doing!"

"Go to sleep," he said gently.

She was suddenly encouraged. And indicated the bed. "Here?"

"Where you wish."

She excitedly turned from him to ready the bed for the both of them. "Lady Hwang promises not to make any more sounds this night. So Your Majesty may⋯."

She turned back to him, but he was gone. He had slipped out while she was talking.

"⋯Sleep." She finished the sentence.

She was alone in the bedroom. With only her thwarted desires for company.

The King had taken the few steps it took to enter the Chamber of the Water Clock, a marvelous, even miraculous invention whose inventing he himself had directed many years before, and only recently had ordered moved to its location across the corridor from where he slept and dreamed. The palace staff assumed he was on a tight schedule of study and government business, and so required the close reckoning of the time that the clock provided. But it was more than that.

He stared up at the massive wooden and metal construction that towered over three times his height, nearly up to the ceiling: an intricately engineered apparatus of clay pots and bronze cylinders; wooden troughs and levers; flowing water and rolling metal balls and painted dolls. The 15th century Korean equivalent of a Rube Goldberg contraption on first glance — a closer look would reveal one of the most advanced time-keeping devices in the world.

Sejong considered it just as he would a living being. Familiar. Like an old confidant or even friend. He called it by name.

"Yeong Sil. Why must you hurry so?"

This was the real reason the King had moved the clock across from this bedroom. He missed the man who had invented it. A servant who had been elevated by way of the King's shockingly contemporary ideals of meritocracy into a position of great power and responsibility: Essentially, Chief Scientist of the Joseon Dynasty.

And, with the exception of Choe Malli of the Confucian Academy, Sejong's only true friend in life. And in death. Politics had ripped Yeong Sil away from the King, sent him to prison and out of the historical record.

But here, in every formed and shaped element of wood and metal, clay and water — formed and shaped by Yeong Sil's own hands — seemed to Sejong were the very bones and blood of his dear friend.

He slowly ascended the wooden stairs leading to the upper level of the device. And as he went, the water flowed past him, from clay pots to bronze cylinders; various levers were struck by the falling water; which turned wheels and sent metal spheres coursing along, in accord with gravity's song.

"It is said," mused Sejong, "That the life of a human being is all but over even before it is begun. Like glimpsing a horse through a crack in a garden wall, as it gallops past⋯."

He reached the top level even as another small metal sphere was dropped with a clack onto a wooden trough and rolled past Sejong, fell through a hole at the end of its passage, and dropped to land with a louder clack below, triggering the next scene of this temporal mechanical pantomime.

"Can you not⋯slow down?" He said softly. As if his dead friend was Time itself.

Three carved and painted wooden dolls went into motion — the penultimate stage in this process. One banged a drum, the next struck a cymbal, the next hammered a gong.

"Just a little? For your King? For your friend?" The figures continued sounding the hour. "I need more time. Or I will fail."

It seemed that the spirit of Yeong Sil — if indeed spirits exist, if indeed one might inhabit a room-sized contraption for banging out the hours — was the only entity other than the Queen who knew what the King was so desperately trying to accomplish. The last thing he must do, before he could allow himself to die.

The clock did not answer him.

Sejong descended the steps as the climax of this process — the actual registering of the exact time — was finally activated:

A small door opened on the side of the device, and

a 12-inch-tall wooden doll emerged into view, holding the hour marker in its hands.

The face of the doll had been carved to look like Sejong.

That detail had been a whimsical suggestion from the King to his friend the Inventor — but now, as he felt time running out, it seemed a kind of cosmic mockery.

As he exited the room the massive clock shut down behind him with a series of clanking movements — the dolls went back into their resting positions, the balls stopped falling, the levers were still. As everything reset for the next cycle.

And a young eunuch stepped out from the shadows of the room where he had hidden himself from the King. He held a rag and jar of oil in his hands — was here in the dead of night for upkeep on the Water Clock, as punishment for neglecting this task during the day.

He resumed the assignment, rubbing the oil into the wood of the support beams. But he was no longer thinking about all the other things he had been thinking about other than the repetitive job in front of him. He was thinking about what kind of a ruler talks to a Water Clock in the middle of the night.

Sejong had gone outside to stare at the reflection of the sliver of moon in a small pool of water built just for just that purpose. His own face stared back at him in frustration. Like an artist who could not figure out the one last step to the masterpiece he was painting.

He reached out and moved his hand around in the water, tracing a circle — sending the moon and stars into a kind of dance across the reflection of his face.

Then moon and stars and face dissolved into the same dream image that had both haunted and comforted him since before he had learned to walk: the gently falling green leaves⋯.

"Your Majesty!" Dong Woo found him lying unconscious next to the pool. It was dawn. The Water Clock had sounded the pairs of hours all through the night. Not once had the King stirred.

"Ah⋯. Good morning," said Sejong.

But there was nothing good, thought the eunuch, about finding the King like this.

The Royal Physician palpated his royal patient's wrist, checking his pulse. Then he observed the eyes, the pallor, the breath.

"Your Majesty has not been entirely revelatory to his subjects," he told the King.

Sejong considered his own wrist. "My pulse does not lie."

"No, Your Majesty. It does not."

"Master Confucius claimed that three things cannot long remain hidden: the sun, the moon and the truth." Sejong gave a sigh of the inevitable. "Who am I to say he was wrong?"

The highest-ranking members of Sejong's government had been called to the Assembly Hall for a special announcement by the King. The ministers wore red; the scholars blue. Sejong stood before them in Royal yellow, wearing the filigree gold indicator of rule that was more a headdress than a crown.

Everyone was properly deferential in demeanor as he spoke. But to be a King of the Joseon dynasty in 15th century Korea was not at all to be an absolute ruler or what the world would eventually call a dictator — nothing at all like the all-powerful Chinese Emperor in Beijing, sixty days ride from here.

For Sejong's political power was checked on all sides — from his ministers and his advisors; from a powerful aristocracy and the bureaucracy whose official positions they all filled — to the academicians and scholars who made up the Hall of Worthies he prized so highly. All of them inevitably had something to say about the way things should be going. The way the King himself should be performing his duties. That was part of their job description. And they wouldn't take without objection what the king now was saying. He expected as much.

"The infirmities of advanced age and the insults of multiple afflictions have deeply diminished the ability to fulfil my duties to the administration of this state. Indeed, I am now unable to continue in full capacity as your King."

He paused, and the wind could be heard across the flagstones, in the snapping of the flags and the rustling of the robes of all those assembled here. But the faces of those present were in shock.

Choe Malli was more stunned than anybody. He

glanced at Chief Councilor Hwang Hui who gave him a puzzled look. This had caught both of them completely off-guard.

But it hit Choe harder. And personally. How could the King — his King, give up the throne? And how could he, Choe Malli, the tutor of Sejong's own sons, the King's advisor and even friend — how could he not have been told earlier? Not pulled into the decision-making, asked for the advice he had always given?

"From this day forward, the Crown Prince will rule in my stead," continued Sejong.

Seated at his side, the Crown Prince had a face as kindly as his father's — but he was in his 20s and not even remotely capable of what the King was now proposing. He did his best to keep his features firm but not unshakeable. A facial expression he hoped would generate confidence in his abilities and accord with what the King was now proposing. He was, however, terrified.

"I will step away from the throne," continued the King.

"To an advisory capacity only. On military affairs. And anything else the Crown Prince will require of me. As I retire, and wait for my death." He paused and steeled himself for the vociferous reactions he knew were coming. "It has been my pleasure to serve as your King"

"Your Majesty. Please withdraw this proposal." Choe's was the first voice to be raised in objection. He kept his tone quiet but strong. Giving expression to all those here present who did not want to see the King abdicate — but were too timid to be first to challenge him.

Everyone swiveled their eyes to stare at Choe without turning their heads. Several silent, intense seconds passed. Then suddenly the crowd erupted.

"Your Majesty is still young! Please withdraw this proposal!" shouted an official.

"Your Majesty's good health is for all to see! Please withdraw this proposal!" chimed a second.

A scholar leaned forward. "Your Majesty! A divided rule is unwieldy and problematic. The history of our own Kingdom attests to this fact"

Sejong flashed with a rare display of anger. "Am I a liar then? And a fool? How can this be a mere difference of opinion?"

Scattered and increasing shouts came from the Assembly as members became more emboldened by their combined resistance, and started throwing themselves onto the ground for emphasis.

"Withdraw this proposal, Your Majesty!"

"Your Majesty, reconsider!"

"Your Majesty, please!"

Choe spoke with great conviction.

"May Your Majesty reign for a thousand years."

Those nearby echoed that stock phrase:

"A thousand years! A thousand years!"

Until the entire Assembly shouted together,

"A thousand years!"

Even the Crown Prince could not resist, adding his voice with tears in his eyes. "A thousand years!"

Sejong just stood there. As the chant continued. He had lost this battle. But the war — for whatever his personal agenda might be — was not over.

Sejong and Choe locked eyes: King's number one scholar and biggest supporter had just set himself on a collision course with his sovereign.

A conflict that could only end in death. And both seemed to realize that at the same moment in time.

CENTENARY

A massive camp on the eastern Steppe had formed across the prairie composed of the clans of the west and the clans of the east — like great schools of fish brought together by the ocean currents.

In this case, that prevailing and undeniable flow was the impending marriage of the Eastern Khan to a new wife intended to fortify his alliance with a tribe whose territory occasionally overlapped with his own — enough, given the eddies and tides of those loosely defined borders, to cause conflicts the Eastern Khan had no patience for. The days of world-beating glory were past, he believed, but the resumption of local bloodshed and bickering seemed to him a chore — and a bore.

These days, it was practically a sport: every clan uncle and tribal cousin sought to claim some kind of descent from Genghis Khan — dead now for over 200 years. But now that he had achieved the highest rank that seemed possible in this life, the Eastern Khan wasn't interested in playing the game any longer. Two centuries had been long enough for the human being behind the legend to be mythologized to such a degree that at times the greatest conqueror the Mongols — or any nation — would hope to field had taken on the dimensions and reputation of Tengri himself, God of All the Sky.

Why live in the past or the future, thought the Eastern Khan? When he owned ten thousand horses and slept with ten times ten wives and had produced offspring beyond counting. And now, a new wife about to hove into view. What could be better than life now?

A boisterous, celebratory atmosphere prevailed. The Khan of the East and his Taishi/Second-In-Command — a would-be warrior with no battlefield in sight — shared fermented mare's milk with the Khan of the West, drinking out of a cup made from a human skull, embossed with intricately worked silver. All that remained of a long-vanquished enemy chief, worked with a typical combination of Mongol brutality and extreme workmanship and even artistry.

And as the celebrants celebrated, Mongol Chieftain Esen of the West passed a cup to his warrior companions. But the ever-watchful Mongol Agent took note that Esen himself had touched it to his lips, but did not actually take a drink.

A sudden cheer went up at the first sight of the arrival of the train of the Bride, as it rounded a nearby rise in the plain.

And when the cheer fell away — another sound pierced the air — the terrible whistling hum of Esen's 'singing' arrow.

That arrow sprung like magic from the chest of the Khan of the East — where it found its mark. In fury, he jerked it out with a bellow, turned to look for his would-be assassin. But in a heartbeat, eight more arrows struck him — as Esen's comrades acted without question.

Their Chieftain's 'game' had been leading to just this moment — the assassination of the Eastern Khan.

As the older man fell dead, the Esen leapt onto a horse, and was instantly surrounded by his companions, weapons out. They in turn were surrounded by a sea of warriors. And no possible escape. But escape was not part of Esen's plan.

He shouted a battle cry.

"Death to the Ming! Take back China!"

His men followed suit, adding their voices.

"Death to Ming! Kill the Emperor!"

The unspoken truth — that the Khan of the East had been utterly opposed to such a path — was known by all. Esen was only giving voice to the collective desire of the Mongols for vengeance on the Chinese dynasty that had denied them what their ancestors had stolen. And counting on that desire being strong enough to overcome the knee-jerk impulse to avenge their newly deceased leader.

"West and East! We are invincible! China is ours!"

There was a moment of silence and then the crowd roared along with him. The Taishi of the just-murdered Eastern Khan — who now took his place — did not fight against the tide of the moment. On the contrary. Esen had just done this man's dirty work for him.

The newly minted Khan of the East pulled his sword and stabbed it into the air with a great cheer.

"The world is ours!"

The Bride arrived in her train — and was escorted out of the painted wooden carriage — a baffled and frightened look on her face.

Esen leapt over on horseback, reached down and yanked her up next to him. Then pranced the horse through the cheering crowd to new Eastern Khan. By passing her designated bridegroom who was literally dead at their feet. Handing the Bride over to her new husband.

The latest Khan of the East was pleased as could be by this situation. He roared with gladness.

The Western Khan — not at all happy by his underling taking business in hand — could do nothing to change this new political reality. As the roaring crowd attested. He had challenged Esen with a seemingly impossible task – and the Chieftain had pulled it off. The Mongol tribes of the West and the East had been reunited. The fall of Ming China — and all its allies — would follow soon enough.

The small boy called Pup sat on his haunches at the
edge of a tide-pool on the island in the Seto Inland Sea
where his father served the Red Sea Lord, watching
a tiny crab make its way along the zone between sand
and surf. Equally not at home, it seemed to the child, on
both land and sea. Just like he was. Or was made to feel.
By those who lived on both land and sea. By all save his
father, whom he looked at like a god. Pup knew his father knew nothing of what was inside his head. Nothing
of what Pup wished he could express. A thought into···
words? He did not even know what a word was. But he
knew, felt deeply as he now felt the warmth of the sun on
his face, that what was inside should be outside. Sometimes, at least. Certainly, should be conveyed, somehow,
to his father. It was the earliest and longest lasting wish
he had ever had. When he first understood what a wish
even was. That is what he wished for.

A chubby bare foot kicked a load of sand onto the little
crab, causing it to flip over and struggle on its back.

The chubby foot belonged to a much larger boy.

Pup had not heard him approach, of course, as he was
without hearing since birth. Pup had not objected to the
abuse of the crab he had adopted — as Pup had been

without speech for just as long.

The larger boy was here to bully — his smaller brother was with him to watch. The bully considered Pup for a moment, like a painter before a blank canvas···.

A short time later — long enough to bury a child — the pirate samurai known as Shark arrived to find his son buried up to the neck in sand. Shark carried a wooden plank he had just been shaping for use as an oar, but was otherwise weaponless. He calmly moved to his child and dug and brushed the sand away to free him, using the oar as a makeshift shovel.

Then he considered the two boys who still laughed nearby — and their tough-looking beach Ronin father now with them, seated on a rock and chewing on a large crab he had caught and broken open.

Shark moved closer. His voice was quiet.

"You watched and did nothing."

No answer. It seemed like the two boys were waiting for their father to rise to the occasion. The man did not disappoint — he grunted, tossed his crab and pulled a sword — but Shark didn't move.

The man lunged, Shark ducked the slashing blade and riposted with his wooden oar — so fast that it was impossible to tell if the blow even landed. But it did. The man suddenly tumbled into the tide pool — skull crushed.

The bully and his brother rushed to the man's side, wailing.

"Come here," said Shark.

His voice was so commanding that the boys obeyed in spite of themselves. They stood before him weeping quietly, terrified at what he might do next. But his voice was matter-of-fact and not without sympathy.

"To be an orphan is difficult. But it is better than being raised by an inferior father. Find me when you are ready. And you may take your revenge."

He turned away from them to his son, leaving the brothers to rush back and cry again at their father's body.

Shark took Pup by the hand and they moved off.

Pup's expression was blank as always. His father did not know whether his son had understood anything at all about what just happened. But he had long since given up any thought that he might have. Only silence had ever been between them. Surely, it would always be that way, until death claimed one or the other of them. He hoped his son died first, for the boy's own sake. Knowing this was a hope no parent should ever have to live with.

Four scholars were seated on the floor of the Chamber of the Water Clock, each at a writing desk hosting a single piece of writing, a pile of blank pages next to that, an ink pot, and a brush.

❖ **Hungry Scholar Hyollo**: A plank of wood covered by painted Tibetan script, the 30 consonants plus vowel radicals composed of distinctive knife-like downward strokes.

❖ **Book-bug Yi Gae**: A tanned sheepskin adorned in the flowing Old Uighur symbols used for centuries in Turfan along the Old Silk Road, with tiny ax-like marks that represented the consonant sounds of the vowel-less writing system.

❖ **Linguist Pak Paengnyeon**: Embossed bronze adorned with the squarish script developed by the Tibetan monk 'Phags-pa by command of Kublai Khan, derived from the letters of Tibet.

❖ **Scholar Shin Sukju**: A leaf of paper displaying the Japanese tri-part writing system of Chinese characters known as Kanji and pieces of the same repurposed as a pair of syllabaries — the symbol sets called Hiragana and Katakana.

Sejong stood between them and the massive, room-sized Water Clock that loomed above. All seemed to be waiting. Then: Clack, clack, bang, bong — the mechanism went into its elaborate dance of levers and gear; flowing water and falling ball bearings. Until the mechanical dolls finally pounded their instruments and announced the time.

"Please begin," said the King.

The four scholars started writing. As quickly and smoothly as they were capable. Sejong paced behind them, observing, as each contestant copied the manuscript in front of him.

For this was indeed a contest: a calligraphic 'speed trial' — even if the contestants had no idea that was the case.

As he slowly moved past each desk, the King lingered long enough to renew again his appreciation of the vast differences in writing systems — even between just these four — as well as some of the apparent similarities. Renewed, too, was his admiration for the scholar's high levels of calligraphic skill. And the sheer beauty of the lines they were making on the page.

Two hours later, those lines had added up. The great clock again sounded its mark.

"Please set down your brushes," said the King.

The four scholars did so.

"Count your pages."

They each complied, counting the pages they had managed to generate. When they were finished, the King continued, "Tell me."

"Five," said Scholar Shin, regarding the Japanese he had copied.

"Four pages," said Hyollo, of his Tibetan.

"Seven," relayed young Yi Gae, indicating the Old Uighur.

"Ten pages of the Phags-pa alphabet," announced Linguist Pak, picking his words carefully, considering the implication as he spoke.

Sejong took this information in stride, as if processing it according to some mysterious inner formula. The scholars had no idea what he was thinking.

"That is all for now," said the King. "Thank you."

He turned away from them and left the room. The four scholars just sat there for a moment. Then all seemed to talk at once.

"Madness?" wondered the Book-bug, who seemed to be rattled by the seeming pointlessness of this latest exercise.

"Divine Madness," insisted Scholar Shin. "By definition. A sovereign with the Mandate of Heaven can do nothing else."

Book-bug looked grave as his youthful face allowed.

"The Mandate of Heaven may be withdrawn. Heaven's support is not guaranteed for the life of a ruler. Or a dynasty."

"Those are words of rebellion," said Scholar Shin.

"There is nothing controversial in stating a fact." Book-bug stood and exited the chamber.

Hyollo turned to Shin, as if to dispel any lingering tension, "Have you eaten?"

Scholar Shin just looked at him. They both stood and went out the door — leaving only the linguist behind.

The inquiring mind of the young man considered the four stacks of pages, the looming presence of the Water Clock, the 'race' he just 'won'.

Where someone else might have dismissed the last two hours as yet another capricious intellectual exercise from an increasingly whimsical sovereign, Pak, whose area of study had revealed order and rule underlying the most chaotic-seeming tongues and the symbols used to record them, searched now for recurring patterns in the King's recent behavior. He knew in his heart that there was order here. Method to the madness. Which suggested to him that the 'madness' was not that at all. But something else.

Deception.

His thoughts continued in that direction. Who was being deceived? Everyone. What was the true goal? Unknown.

Over the past few years, the pieces of exotic and strange fragments of knowledge sought by the King had escalated to the encyclopedic. Enough to fill one library and start another. The breadth of interests was vast — seemed to include all possible areas of knowledge, ancient and current.

It seemed the King had been obsessively chasing after so many things: military advances of new gunpower formulas and weaponry; astronomical data for tracking the movements of the heavenly bodies and predicting eclipses; Pharmaceutical knowledge for the health of the nation. But key advances in the King's pursuit of these various fields had been accomplished by him and the Hall of Worthies decades ago. Why revisit these areas now?

With this morning's curious 'time trial', the young scholar's thoughts went to his specialty: Language. And more specifically today: Writing. The method by which language is recorded, and more, by which thoughts are thought. Pak knew from his own experience, that to write was also to think, that a thought did not necessarily seem to proceed from the heart/mind to the hand to the page — but instead, at times at least, seemed to take shape in that space between the tip of the inkbrush and the surface of the paper.

And so, the means by which that composition/thought took place — the specific writing system in use — was utterly crucial to civilization and to the identity of an entire people.

What if the vast array of records the King had been collecting had nothing to do with the content and everything to do with the method of recording?

The young man let his thoughts pursue this internal dialog as far as it would go. Even if it meant reconceiving his King as a ruler filled with deceit.

Consider a possibility: The subject matter was a ruse, a cover story, a way to throw an outside observer off the scent. To hide what the King was really doing. The time-trial was the key. The first time he had shown his hand. The information that had been faithfully recorded by those foreign characters, those letters, those symbols

— a Tibetan Buddhist tract, an Old Uighur tale of Geng-his Khan, a Yuan government proclamation in Phags-pa, a comparison of death poems in Japanese — that was irrelevant.

The conclusion seemed unavoidable: Which of those four writing systems was faster? Which more efficient? That is what the King had wanted to know.

King Sejong's area of inquiry was writing itself.

Pak was shocked by his own conclusion. And more: The tipping of his hand by way of this experimental test-trial surely indicated that the King was getting closer to his goal. In the same way a General engaged in a diversionary tactic against an enemy must finally execute the actual attack.

But did the King believe that the risk to his true goal was so extreme; the end itself so crucially important that he must hide it from even his most faithful collaborators? Was the King going into battle alone?

That, thought the young scholar, was unacceptable.

๑๑๑๑๑

Interpreter Maedu had his eye out for the 104 tiny bells of the Sokka Pagoda before he and Pyonghwa even reached the temple nestled in the mountains of Myo-hang. Their regular stop on the way to and from China. On their regular missions for King Sejong. The green, mist-decorated mountains were as lovely as they had ever been, but Maedu thought of nothing but his ongoing dis-agreement with the bells.

The chimes were still.

"No welcome? What a surprise," said Maedu.

"And if they did ring, you would complain about the racket. Or the quality of the tone," observed Pyonghwa.

They paused at the base of the pagoda as always. Maedu considered what his partner just said.

"Well, yes." Then he plopped down and kicked back for a nap.

꧁꧂꧁꧂꧁

Above the doorjamb in a rough part of the Korean capital was a stone cross. Unmistakably Christian.

Sejong, in his 'commoner' disguise, had gone to Church. In a manner of speaking. Centuries before the establishment of Christianity in Korea.

The small room featured a makeshift altar and the trappings of a mass: Chalice, censor, candles and a tiny altar bell. And the same distinctive cross hanging on the wall.

The tiny room was a Nestorian Church. The only one in the Korean capital. The only one left in Asia.

This particular branch of Christianity was considered heretical by the Pope in Rome for considering the divine and human aspects of the Christ to be completely separate, in opposition to accepted theology. Following China's Silk Road nearly 4000 miles from west to east, across mountains and over deserts, Nestorian missionaries reached the Chinese capital and the first Tang Emperor as early as the early 7th century by the European calendar. A few churches were established; allowed to exist but not particularly encouraged. Another growth period had occurred under the Mongols with their Yuan Dynasty — to be purged when Genghis Khan's legacy was finally tossed from China by the Ming rulers.

Natural selection might suggest why Christianity did not take hold without European armies and navies to force the prospect. Both Buddha and Jesus provided similar relief to common people who might have felt excluded by official state religious practice. Promising a far more personal relationship not just with ceremony, but with divinity itself. But as a given savannah can support a lion species as top predator but not something else that is too much like a lion; as a certain field can support apple trees hung with rich red fruit but not another something too much like an apple tree — so Buddhism and Christianity may have been a little too much like each other in what they most offered. And in China — in Asia — Buddhism had gotten there first. But that didn't stop the missionaries from trying.

The Nestorian Priest was middle-aged with dark, wavy hair, and mixed Asian and eastern Mediterranean features.

He rummaged in a small wooden chest containing a pile of documents and found what he was looking for: A stone rubbing.

"I count three variations," said Sejong, who stood at a small table and compared the writing on several different tracings from gravestones that the Priest had already provided him with. All were written in the Phags-pa script that just 'won' the time trial in the Chamber of the Water Clock.

"Here is a fourth," said the Priest. "From a stele dating back to the Tang Dynasty. Or so it is considered." He stared with appreciation at the inscription. "The straight lines and simple angles make the letters of the Monk

Phags-pa amenable to being carved into stone."

"Those same qualities make it amenable to the page as well," responded Sejong. "Faster and easier to write."

"In the light of eternity," smiled the Priest, "What are a few additional moments, here or there?"

"I will not say that you are wrong," said the disguised King. "But my concerns are more time-bound. And practical."

"Alas, my own have of late become so as well."

Sejong glanced up, puzzled. "Why is it?"

"My Church has been completely purged by the Ming," lamented the Priest. "All my fellow believers in China have gone into hiding or even now walk the Silk Route back to the West. I alone remain here in Joseon. By the grace of God — and the indulgence of the Korean King." He continued with a twinkle in his eye, "Please convey my gratitude. If you ever meet that esteemed gentleman."

Did the Priest know who he was? Perhaps he did. Regardless, plausible deniability seemed the safest position in this case. For both of them.

But Sejong was staring at the tracings, comparing the variations. One symbol in particular had his attention: Two strokes, horizontal and vertical. Looking a bit like the numeral '7'. Simple.

Something about it had started his thoughts into motion.

"I have a partial copy of the Sutras of the Buddha Jesus," interrupted the Nestorian.

Sejong glanced up. His concentration broken.

"Written in yet another variation," continued the Priest.

Sejong's face lit up at this. He was not interested in the contents, only the method of recording it — though the Priest didn't know that. With sudden solemnity, he revealed an exotic-looking sheaf of papers. The King's gaze focused on yet another variation of the '7' looking letter distributed among the rest of the character set.

"I cannot take such a treasure from you," he said.

"This treasure belongs to all," insisted the Priest. "The Buddha Jesus has broken the wheel of Karma. Broken the bonds that tie us to this world."

Sejong just looked at him. His voice serious as the grave. "I would, instead, be further bound."

The Nestorian didn't understand what the King was doing with all these writing samples any more than anybody else in the Kingdom did. But that didn't matter. He seemed to admire him just the same — just like everybody else. And wished — just like everybody else — that he could ease his burden even a little.

He gently indicated the stone cross above the altar.

"Heaven will be waiting for you."

And handed the King his priceless Sutras.

⚙⚙⚙⚙⚙

No one went in or out of the west gate of the Palace at this hour of the night. But the gate remained open. And the Old Guard still on duty. Just in case. Just in case of a case just like this one: a lone supplier of dry goods, pushing his two-wheeled cart.

It was enough for the Old Guard to spot the small piece of yellow fabric tied to the crossbeam on the front of the cart to know to avert his gaze — as he had done countless times before — and wave the visitor through. In the knowledge that this rustic tradesman was the King in disguise.

As the King passed by, the older man could not help but glance after him. With a quiet wistfulness in his gaze. For the Old Guard was old indeed. How much longer would he be allowed to keep this job? Until retirement or death took it from him? Took the King's face from his sight?

That night, in the barracks of the Guards, everyone seemed asleep but the Old Guard and the New Recruit he had kept up with his reminiscences.

"Two times over the years, I have myself saved the life of the King," he said in a quiet voice.

"Is that true?" asked the Recruit, not much older than a boy.

The older man nodded proudly. "The first time, was my very first day on the job. Same age as you. The King was five years old. Not even Crown Prince yet. He was all dressed up. Looked like a little man! He ran to catch something he saw falling through the air. I don't know what it was. He tripped. I caught him!"

"You touched the King?" The Recruit was astonished.

"He could have cracked his head on the ground! And he wasn't the King yet. Like I said."

A Sleepless Guard rolled on his pallet. Not happy about having to overhear this anecdote yet again — and again and again over the years.

"The second time he was twelve," continued the veteran. "Trying to escape the palace over the western wall."

"They say he still does that!" exclaimed the young man.

"They say a lot of things," said the Old Guard, in an

attempt to cover for the King. "Anyway, he fell back-wards. And I caught him that time, too. Knocked me right over. And he said: 'Ten thousand pardons, Sir'!"

The Old Guard laughed at the thought. "The Crown Prince of all Joseon called me 'Sir'! Can you believe it?"

The open look on the younger man's face said he probably would believe anything.

"'Ten thousand pardons, Sir'!" repeated the Old Guard. Then he settled back on his pallet. Happy for a moment — in the loneliness that was his life — comforted by those memories that meant so much to him···. the memories of his King.

And as he drifted off, in the little death that is sleep, he thought that when the thing itself finally came — ac-tual death — he hoped the face of the King would be the last thing he saw.

⟨⟩⟨⟩⟨⟩⟨⟩⟨⟩

The King and Queen were being carried in decorated palanquins out of the Palace gates and down the main street, accompanied by tens of officials and scholars, guarded on all sides by security forces — all dressed in ritual finery, all stared at by masses of common folk pushing forward for a better view.

It was another Confucian public rite that required the King's performance: to function as the human bridge between Heaven and Earth; as a living example of the order of the Universe.

As always, Sejong kept his expression magnanimous but dignified. None could see the weariness behind his eyes. Not even his wife.

When they reached the designated plot of farmland outside the city, the palace denizens were arranged according to rank, as musicians played on traditioal courtly stringed and percussion instruments hauled out for the occasion.

The juxtaposition of royal personages and this rural setting was jarring. Even more so when Sejong, in his ritual vestments, started to plow the field.

He set hand to handle and guided the wooden implement as it was pulled by two large oxen, who were in turn guided by a pair of local farmers given the honor of this task.

The King only went a short distance, enough to make the ritual point. Then he let go of the plow.

A decorated blue box was brought to him by Choe Malli and Chief Councilor Hwang Hui as the next step in this ritual. The box was opened, revealing seed grains within.

The next move was to be the King's, but the King didn't move.

His attention was still on the plow before him. His gaze followed the lines of the wood, the handle and the share — which made a near right angle to each other. Vaguely in the shape of the numeral '7'.

Again, that shape.

Then his eyes drifted towards the source of the accompanying musical sound: The stone percussion instrument — the lithophone called the *pyeongyeong*, hung with two rows of eight stone chimes. Carried out here at great trouble and effort, because its sound was unmatched by any other musical device. In every Confucian ceremony since the start of our story, this instrument had been in use, so much part of the essential ritual atmosphere that Sejong no longer took any special note of its presence and effect beyond his typical musical appreciation.

But this time, the King's sudden attention was fixated on the fact that the chimes, too, were cut into a similar '7' shape as the plow.

The percussionist struck one of those stones, sounded

a tone — and suddenly time seemed attenuated. Stretched out. Giving Sejong's senses a moment of synesthesia — as if that '7' had a color and a sound of its own — as if shape itself was a source of music and light.

The sound a low booming: wood and stone seemed wood/stone, one substance, cut from a tree that held up the world; and the light: The pure sun.

Choe Malli was first to realize something might be wrong. A split second before the Queen. As their facial muscles contracted, as the very first indications of concern emerged into view, before their decades of Palace experience could mask those cues — the King had turned to them and smiled.

And proceeded with the ritual. He took a handful of seeds from the box on offer, and sprinkled them into the open earth of the row he had just plowed.

Then he exchanged a glance with Choe that managed to convey both warmth and ritual dignity. If Choe had been concerned about the King's apparent mental distraction, any doubts vanished with that look. And Sejong's almost preternatural ability to bind people to him with sudden graciousness.

The King then locked eyes for a moment with his wife the Queen: the look on her face of both question and answer made it seem as if she knew exactly what he had been fixated on few seconds ago. As if they shared a single heart/mind.

Then he took another handful of seeds and tossed it across the air — where the sunlight illuminated the mote-sized kernels as they arced towards the ground in a rainbow of gold.

For that instant, the ritual choreography became the very Confucian embodiment of high and low: The archetypal movement of Heaven, Earth and Human Being.

࿐࿐࿐࿐࿐

The Joseon capital city, Hanseong, was nestled amongst hills and mountains; a large river and countless trees, with multiple palaces and thousands of common dwellings placed according to ancient geomantic principles of the flow of wind and water; the invisible but still felt senses of balance and harmony with respect to object and surroundings.

From one of the any of several mountain tops around the city, in the moonlight, the capital looked like a classical landscape painting, a perfect dynamic between nature and human structure.

This particular night, across this pretty scene floated the sounds of a Korean zither-type instrument called a geomungo. The strings plucked out a hypnotic yet strong sound. Like a waking dream. Both otherworldly and very much alive.

The city was asleep, but a few late-night denizens who wandered the abandoned streets noticed the sound — it seemed to add a note of comfort to the thoughts one might otherwise expect to entertain at this hour, drinking alone with shadow and moon.

The eunuchs in their palace sleeping quarters were all awake and listening.

The Old Guard on his pallet seemed warmed by the sound, as if the notes were the only blanket he needed.

Lady Hwang turned over in her sleep, as if hearing the music in her dream.

The sound originated at Gyeonghoeru — the lovely, open pavilion in painted wood and stone that seemed to float on the artificial lake in the middle of the Palace grounds.

Sejong was seated in the center of the otherwise empty space, playing the instrument, deep in thought.

Scattered on the stone tiles of the floor around him were the Tibetan anatomical treatises brought to him by his long-traveling interpreters — Pyonghwa and Maedu — who even now were entering China yet again on his behalf.

The Phags-pa gravestone tracings and the 'Jesus Sutras' had been laid out next to the anatomical figures. And next to that, sketches of the plow and the stone chimes — the '7' shape that had so grabbed his attention of late.

It was if Sejong was trying to make some connection between these seemingly disparate classes of objects. And hoped the music would help both focus and free his heart/mind.

As if he wrestled with an intractable mathematics formula — or was attempting to accomplish the 15th-century Korean equivalent of splitting the atom.

Queen Soheon, when she appeared, appeared to almost float over the delicate stone bridge that spanned across the lake to the pavilion. She was stunning in the moonlight. Flanked by two maids. Like a goddess carried by a pair of swans. A Seraph winged by Seraphim.

The King played on, eyes closed, concentration intensifying — when suddenly the Queen was next to him, leaning close his ear.

"Our prayers have been answered," she whispered.

"Someone has been murdered."

Sejong opened his eyes and took his fingers off the strings. He glanced once at the Tibetan anatomical treatises at his feet. Then nodded at his wife. And set the zither aside. Their inexplicable apparent enthusiasm for homicide had stopped the music. For now.

രുജ്ജ്ജ്ജ്

A dead body lay face-up on the table in the Morgue. The Magistrate of the Capital stood by in his official capacity as Coroner. But the hands-on job itself fell to a specialist with practical experience — the Ojakin, an Inspector of Forensics. Who even now was concluding his investigation.

"I understand a man with no family has been killed," said a voice. "In an alley. In the dead of night." It was the voice of the King.

"Your Majesty!" The two men hovering over the recently deceased bowed quickly and in alarm. Sejong's unexpected if not unprecedented arrival was the last twist in this minor murder mystery that they would have expected.

The King entered, flanked by the same Constable who

had rousted the Shamaness and her celebrants at their illicit ceremony a few weeks previously. Sejong wore royal 'working' robes — no need to be in disguise despite the location outside the palace, as this was technically official business. No matter how unusual his direct participation.

"Show me," commanded the King.

"Pierced by a blade directly to the heart. Once. Between the ribs, here," indicated the Ojakin, somewhat nervously. Not because he was in the presence of the ruler of Joseon, or not only, but because the King was an expert in this field — had written the book on it, in fact. Or at least, had re-written the book on it: edited and annotated the classic book of forensics medicine compiled in China during the Yuan Dynasty in the era of Kublai Khan.

There was no one in the Korean Kingdom who knew more about forensics than the King.

"And the murderer?" he asked.

"There is little to mark the killer's traces," answered the magistrate. "In the alley where the crime occurred. Or on the body itself."

Sejong nodded and considered, musing aloud. "No one to pray for him, no one to bury him, no one to thank him for his service to the State of Joseon, to his King."

The others shifted awkwardly at these strange words. The King might have a bit of an eccentric reputation, but what was he going on about?

"Those duties fall to me," he concluded.

"Your Majesty," objected the others in unison.

"Leave us," ordered the King, referring to himself and the dead man. "Prayers first. Then interment." He sighed and gave a weary smile. As if this was business as usual rather than a completely contrary set of circumstances.

"It will be a long night."

He paused and waited, until they all realized that here, in the middle of the night, with all other the officials of government asleep at the Palace or their homes, they had no real choice but to let the King be the King. Nomatter how eccentric or immoral or even illegal the behavior. The three men nodded and withdrew, sliding the door closed behind them.

Sejong turned to the body. He put his hands together in Buddhist fashion, and recited a mantra for the dead.

Then he took a slender blade from inside his garment where it had been kept hidden and moved closer to the corpse.

This was, of course, absolutely taboo. The Book of Filial Obedience, one of the cardinal texts of Confucianism, stated that every part of the human body had been gifted, as it were, from a mother and a father — and therefore, by extension, any harm or impairment committed upon it was an assault against those parents. And for a strict Confucian — and Confucian culture — the parental bond was sacrosanct.

That meant no surgery on a living person, and no dissection of one dead.

The King of Joseon, by his very nature, did not just know all this, he was, in fact, required to be the very embodiment of correct Confucian behavior.

And so it was in full knowledge of the outrage he was committing that he inserted the blade of the knife inside the dead man's mouth⋯.

魚魚魚魚魚

The door slid open to reveal the magistrate, the Ojakin, and the Constable still waiting. Sejong nodded for them to come in — the body on the table behind him was now wrapped tightly in linen from foot to head.

And anything the King might have done to the body

had been hidden from view beneath the wrappings. But were those bloodstains in the fabric over the throat area — or a trick of the light? The three men stepped into the room and did their best to ignore it.

Two hours later, the same trio was moving alongside a horse that had the dead body draped over its saddle. Sejong had guided them to someplace just outside the city he seemed to be familiar with.

The King paused at a spot he apparently found appropriate, having felt a breeze and heard the bubbling sound of a stream nearby.

"The wind and the water are auspicious here," he said, taking a moment to appreciate the comforting nature of the setting. Then he took a shovel from a pack dangling off the horse, and pierced the ground.

The sight of Sejong the Great - King of Joseon Korea — digging a grave in the middle of the night in the middle of nowhere was more than a little shocking.

The other men scrambled to grab implements and assist him. But the looks on their faces were easily read: Surely this was insanity.

The King held his stained hands — by blood or dirt even his wife could not tell — in a small basin of water. As the Queen gently helped wash them off. Sejong seemed dazed from this exhausting but exhilarating night.

"A man with no name, no family, no wealth, no learning, no expertise, no political position···. A man with no breath," said the King, almost in amazement. "And half his blood spilled onto my hands. Has served me more than those who have everything."

The Queen dried his hands with a small cloth.

"How can I not return the favor?" he continued. "To those just like him? Who still live? Those who have no voices. No means of making themselves heard. Making themselves known to the world. And the world to be — centuries after they are gone. After we all are gone."

A confidence had crept into his voice. His wife picked up on it.

"Does this mean···?" she was almost afraid to ask.

"Yes," he answered.

The Queen gripped his hand tightly, her eyes glistened with hope. "Yes?"

"Almost," he said with a smile.

"Tell me!"

"Not yet. To tell is not to do. All the elements, all the constituent parts, are nearly there. I only must connect those parts. I can feel it." But still, the doubt was in his voice.

"It is all there already," said the Queen.

Sejong looked at her, trying to follow.

"In Heaven's heart," she continued. "Like a dream you have forgotten. You do not need to 'invent' anything. You must only remember. Remember what you have forgotten. What Heaven knows. What you have always known."

Something about her words greatly eased his mind, relieved him of the burden the pursuit of his mysterious goal had placed on him. He put his head on her shoulder, and drifted into a reverie.

Of the falling green leaves. Always mysterious. But now, for a moment, somehow comforting.

Sejong opened his eyes. And knew what had to be done.

ை௳௳௳௳

In the pouring rain, an unmarked but hefty-looking carriage careened along the road, pulled by a team of strong horses, leaving the city gate and the capital behind.

Sejong sat inside the speeding vehicle, dressed for travel; on his lap were all the documents his two interpreters had smuggled to him out of China; in the carriage around him were stacks of books and manuscripts. This was what might be called a 'working holiday.'

Or the race to the finish line.

༺༺༺༺༺

Government Officials and Palace Scholars were gathered in the Royal Council Hall where typically the King hosted a brief assembly first thing every morning. But the King was not here. The Crown Prince appeared instead, assuming the King's place at the head of the room. He addressed them with as firm and confident a voice as he could manage for his youth and gentle demeanor.

"Good morning. I trust you have eaten well. Let us proceed with the business of the day."

But Choe Malli was not having it. "Crown Prince, where is His Majesty?"

"The King is indisposed," responded the young man, calmly as possible.

"Crown Prince, what is the nature of the indisposition?" asked another scholar.

"A matter of health"

"His Majesty's petition for a substitute Reign on medical grounds was soundly rejected by this Assembly," said Choe, cutting him off. "And yet, here the Crown Prince is before us. And our King, nowhere to be found."

The Assembly was a sudden cacophony as everyone tried to talk at once and the Crown Prince had to shout to be heard. "This is a temporary situation. Please proceed with the business of the day"

But those assembled were no longer paying him attention. The discussions and shouting between each other continued to escalate. In a matter of seconds, the Crown Prince already had lost control of the government.

He turned and exited the Hall — leaving them to their 'deliberations.'

Choe Malli and Chief Councilor Hwang Hui exchanged a look from across the Hall. Both knew that from such small beginnings entire governments could end. As quickly as this Assembly had fallen apart.

Liaodong was the largest small city on the eastern edge of the Chinese empire, lying just north of the Korean peninsula. The latest destination for Pyonghwa and Maedu.

They had reached the home of the man that Sejong had sent them to visit, and were led by a servant into a small, walled garden. The servant left them there and disappeared into the adjoining house.

Pyonghwa calmly waited; Maedu glanced around impatiently. After several minutes of this, a man was before them. This was the mysterious scholar Huang Zan, exiled from Beijing for reasons lost to history.

He wore nightclothes, as if just roused from sleep. Maedu glanced overhead to confirm — indeed, it was past noon. The Exile noticed. And declaimed a seemingly spontaneous poem in rhyming Mandarin.

"The life of an exile. Means no sundial." He indicated his rumpled, slept-in clothing. "And no style."

He went silent. And waited for a rhyming response from these two Korean visitors. Maedu was too famished to pick up on that.

"No rice, either?"

Exile Zan frowned at this. Shifted to his guests' native

tongue, improvising a couplet in perfect Korean.

"Travelers who to their host / Are taunting / Will go wanting."

Maedu gave Pyonghwa a look of annoyance. But his partner had just caught onto the Chinese scholar's eccen-tric rhyming game.

"I have a hunch," proffered Pyonghwa, "There will be lunch."

The Exile smiled.

By mid-afternoon, the garden table held only the remains of the shared meal; and the scholars were deep into the business at hand. Exile Zan read aloud from a list of items that Sejong had requested; shifting easily between multiple languages to do so.

"Three maps mapping lands to the west; a prayer flag from a kingdom of the south; a rhyming dictionary from the Mongols up north⋯. Does your King want, as well, a piece of the sun that rises in the east?"

"Truly, His Majesty's⋯enthusiasms do indeed range-wide," agreed Pyonghwa with sympathy. "Forgive us the imposition."

There was a long silent moment as the Chinese intellectual studied their faces. Then he dropped all verbal games gave his cold analysis of the situation.

"'He deceives the sky to cross the ocean'."

The next day, Pyonghwa and Maedu were on the road back to Korea, their cart loaded down what they had acquired from the Exile, the mission a success. But Maedu was still angry.

"How dare he insult His Majesty."

"You daily do the same."

"His Majesty is my 'His Majesty'. It is my right to do so. All day and every night, too," insisted Maedu. "Not to question the King of our Kingdom is to deny our duty as subjects."

They continued in silence for a moment.

"It was not an insult," observed Pyonghwa. "But an ancient observation about strategy."

Maedu was listening. Quietly, for once. Pyonghwa continued the thought. "Suggesting that His Majesty hypothetically could seem to have a hand in everything in order to disguise the one thing he is actually aiming for."

"And which one thing would that be? 'Hypothetically'?"

"I do not know. Do you?"

Maedu thought for a bit.

"This I know," he finally said. "I don't like being treated as the King's fool."

◈◈◈◈◈

The two most powerful individuals in the kingdom who were not the King — Choe Malli and Chief Councilor Hwang Hui — strolled the Palace grounds and took stock in the wake of the debacle of the Daily Assembly.

"I read the Royal Physician's report," said Choe. "Admittedly, His Majesty is not well. But these are nothing but the accumulating afflictions of age and a life of royal duty. No reason yet for the dereliction of that duty. Let alone abandoning the throne. I will object to these sudden attempts at abdication until my brains pour from my forehead and pool at his feet. If I can find him," he concluded ruefully.

"His Majesty, even now, is in a carriage, racing to the waters of Chojeong."

Choe was annoyed at that news — and growing more concerned.

"What else do you know? That you have not seen fit to tell me?"

"There is nothing the King of Joseon does that I do not know."

The Chief Councilor had eyes and ears everywhere in the Palace — and beyond. An intelligence network that Choe saw as a threat. Even if now it might provide answers to Choe's own questions.

"Then say it."

"His Majesty spends his days reliving the fixations of his youth: The fire arrows; the medicinal pharmacopeia; compilations of rainfall and flood records, the movements of planets and constellations. And his nights"

"His Majesty's personal···proclivities are of no interest to me," insisted Choe.

"His nights praying to the Buddha with the Queen. And talking to the Water Clock — calling it by the name of its inventor."

Choe was taken aback. "Yeong Sil?"

"Yes. As if the soul of his dead collaborator inhabits the contraption itself. And so the King speaks to it, bemoaning the advance of time."

Choe considered for a moment. But did his best to downplay the worst. "Time slipping away? That is humanity's oldest complaint"

"And yet we do not wander the night, you and I, talking to ghosts. Or taking refuge in the religion our own government has banned."

"Tell me again that the King has gone mad," said Choe,

"And I will consider your words treason."

The Chief Councilor ignored the threat and pushed even further. "You yourself prevented His Majesty from officially abdicating the throne. But now he has taken matters into his own hands. To outflank you. I say: let him go."

"And who will replace him? The Crown Prince is too young and···." Choe picked his words carefully, "Not formidable."

"A more suitable candidate may appear."

Choe just looked at him. His voice was dark. "Those who would seek the chaos of a premature succession···," he left the threat unspoken.

But the Chief Councilor didn't back off. "Yes?"

"Will not find an ally in me," said Choe. "Or in those who follow me."

The Chief Councilor studied him for a moment. "Then I will wait," he replied, diplomatically. "Until you think otherwise."

"You will be waiting a very long time." Choe motioned into the far distance. "His Majesty has gone for a holiday? So be it. Let him rest in the waters. And when he becomes restless? I will persuade him to live out the rest of his life on the throne. As productively as possible. In preparation for a stable and orderly succession of power."

"I do not share your confidence in the King."

"My confidence is in myself. When has His Majesty not followed my advice?"

The Councilor didn't dispute the point. But he silently wondered when Choe's overconfidence would come back to haunt all of them.

Three wooden launches swirled towards each other, guided by three pilots who each stood at a long wooden oar, carried by the three currents of the whirlpool that churned equidistant between the three island fortress bases of the three Murakami pirate clans. On each launch sat a Sea Lord — Red, Green and Blue — flanked by a bodyguard. The middle of this whirlpool was the only meeting spot they could ever agree upon. Only here — surrounded by water, with a threat of being pulled under should the currents do something unpredictable — was the chance of ambush zero.

Or close enough.

Sea Lord Red, with Shark at the oar behind him, waited for the others to open the conversation.

"I have heard it told," said Sea Lord Blue, "That the King of Joseon is attempting to abandon his throne."

"They say he is no longer fit to rule," added Sea Lord Green.

"Even a tiger gets old," said Sea Lord Red, with grudging respect. "And wants only to find a cave, and lie down."

The boats continued to circle, as the Lords eyed each other with the mistrust that was part and parcel of the pirates that they all were.

"We were youths," said Sea Lord Green, "when that Tiger chased our ships from the shores of Korea."

"Lords of the Sea now," added Sea Lord Blue. "Why do we hesitate to take advantage of this situation?"

"The knives we would put into each other's backs, at the first opportunity," said Sea Lord Red without humor, "Is cause for hesitation."

They circled in silence for a moment, knowing that statement to be true. But the time for words was over.

Sea Lord Red suddenly pulled a knife. Then cut the palm of his own hand. And let the blood drops fall into the spinning water.

The other two Lords watched his action. And silently

agreed with the sentiment. They both followed suit, out came the blades, down dripped the blood from their own hands.

The drops of crimson swirled together, caught by the currents of the whirlpool, sealing the pact, the silent promise to combine forces against King Sejong — with a promise of bloodshed to come.

ᙥᙥᙥᙥᙥ

The Imperial Palace in the Forbidden City in Beijing was the largest such structure on the planet. Dwarfing anything in Europe or the Americas. A flock of cranes flying not just overhead but across time as well, would have to range far to the west, over the Sahara, over two thousand years earlier to look down and see something comparable. Like those Pharaohs of Old Egypt, the Emperors of China were considered rulers absolute. Unlike those Pharaohs, the Emperors were never considered gods in and of themselves.

"Son-of-Heaven" was the best an Emperor could do. And that was quite good, if one's aim was power unquestioned. To aim is not necessarily to hit the bullseye, however. By way of Confucius, checks-and-balances were built into the system. According to the Sage, a sage gentleman scholar — not unlike Confucius had been himself, not surprisingly — should be allowed to advise and question the Emperor in all things that had to do with good government. And everything, for Confucius, ultimately had to do with good government.

But more significantly, as a nod to Taoism, with its mysterious Way — the give and take rhythms of the seen and unseen natural universe — Confucius allowed that the Mandate of Heaven can be withdrawn. Taken away from any given ruler like a rug pulled out from underneath — and conferred upon someone else. Anyone else. Not necessarily — even not likely — a member of the same royal family. Or indeed any member of the ruling class. A commoner had taken the Dragon Throne before. A commoner, a Mongol, even a eunuch could do it.

Or at least, that was at the back of the mind of Eunuch Wang Zhen.

Minister of War Yu Qian stood with his head bowed before the Dragon Throne. Everything about this setting conveyed power — the intention here, as everywhere in the Imperial Palace, was to over-awe. But Yu Qian had been favored by the previous occupant of this throne, and the current lad had none of his father's greatness —

or indeed, seemingly any interest at all beyond the aesthetic. The Minister of War showed his respect as was expected, even if awe was out of the question. He did, however, fully recognize the danger of the individual who stood at the Emperor's right hand. And he knew that to request readiness for battle would be a battle uphill.

"The Mongols of the West and the Mongols of the East," said Yu Qian, "Have settled their differences."

"Why should that wrinkle the brow of the Great Ming?" responded the eunuch in the Great Ming's stead.

"We are not prepared for the inevitable," continued the War Minister, "Training forays are needed along the entire northern border"

"A waste of resources," interrupted Wang Zhen.

"And the Joseon King must provide not just arms, but armies"

"An over-reaction to the drinkers of horse milk our grandfathers chased from this land. With their horse-tails between their legs."

At least, thought the Minister of War, those men had something between their legs. The eunuch seemed to hear the silent thought. Such was his ability at reading expressions. And his own buried anger at the mutilation that was done to him as a boy.

The boy now seated on the throne suddenly stood and moved into the rays of the sun from the oculus above. If there was any awe to be had in the room, it was from Eunuch Wang Zhen as he beheld yet again how very handsome the young Emperor could be, light source depending.

And how good-humored, thought the Minister of War, as if taking up some silent dialog between them. The young man, now twenty, had been made Emperor as a child, and had always been overly comfortable in the role. Like it was playtime.

"We hate when our two favorite subjects fight," the Son of Heaven said brightly.

The eunuch and the Minister of War both nodded their heads in deference. But they could not help but be charmed. The Minister grudgingly so; the eunuch seemed almost smitten.

"Bow three times to each other and make peace," continued the Imperial lad. "Or your Emperor's day is ruined."

The two in front of him hesitated. The young ruler stepped down to them, and touched them both on one shoulder.

"One," he lightly guided them into the first bow he just

commanded.

"Two," the second.

"Three," he forced them to complete the cycle.

"There," he smiled genuinely. "Not so difficult as all that?"

In the corridor outside the throne room, Eunuch and Man of War confronted each other in a way that they could not have in the presence of their ruler.

"My properties extend northwest beyond the Great Wall," said Wang Zhen. "Have you forgotten? I will not have the army trampling them underfoot."

"You chose to build along one of the main routes into China."

"Do you challenge me, Minister? That is not a war you will win." The eunuch indicated the great palace around them. "Within these walls, I am in command. And the next time the army is sent into battle, beyond these walls, beyond even the Great Wall — it is I who will lead it."

Yu Qian reacted badly. Even as Minister of War, this was news to him. The eunuch had obviously won the young Emperor over completely, to be able to convince the boy of this.

"You may defend the rear, if you'd like." The eunuch meant it to sting. Then he turned and headed away, leaving the War Minister alone, face grim, without any strategy to counter what he knew was a disaster in the making. The worst kind of disaster. One that can be seen as clear as day. And not avoided.

⁂

A veritable horde had gathered on the Steppe. The likes of which had not been seen since Genghis Khan had brought them together two centuries previously.

Horses were raced, archery practiced, swords sharpened — the Mongol clans of the west and the Mongol clans of the east had joined forces and were practicing for battle.

Inside the main pavilion, Chieftain Esen Taishi — whose murderous gambit had reunited the tribes and set them on the road to war with China — was quietly fashioning an arrow sleeker and more accurate than the 'humming' missile he had put to terrible use before. But the new model was no less lethal.

"We studied the strategies of their long-dead masters,

when we ruled China," he said. "We learned all they knew; all they have now forgotten."

Only the Mongol Agent was here with him, silently listening. Waiting for the deadly assignment he knew would soon be tasked with. Even if he didn't yet know the details. Why else would he summon here to the empty pavilion? While his boss fiddled with yet another wicked missile?

"Now it is time for a new game: Turning their own strategies against them."

He notched the arrow and drew the string, taking careful aim at a target on the other side of the pavilion.

"As the old masters once suggested," he suggested, as the arrow flew across the air.

And buried itself into the throat of a life-sized portrait of King Sejong.

The same type of garish painting Sejong himself saw in the mudang's hovel during the shamanistic ritual. Stolen out of Korea by spies Esen had sent for just that purpose.

"'Remove the firewood from under the cauldron'," he quoted.

The Agent quietly considered the King's portrait as the Chieftain walked towards the target and explained.

"Ming will observe the gathering of our forces. The Emperor will call upon the Joseon King for support. But if that King has an arrow through his throat, and the Korean capital is in chaos? The fuel for Ming's fire will be gone. China will face us alone. And be ours. Again."

He restated for emphasis on the ancient Chinese war stratagem, savoring the words as if he could taste them. "'Remove the firewood from under the cauldron'."

Then he reached out and yanked the arrow from the face of the King of Korea.

⑳⑳⑳⑳⑳

Expecting to see that face in the flesh despite the lateness of the hour, Pyonghwa and Maedu, having finally returned home, were blocked from entering the Royal Palace. Even Maedu didn't have time to announce his outrage before one of the Security Staff pulled them aside.

"Come with me."

"Our business is with the King," said Pyonghwa.

But Security didn't explain themselves further, only indicated the way. Away from the Palace. The undercurrent of threat and tension was unmistakable.

Pyonghwa hoisted his traveling bags full of items received from Exile Zan in China, and moved to follow. Maedu had no choice but to fall in alongside.

Pyonghwa and Maedu soon found themselves on horseback, galloping along with a quartet of Security. Neither of the interpreters was trained to ride like this, and their lack of skill was apparent. But the King's men didn't care. They goaded their horses to go even faster. The translators struggled to keep up.

A night of this brought the small party to an isolated and rustic villa — the mineral springs at Chojeong, a recently discovered water source reputed to have healing qualities. Pyonghwa and Maedu guessed where they were, never having been here, but were mystified as to why.

After they dismounted, they were met by a eunuch they had never seen before, who moved them into the complex itself.

There were stones and mist all around. They heard the sound of struck tones on a lithophone; plucked notes on strings.

And the eunuch had vanished.

Pyonghwa and Maedu were alone, lost in the mist and the mystifying surroundings. They followed the strains of music. And heard a familiar voice.

"Please. Come in." It was the King.

They moved a bit further, hesitantly. And began to pick out figures in the mist — musicians playing their age-old instruments, an armed guard, another eunuch.

And then suddenly the mist billowed, revealing:

Sejong.

Submerged up to his shoulders in a room-sized hot spring bath of wood and stone. He still wore his royal robes. Which were soaked up to the neck. As if he had forgotten he was wearing them when he hit the water. Or just did not care.

Pyonghwa and Maedu reacted. Had the King truly lost his mind?

"What have you brought me? This time?" said the King, pleasantly. As if they were back at the Palace, in the library or strolling the grounds.

The two travelers were exhausted, but this strange situation had somehow energized them — made them giddy.

"All that you asked for, Your Majesty," volunteered Pyonghwa.

"The Mongolian rhyming dictionary?"

"Along with everything else."

But clearly, the dictionary was what the King was after.

In fact, it was the only thing the King was after.

"'He deceives the sky to cross the ocean'." Maedu quoted the Exile in Mandarin Chinese.

Pyonghwa shot him a look. But Sejong just laughed pleasantly.

"You have always hated loving me," he said to Maedu.

"I am your loyal subject," said Maedu. "In all ways. Including dissent. When necessary. What does 'love' have to do with it?"

Pyonghwa glared at him, horrified. But the King only smiled. "Confucius would have agreed with you," he said.

The King tried to look at him. And that is when both of the newcomers could not help but notice that he was not making eye contact, but only looking in the general direction of their voices. Not able to make eye contact. They both realized:

The King was blind.

"Read it to me?" Sejong asked.

Pyonghwa was hit hard by all this. His voice shook.

"Your Majesty⋯."

Sejong indicated his eyes — with which he could only perceive the blurred outlines of his visitors.

"The Royal Physician believes my condition is possibly⋯temporary."

The King said nothing more about it. But motioned to indicate the steamy water.

"You must be weary. From your travels." It was an invitation — and also, a command.

In the time it took to awkwardly yank off their garments and awkwardly settle naked in the bath with their sovereign ruler, they awkwardly did so. Both thankful that court propriety dictated against ever staring directly at the King's face. They gladly and pointedly did not do so now.

Sejong rested the back of his head against the edge the pool, a small towel over his eyes — as if part of some treatment for his blindness.

"The Rhyming Dictionary of the Mongols seems to follow the Chinese character-mother pattern quite closely," said Pyonghwa, as Maedu held the precious book above the waterline so that his partner could study it. "And is, of course, written with the alphabet of the Phags-pa Lama."

"Of course," said the King. The character set created under Kublai Khan by the Tibetan monk was precisely the thread Sejong had been so avidly following over the past several months. "Please read."

Pyonghwa got his bearing in the text, and then began

to read aloud a series of rhyming syllables. The dictionary had been compiled over a hundred years previously, as a way to record and recreate so as to standardize the sounds of the Old Mandarin dialect using the new alphabet of the Mongols — as a reaction to the variety of spoken language changes that China had been inundated with in the wake of the Mongol takeover and the establishment of the short-lived Yuan Dynasty.

But to hear Old Mandarin was not Sejong's interest. He was interested yet again, not in the subject matter, but in the method. In this case, the efficacy of the Phags-pa system in recreating sounds, and in the efficiency of one or two or a half-ten of its letters⋯.

Sejong's eyes were unseeing of the outside world, but gazed inwardly with great intention.

And a reverie took him away:

All was blank. A grey open space where nothing was defined, all flat, featureless, even. Sejong, wearing the royal clothing of a typical day, was at a writing desk, ink brush and paper in front of him.

Pyonghwa's voice continued to come to him, entering this space, reading aloud the foreign rhymes.

Sejong wrote in Chinese and Mongolian characters what he heard — duplicating exactly the dictionary entries that Pyonghwa was reading. Here, in this imaginal space, he still could visualize.

The King stared at the lines he had written. Something struck him as notable:

"Why does the vowel always stick to the consonant?"

In the bath, it appeared to the soaking interpreters that Sejong was thinking aloud. "I have noticed this before, of course. With rhyming dictionaries," he continued.

Pyonghwa nodded. Staring closely at the dictionary entries in the book his partner still held above the water.

"Yes," agreed the interpreter. "It seems universally the case."

The King appeared not to have been aware of Pyonghwa's reply. He seemed lost in his own inner thought processes.

"But I never thought to ask why," continued the King.

In his state of reverie, Sejong stared at the exact duplication of the book — visualized by his memory and imagination.

"Why must a syllable always be divided by such methods? Does a vowel not sometimes stand alone…?"

In the steamy water, both Pyonghwa and Maedu reacted to this statement — which struck both of them as a profound insight.

"As a human being stands between earth and heaven," said the King aloud.

A look of "Eureka" appeared on his face. The same expression Albert Einstein might have had upon deriving $E = mc^2$.

Pyonghwa and Maedu looked up and stared directly at him — propriety overcome by the overpowering moment of realization.

"Ah. What have I just said?" said the King.

Now Sejong found himself walking along an infinitely flat, horizontal plane. A huge, cloudless, blue sky overhead, with a bright, beaming sun.

The King was the only vertical figure in this entire landscape: Flat earth, round sun and upright human being.

In the far distance appeared another solitary image: The *pyeongyeong* percussion instrument we first encountered at the ancestral rite. With its numeral '7' — or upside-down 'L'-shaped — carved stone chimes. The stones sounded — struck by a percussionist whose iden tity Sejong could not discern at this distance.

Sejong walked towards it, with a hyper-deformed sense of time that could have been ten heartbeats or ten thousand years. Until he was close enough to see that it was the Queen who played the instrument. With a small smile on her face as she softly struck another of the stone chimes.

Sejong momentarily fixated on the outline of the hanging stone — the '7' shape.

Then he was walking again across the imaginal landscape. The Queen and the *pyeongyeong* vanished behind him. But the sound of one lone stone chime continued to reverberate after, as if following him.

Then moving alongside him, he saw Choe Malli, guiding a plow pulled by a pair of oxen — just as he had during the rite of planting. And again, Sejong fixated on the outline of the plow: Yet another example of the vaguely numeral '7' shape.

And again, he found himself walking alone, and Sejong repeated a version of what he had said before.

"Between Earth⋯."

The ground at his feet became an unending straight line⋯.

"And Heaven⋯."

The sun above became an immense circle⋯.

"Stands a human being."

He stopped in his tracks. Suddenly, it wss as if Sejong himself had vanished, or rather, been replaced. By a single, vertical line that joined the horizontal below and the circle above.

As if this image: Earth, Heaven and Human — horizontal, circle and vertical — was the key to the solution that the King had been searching for.

๛๛๛๛

The same carriage that had brought the King to the hot springs raced back towards the capital, pulled at full gallop. Flanked by the same riders as before.

Sejong sat inside. Dressed and dried-off, and apparently sleeping. Someone had taken him from the bath and prepared him for the trip home.

A jolt woke him. He glanced around. Then down — reacted to the sight of his own hands. And confirmed: His vision had returned.

The King's eyes were clear and full of resolve.

As the royal carriage raced through the Palace gate it was under the eyes of the Old Guard, posted here tonight. He watched the carriage go by, then stepped out into the path as it passed to watch it continue into the palace grounds. As if, after all the years of witnessing the King's comings and goings, he sensed some great import this time, some kind of epiphany.

The Queen too had sensed it. Though she should be in her bedclothes, should be sleeping, the Queen was dressed and sitting quietly. As if waiting for what she knew was coming.

"The King approaches!" shouted a eunuch from the corridors outside.

The Queen glanced at the door as it slid open and the King entered the chamber. The Queen and the two attendants accompanying her all bowed.

Sejong moved to his wife and took both her hands in his.

"It took so long," he said, "To see what was so near. Always so near⋯."

The Queen smiled. "To see one's own heart⋯is perhaps not so easy."

The King wanted to tell her every last thing. The words spilled out. "Three shapes⋯that was key. Corresponding to."

But the Queen put her finger on his lips, to stop him from continuing.

"Save your strength. For tomorrow."

"Yes. Tomorrow," he agreed. "The announcement will be tomorrow."

He kissed her hands.

"Now, I must prepare. Sleep well."

The Queen nodded. The King left the room. When the door slid shut behind him, the Queen slumped forward, stifling a cough. The two maids rushed to her side. Her eyes appeared glazed and watery. She was obviously very ill. And had just as obviously had been hiding this from her husband.

"You are not to leave my side," she insisted to the maids.

"Your Highness, we must call the Physician."

"No."

Then she tried to put on a positive face. "All will be fine. Tomorrow."

She was speaking of something much more than her own health. But the two women taking care of her had no choice but to obey. And remain with her through the dark night.

༺༺༺༺༺༺

There was an ancient stone water well behind the Assembly Hall, just beyond the Inner Palace. A liminal point, as it were, between public and private spaces at the Royal Palace. Easily accessible to the King, whenever he woke in the dead of night with an inspiration; a bit more of a stretch for the handful of young scholars of the Hall of Worthies or the translators of the Interpreter's School to reach after a scramble to throw on proper clothing given the possibility of rain, moon, or even snow, as inspiration knows no weather. But there was not one of those young men who did not think of the well with deep emotion. And imagined, in a kind of exercise of future memory, a time when they would say to their own grandchildren, "That is where your grandfather and his friends would meet with the King." And to a time when they would say to themselves, "I miss those nights so very much."

But on this night, with a chill in the air, escorted by security officers and roughly deposited at the well-head, future fondness was the last thing from their thoughts. "Are we being arrested?", "Why are we here?" But the officers hadn't answered and before they could speculate amongst themselves, King Sejong had arrived.

All bowed in response, but he was all apologies. "Ancient wisdom says that the loyalty between ruler and ruled goes both ways. If you are to be the hands and feet of this kingdom, then I as King, must be the heart."

He smiled at them all, but there was a great weariness in his eyes. "You have walked far for me; made much, with what I have sent your way. But I have not kept my side of the promise. I have not revealed my heart to you."

Silence. Nobody had expected to hear anything like this…confession.

"In a few hours, that will change," he continued. "And I will need you more than ever."

His voice lightened for a moment. And for a moment, he became again the much younger man who had once gathered them all here to write poetry by the light of a mid-summer meteor shower. "Now please forgive one more time the 'tyrant' who has dragged you from your dreams."

Then he left them.

When he was gone, they just stared at each other — more mystified than ever.

One by one they returned to their chambers. Until only Pak Paengnyeon remained. The young Linguist would stay here, his mind working over and over again every piece of information that had transpired between the Hall of Worthies and the King over the past few years, honing in on the past few months, unable to stop his thoughts from attempting to recreate whatever the King seemed to have accomplished. Whatever was behind the King's promise to reveal all tomorrow morning.

Until the morning came. As the dawn broke, and its first rays struck the stones of the well-head, Pak, giddy with lack of sleep, suddenly seemed to know.

"No. Not possible," he thought. "Is that what His Majesty was doing? Who would even attempt such a thing?" Then, aloud, as if to the morning sun. "Only him."

The young scholar heard the sounds of the crowd now gathering outside the Royal Assembly Hall, and rushed to join them.

༺ঔৣ৾ঔৣ৾ঔৣ৾༻

The expansive steps in front of the Royal Hall were filled with government officials, scholars, and officers by the time the young linguist found his place among the rest of the Hall of Worthies, and turned to face the now empty royal throne, awaiting the King, knowing that nobody else knew what to expect. The very idea of what Pak was now certain the King had accomplished filled his heart/mind to such a degree he felt faint, felt as though he might actually die. But he could say nothing. Could only wait with the rest of them.

As the King, in his chamber, was dressed by the dressers of the Royal Wardrobe Department. In the full, visually arresting, Royal robes of yellow and red, silk and stone that were demanded by this occasion, and this objective: To overawe. To so compel with his presence and charisma as to evoke the sense of Heaven nodding in approval over his shoulder and break apart the walls that surrounded each heart/mind — that his message would be received at the depths of their being. Rather than precipitate a coup that could have him dead by the end of the day.

Lady Hwang stepped inside the Queen's quarters, unsure of why she had been called here this early. The Queen was seated, flanked by her two maids.

"Lady Hwang, I want to hear the King's announcement today."

"Yes, Your Highness!" was the consort's puzzled reply, as she wondered what she had to do with it.

"We can all watch from behind."

"I will be staying here," the Queen cut her off.

"Please find a way to convey."

She suddenly coughed, explosively, before she could suppress it. One of the maids handed her a small cloth to cover her mouth.

Lady Hwang then noticed a pile of folded clothes tucked away behind them — all with blood on them. She was alarmed.

"Your Highness! Does His Majesty know?"

"He must not. Until after the announcement." Another terrible cough.

"I must tell him now."

"No," insisted Soheon.

Lady Hwang glanced at the two maids — who looked panicked. They clearly wanted her to do something to help. Anything.

"Highness, please."

"Let me die," exclaimed the Queen, with a sudden bitterness that none of them had ever seen before. "You will have him to yourself."

Lady Hwang looked appalled. But the truth of those feelings hurt her even more. The Queen was not entirely wrong.

"What kind of person do you think I must be?" said the consort quietly.

"One who is in love with the King."

"How does that make me different from anybody else? Who does not love the King?" Tears fell from her eyes. Lady Hwang continued. "Even the ones who speak against His Majesty. I think they love him more than we do! They can't help it! That is what they hate most!" She moved to leave. "I will not let you die. I will not hurt him like that."

"If you stop him now from doing what he must do, you will destroy him."

Lady Hwang considered this for only a moment — then she was out the door.

And rushing along the corridors to find the King. She suddenly caught a glimpse of him, dressed in his royal best, moving stately along towards the assembly. He looked magnificent and she stopped in her tracks, overcome by awe.

She just watched. Wanted to say something. Could not. Then, summoning some kind of great inner force, she shouted, "Your Majesty!"

His concentration was broken. He turned, saw the look of anguish on her face.

In a matter of moments, he was rushing along with her towards the Queen's quarters, all decorum, all awe-inspiring effect gone.

Then he was at her side. His wife was dazed, her condition had rapidly deteriorated in the short time it had taken for him to reach her.

"I am here. I will not leave you."

"You must."

"No."

"Tell them what you have done…tell everyone…."

"How can I go now?" he insisted.

"How can you not? I…I will wait for you."

They looked into each other's eyes with deep understanding. Then the King nodded assent. Lady Hwang and the eunuchs were in tears.

The King leaned forward to hold her once more. She whispered intensely in his ear.

"Do not just tell them. Show them. Show the world."

In all his majesty, His Majesty stepped into view, in front of the throne, out from beneath the overhanging roof, before the entire government, the daylight striking him as if the sun itself had been waiting.

The hundreds of Officials, Scholars, Ministers all went rigid with attention.

The faces of those who knew him best did not know what to expect: Choe Malli and the Chief Councilor and his cohort; the heads of the Military and Domestic Security; the scholars of the Hall of Worthies; the eunuchs watching from the sidelines; and Lady Hwang and two maids from behind the scenes.

All had no idea what is to come. Only Linguist Pak — who now felt as though he could no longer breathe — was certain of what Sejong had wrought. A realization that threatened to overcome him; drop him right where he stood.

The King stepped forward to face the crowd. Paused for a long moment. Then, in a voice that seemed directed not just at the hundreds here gathered, but at everyone beyond — beyond this space, beyond even this century, he spoke.

"The sounds of our language are different from the sounds of China, and so cannot be expressed in the writing of China. Consequently, the uncomplicated people of our Kingdom are unable to make their concerns understood⋯by those of us who are educated."

There was no other sound but his voice.

"This makes me sad."

A long pause. Then came the revelation, the truth of all he had been doing in secret, hidden from everyone but the Queen.

"And so I have newly made twenty-eight letters."

It was as if everyone assembled had stopped breathing. As if Time itself had collapsed, taking the air with it.

"I hope this alphabet will be easy to learn and used every day, whenever the need should arise."

He held out both his arms, opening his hands. Not dramatically. But pragmatically. At that pre-arranged signal, two eunuchs rushed into view. One put a mop in his hand, the other a bucket of black ink.

The King moved forward, to the open flagstones separating him from the assembled crowd.

He dropped the bucket onto the ground, then shoved the mop into it, soaking the mop.

"'k' — the molar sound, the shape of the root of the tongue closing the throat···."

He stabbed forcefully downward to draw the first letter of his new alphabet right in front of them, splashing the flagstones with black.

"Comparable to the first spoken phoneme of the Chinese character 'kun'···."

The King's new creation is his own version of the right-angled '7' shape he has been so fixated on during the course of this story.

Off to the side, hidden from view of the crowd, Lady Hwang watched with two maids. She quickly turned to them and sent them rushing off back to the Inner Palace. As if on a crucial mission….

The King slashed the mop to make the second character: A '7' shape with an additional horizontal mark halfway down the vertical.

"'k', molar sound," he emphasized the hardness of the letter as he voiced it. "Not unlike the first spoken phoneme of the character 'k'oai'." Sejong proceeded using a method similar to the rhyming dictionaries he had consulted: establishing and identifying a character by referencing something already known. In this case, the letters of his new alphabet by comparing them to Chinese syllables all those here assembled already would be familiar with.

The young linguist watched, his prediction confirmed. This was it! He suddenly could not stop himself. And moved from his spot in the Assembly rushing along in a half-crouch fast shuffle walk — trying to keep the bowing position even as he moved as quickly as possible to get closer to the King. The better to see these letters that no human being but the King had ever seen before.

"'ng', a molar sound, not unlike the first spoken phoneme of the character 'ngep'." The King swiped a large inked circle as the third consonant.

The two Maids Lady Hwang had sent rushing back to the Inner Palace had reached the Queen, where it became clear what the consort had tasked them with.

"The sounds of our language are different from the sounds of China, and so cannot be expressed in the writing of China. Consequently, the uncomplicated people of our Kingdom are···, are···." The Maid could not remember the rest.

Her partner jumped in. "The uncomplicated people of our Kingdom are unable to make their concerns understood by those of us who are educated···."

The other maid chimed in to complete the King's line, "This makes me sad!"

The Queen was deeply moved. Her eyes teared up. As the maids continued, passing the King's announcement back and forth between themselves as they could recall it.

"And so I have newly made twenty-eight letters···."

Seeing the tears in the eyes of the woman they both adored made them both start to tear up as well.

"I hope···. I hope···."

"I hope this alphabet will be easy to learn and used every day, whenever the need should arise!"

All three women were weeping. A sad, sweet, and even

comical moment. As the tears gave way to joy and smiles. This was everything the Queen wanted to hear.

The King continued to rapidly but directly make his way through the letters. More and more scholars and even minor officials could not help but do the half-shuffle bowing move to get closer to the King and see what he is doing.

The ink had splashed onto the King's fine robes with the effort, but he took no notice.

"'n' — lingual sound, the shape of the tongue in contact with the upper jaw⋯."

For the onlookers, the performance was dizzying. As they sought to grasp, some more quickly than other, the importance — and the portent — of what took shape beneath the King's bold, slashing calligraphy.

"'m', the shape of the mouth⋯."

"'s', the shape of the teeth⋯."

Then he was on to the vowels — as if this presentation was a piece of music rushing to the climax.

"'a', not unlike the middle phoneme of the character 'ttam'⋯."

"'u', not unlike the middle phoneme⋯."

"'e'⋯.

"⋯phoneme⋯."

"…character 'zyang'…."

"'ya'…."

"'yu'…."

"'ye'…."

Until the mop that was his ink brush finally stopped moving. Nobody said a word.

"I call this system, 'The Correct Sounds for the Instruction of the People'."

Again, no response. Dead silence.

Finally, Linguist Pak, who was now close enough to whisper and be heard, struggled to find his voice, barely getting it out. "And for the final phoneme…of any given word?"

"Just use again," answered Sejong, gently, "The first sound: The initial consonant or vowel. To begin or to end, is the same."

"Of course," said the young man in awe. "Simplicity itself."

Then the King turned and vanished towards the back of the Hall.

After he was gone, nobody moved. It was as if they were frozen or in a state of shock. A wind now was heard. The only sound. Many heartbeats came and went. Still, nobody said a word.

Then one scholar began to laugh — he couldn't help himself. Seemed beset by a kind of hysteria. His laughter suddenly turned to crying.

An overwhelmed emotional state that seemed to speak for all of them. Nobody knew what to do.

Choe Malli, the King's lifelong advisor and friend, had a look of devastation on his face. As if the King had personally betrayed him.

Twenty-eight letters. The newest on planet Earth. Right there before them.

Mute testimony of the King's intention to change the world.

Chapter II
Promulgation

Soheon was in her bedchamber, in her husband's arms, who held her against the deepening darkness, as she shifted in and out of consciousness, rousing long enough to smile at the ink on his robes.

"What have you done?" she asked proudly, knowing the answer.

"Nothing. I could have done nothing without you."

The Queen's breathing stopped for a long moment. Then started again. Barely enough to speak.

"I think, I must go now."

"No."

Lady Hwang and the Queen's maids were standing vigil nearby, in tears.

"Show me," the Queen said with a small smile, "What you did."

Sejong understood. Took her hand. And 'wrote' into her open palm, using the tip of his index finger as if it were a writing brush, and traced the same letters he made in the Assembly Hall, his lips close to her ear, whispering to her the corresponding sounds as he did so.

"'a'.... 'e'.... 'i'.... 'o'...."

Again, Soheon stopped breathing. This time for all time. The King embraced her, and his tears ran down both of their faces.

Later that same day, a eunuch stood on a Palace roof-top, holding the same nightgown the Queen was wearing when she died. In accord with ritual, he shook the garment strongly, so that it snapped in the wind.

Then he shouted, loud enough to be heard by all those assembled in the courtyard below, loud enough, all here hoped, to be heard by the soul of their Queen.

"Your Highness! Please come back to the Palace! Your Highness! Please come back to the Palace!"

Then he threw the garment off the roof, down towards the ground, where it was snatched from its fluttering descent by the three eunuchs who stood waiting for it. The moment they had it in hand, they turned and rushed towards the Inner Palace.

Racing through pathways and hallways, they finally reached the Queen's bedchamber, entering at speed, and flung the nightgown over the body of the Queen, then repeated the entreaty of the rooftop.

"Your Highness, please come back to the palace. Your Highness, please come back to the palace. Your Highness, please come back…."

They spoke softly, as in prayer, and Sejong, still here watching over his dead wife, silently mouthed the words along with them.

The preservation of the body of the Queen took days.

On the first day, she was placed upon a bier packed with ice to delay decay.

Her body wreathed in the mist vaporing off the ice made it appear as if she was floating in a cloud.

The only living soul who kept watch that night was the King.

The vapor, the lamplight, and his mourning vigil gave the scene a look of transcendence. But he felt utterly earthbound and helpless.

He slowly reached out and touched her cheek.

"Please come back."

In his eyes was utter desolation.

The next day, several women trimmed the Queen's hair and finger nails as the King watched.

And as the Wardrobe Department staff wrapped and covered and draped the Queen's body in a dizzying succession of garments, still the King did not leave.

Until the chamber itself was replaced by the Royal Coffin Hall, a cavernous, otherwise empty structure built to house the Queen's coffin. And the coffin itself placed inside an ornate, portable mausoleum of painted wood and metal panels, with hand rails for carrying, when the time came for her burial ceremony — which would not occur until the death of the King, at which point, they would enter the tomb together.

As the King waited with her, unwilling or unable to leave her alone, it seemed he was waiting for that burial — and so for his own end. At the very least, his withdrawal here, without sustenance or sleep or the comfort of any who might attempt to ease his mourning, seemed likely to bring death sooner rather than later.

Then he heard the sound of hammers on nails just outside. And went to take a look.

What he saw were craftsmen constructing a small, purposefully rustic-appearing thatched shack. Right in the middle of the Royal courtyard. It appeared strange and out of context. Even like something out of a dream. But Sejong was not surprised, though he might have momentarily forgotten. This was the official Mourning Hut. The tiny dwelling inside which the King was now epected to live for the months' long duration of the ritual mourning period — and from which, continue to carry on the business of state, like a proper Confucian ruler must.

"Your Majesty." It was Eunuch Dong Woo, eyes red from days of crying over the loss of the Queen, whom he had known since childhood, for as long as he had served the King. "The First Academician···of the Confucian Academy⋯. Would speak with you."

Sejong just looked at him. It was the last thing he needed right now. But he knew it could no longer be avoided: the business of the Kingdom, this meeting with his old friend Choe Malli, and the fallout from the announcement of the new alphabet.

That night, Choe was led by security guards along the darkened Palace grounds to the now-completed Mourning Hut, and deposited at the tiny entrance.

Choe paused, took in the soft glow from within the thatching, took a deep breath, then stepped inside.

The lamplight revealed the King seated on his royal throne — around which the hut had been constructed — which nearly filled the small interior. It was a jarring sight. The constricting, rough surroundings, the royal throne, and the King dressed all in white.

His eyes stared into space. As if deep in thought. Or in the darkest mood Choe had ever seen him.

Choe took two steps forward — which was as close as the floor space would allow — and stopped. He avoided looking directly at the King, as propriety dictated, even in circumstances such as these.

His voice was quiet. "I mourn the loss of our Queen."

"My Queen," said the King, voice raw with pain.

"She belonged to all of us. Forgive me."

Sejong just looked at him. Choe continued to avert his eyes. "I too loved Her Highness," he said quietly. "Who in Joseon did not?"

That brought a small piece of Sejong back to himself.

"Yes. Of course. Forgive me. Your pain must be…considerable."

Choe dared to glance up at the King — their eyes met. No sound. Just silent tears, as they mourned her together.

Then Choe turned his head away again. And waited for a long time in silence. Then continued to that which could no longer stay unspoken.

"Your Majesty."

"What is it?"

"Please withdraw this…invention. Do not make the alphabet official government policy."

Sejong suddenly was all business. His mourning set aside for now.

"The 'Correct Sounds' belong to the people."

"That is a quaint notion."

"If the government refuses to encourage its use, that is the government's failure."

Choe leaned closer. "The 'failure' will be attributed to

Your Majesty."

"By whom?"

"Any and all who hear of this⋯incident. From now, until the end of time."

Sejong appeared to be listening. Choe continued, emboldened.

"Master Mencius," he referenced the great acolyte and explicator of Confucius, "Emphasized the beginnings of things: Of benevolence, of righteousness, of wisdom, of courtesy. All of which you have demonstrated almost in excess. In all you have accomplished. But are not endings equally significant?"

"Endings?" Sejong went on the attack. "Do you speak of my death? That in itself is punishable by execution."

"Your legacy," clarified Choe. "Your achievements are too numerous to enumerate. But the memory of your benevolence and wisdom; the respect you have shown towards your advisors — these can be erased with a single bad move."

"'New beginnings are disguised as painful endings', says the Sage of the Tao," quoted the King.

"'The fox who gets its tail wet does not cross the river,' according to the Book of Changes," countered Choe, continuing the battle of the Ancients.

"Confucius said: 'If Heaven is on my side. What harm can you do to me'?" concluded Sejong.

Choe reacted with disbelief.

"Is that what Your Majesty believes? That Heaven is behind this···. this···. childlike diversion you have concocted? Consisting of two lines and a circle?"

"That is a testable proposition," said Sejong in challenge.

"Indeed it is," countered Choe. "The Mandate of Heaven can be withdrawn. As history has shown us."

Sejong considered for a long moment.

"Would you put me to the test?"

Choe did not back down. "Withdraw this alphabet. Expunge the record so no mention of it remains. And you will be remembered as a kind and generous sovereign."

"And you, remembered as a paragon of good government? As chief advisor to the most benevolent ruler in the history of the Korean people? A king whose accomplishments, whose very goodness was but a result of careful tending by Choe Malli, Confucian Scholar, Kingly confidant, Academy Co-director, Advisor Extraordinary."

"That is not my first consideration."

"Nor your last."

Choe looked wounded by those words. He was quiet.

"Not even once, did you ask me to join you⋯and the other scholars⋯at the water well."

Sejong was taken aback by this sudden and unexpected admission of vulnerability. His voice softened. "You would not have consented. You would have called it inappropriate. Unseemly, even. To meet in the dead of night. Under the stars. Without proper ceremony. Even before I spoke a single word. Of what was on my mind. And in my heart. Of the thing that had filled my heart/mind to the exclusion of all else. Kept me from sleeping. Invaded my dreams when I did sleep. That has now robbed me of my eyesight. And turned me into an old, broken man, years before my appointed time."

"But you did not even ask."

"For that. I am sorry."

A sad moment between them. Then the fire came back into Choe's eyes.

"I will bury you." The threat, here in this setting, was shocking. But Sejong did not waver. "I hope that is the case. The sadness I would feel at losing you, so soon after my wife. Would kill me."

The words went through Choe like a spear.

That night, Choe stood alone, in the dark, in the rain, at the water well. Droplets ran down his face, mixed with the tears.

On the other side of the palace grounds, in front of the Royal Assembly Hall, that same rain beat down on the 28 letters of the King's new alphabet.

The Linguist Pak Paengnyeon stood a few steps away, staring at them. For as many nights as the King had been mourning the Queen, the young scholar had come here, to the scene of the crime as it were, still thunderstruck by the achievement on the stones. He came just to stare at it. As if by doing so, its genius would penetrate every facet of his being.

The rain beat down on the letters, made the edges of the inked figures start to run.

The young man crouched down, touched the newly wetted ink of the first letter with his finger, the way a worshipper in the West might have touched the blood of a Saint. Then spoke the sound it represented out loud. The sound the King had given it.

These were his letters now. The King's gift to him. To all of them. The moment the letters had appeared on these flagstones, they were no longer the sole possession of their creator.

"'The Correct Sounds for the Instruction of the People'." He said it aloud, thrilling at the words. The scholar was Confucian by indoctrination, Taoist by inclination, might end up Buddhist by the time it was all over, but for now, and for as long as he could foresee, this was his religion. These twenty-eight letters. The ink might be running from the flagstones, but they had been so deeply carved into his heart/mind that he lived and breathed nothing else. This was meaning. And meant more to him than anything else ever had or ever would.

Then he raised his ink-wet fingertip to his forehead, and drew the first letter across his skin, sounding it out once more as he did so. As if to bind himself even further.

⊛⊛⊛⊛⊛

Jeong Inji — the laughing/weeping witness at Sejong's announcement of the 'Correct Sounds for the Instruction of the People' — was one of the most titled scholars of the era. A historian who served his kingdom as Special Advisor, Minister of Education, of Rites, as Royal Tutor to Princes and ultimately Prime Minister.

His understanding of Confucian thought was impeccable and unmatched; his dedication to government service unquestioned.

He was also the best writer in the land. Even if that born and nurtured ability had never been put to the test···.

How could he have so lost his composure in public? Before King and Assembly and Earth and Heaven? His first instinct had been to retreat to his office in shame and contemplate withdrawing even further: To the mountains, where he would become a hermit. Some of the most famed officials and poets of China had done so — the precedent had been set centuries ago. Surely history would forgive if not honor him for doing the same?

And yet, nothing had come of it. Jeong Inji had lost no face after his emotional outburst. If anything, he was admired even more for having given expression to the shock of the moment. As if he had been the conscience of the crowd, the conduit of all who had been present for that momentous occasion.

For momentous it was.

In Jeong Inji's mind, everything had changed.

He had gone for long and seemingly aimless walks.

At all hours. And always seemed to end up here, at the steps of the Assembly Hall. Where the letters still remained, in ghostly outline.

How was it possible that the universe could shift so radically? In the Book of Changes, over a thousand years before, the concept of revolution was examined. It was a cornerstone of the natural world — including the world of humankind. The Old was replaced by the New. In life, and in politics. But these elements were all known quantities. There was nothing new about the 'New'. Previous generations were replaced by the next; even rulers sometimes were replaced not by an heir but by one of the ruled. No matter how radical or violent, the up-ending was still a known pattern, even if the variables — the objects or individuals in question — might all have different names.

But this? This was new. Something that had not existed under Heaven was now here. Or rather, something that had not even occurred to Heaven had appeared in the sky.

A new star.

That's what this was! thought Jeong Inji.

Even more. A new constellation. Of twenty-eight stars. The letters of the alphabet. Blazing so brightly that they outshone the moon; and could be seen even at noon.

And he himself felt reborn.

The alphabet marked the start of the second half of his life. Dividing his time in the world down the middle. There was Before the Alphabet and After the Alphabet.

He stared at what remained of the King's markings on the flagstones.

Then, in the quiet of the Palace grounds, he thought he heard the soft echo of voices⋯.

⁂

The old stone well-head had been here, occupying the borderland, as it were, between the Inner and Outer Palace since before the Inner and Outer Palace had been built. No one actually knew how far back in time the well went. According to ancient philosophy, a well spring was a stand-in for Heaven, with its inexhaustible supply. But even Heaven — the creative principle of the Cosmos — like a well, could fall into disuse with respect to humanity, become muddied and overgrown and useless out of human neglect.

The young scholars who had been gathered here countless times over the preceding years, answering the late-night summons of the King, gathered yet again, but under their own auspices. Deeply educated if not indoctrinated with the knowledge of the classics, every one of them was aware of the metaphorical connection between a well spring and the principle of Heaven. And each believed Sejong had done more than could be expected of any sovereign with regard to keeping this particular fountainhead clear and inexhaustible — metaphorically and actually.

But on this night, the opening sentiment was that the well had been poisoned. So to speak.

"Our talents have been exploited," opined Book-bug Yi Gae, who had become even more radicalized since the last time they had met. "This is not the Shang dynasty of China, two thousand years ago. Or even the Goryeo of our father's memories. Duty does not demand that we tolerate a tyrant."

"When has His Majesty ever been wrong?" asked Scholar Shin. The Book-bug just stared at him and sadly shook his head.

"Allow me to attempt a middle ground," proposed Hyollo the Hungry Scholar, interceding. "The King kept his agenda hidden, even from us, for reasons of practicality. Had he instead acted openly, Choe and the officials would have shut him down. It was a tactical move. Nothing⋯personal."

"Fine," said Interpreter Maedu, his prevailing bitterness on display more than ever. "Then, I personally, have walked my last mile from here to the Great Wall"

"Until His Majesty orders us out again," added his traveling partner Pyonghwa. Maedu just scowled.

"At this very spot," continued Scholar Shin, "His Majesty said he would be needing us more than ever."

"The 'Correct Sounds' are finished," said Maedu, as if wanting to put an end to this impromptu meeting. "What more can he ask of us?"

Linguist Pak Paengnyeon finally spoke, his voice quiet. "Whatever it is. I will do it."

They all turned to him.

"I taught myself these twenty-eight figures in the time it takes to prepare a cup of tea," he continued. "Each consonant evokes the shape of that which produces it: The tongue striking the roof of the mouth, or the back of the teeth, the throat constricted or again, open. And the vowels. The vowels reflect the fundamental combinatorial principles of nature itself. Writing systems of a hundred lands fill the shelves of our library. None are like this."

His colleagues all glanced away, almost embarrassed

to hear this incredible truth stated so baldly.

"I···have learned His Majesty's letters as well," said Scholar Shin.

There were murmurings of agreement from the rest of them.

"Out of curiosity," Maedu grudgingly admitted.

They all had taught themselves the King's alphabet.

"Then I am not saying anything you haven't seen for yourselves," said Pak.

Nobody disagreed.

"The elegance, the logic, the simplicity of these figures is beyond compare," he continued. "How can this be the result of mere study and invention?" His eyes looked haunted. "What then, are these letters?"

Nobody had an answer. Then:

"They are a gift of Heaven." Jeong Inji stepped into view. Everyone stiffened with formal attention — the older scholar was their superior in all ways, and was also the last person any of them expected to see here, in the middle of the dead of night.

His voice was even. "Those with doubts should leave and not trouble destiny any further." Nobody moved. Not even the Book-bug, who for a moment, looked ashamed. "Then we are in agreement," concluded Jeong.

"Our lives belong to the alphabet of our King."

Nobody objected. This statement simplified and clarified everything. Their lives — and even their deaths — were now clear as the water in the well.

ᘓᘓᘓᘓᘓ

In the bright sun of the next day, the letters had been baked into their rain-distorted shapes. And now workmen worked to undo the work of both King and rain — splashing buckets of water onto the stones and rubbing with rags.

Choe Malli and Chief Councilor Hwang Hui watched from a few steps away.

"This cannot go unchallenged," said the Councilor. "The King plays the fool."

"I am the fool," said Choe ruefully.

The Councilor just looked at him. "Then we all are. Not to have seen this coming."

"'Openly repair the roads, then slip through the passage of Chengang'," quoted Choe.

"My recall of ancient Chinese stratagems is not what it was when I was studying for the civil service exams," apologized the Chief Councilor.

"The King has engaged himself with a multitude of activities, 'repairing' his old accomplishments," explained Choe. "To all appearances keeping himself busy with trivialities that were a threat to no-one. Even his attempt to abdicate the throne. It was all a ruse. To purchase time. To divert attention from his true goal: The creation of a writing system for the Korean language. Independent of China or any other nation. For use by anyone who can pick up a pen."

There was another splash of water against the recalcitrant letters that the workmen just couldn't seem to erase.

"That deception worked," observed Hwang Hui.

"Because I underestimated him. And discounted your observations and your doubts. I allowed my affection for His Majesty to cloud my mind. I will not do so again." The threat behind Choe's words was unmistakable. "Understand," he continued, "This is a disaster we may not survive. As an aristocracy. As a government. As a kingdom. Even as a people."

"Twenty-eight letters can do all that?"

"It takes years of study to learn the ten thousand characters of the Chinese language, to gain knowledge by reading, to express oneself by writing." Choe gave a bitter laugh and indicated the letters.

"An intelligent man could learn this 'alphabet' over breakfast. Even a simple-minded slave in less than a week." The Chief Councilor reacted with alarm. He had not thought of that.

"A kingdom of commoners who can read and write, is a kingdom destined for upheaval," continued Choe. "And for the destruction of all propriety. Indeed for destruction, plain and simple."

Yet another bucket of water hit the flagstones. Choe shook his head in wonder, grimly quoting the King's name for his creation. "'The Correct Sounds for the Instruction of the People'."

The letters still did not seem to want to come off the stones.

"Joseon Korea will become a pariah," he continued. "Despised as barbarians by our superiors in China, who will abandon us at the first sign of trouble. We will be alone and vulnerable against all enemies we have kept at bay until now. If China itself doesn't take the lead — and erase Joseon from the map of history."

Again, he considered the letters.

"The King's 'baby' must be strangled in its cradle. Before somebody else does the job for us."

The Steppe here looked like a becalmed ocean, the grass still, save for the single line of force that cut through it like a barracuda.

The Mongol Agent rode south towards the Korean peninsula; his hair had grown out past the shaved sides of the head of the typical Mongolian, as he had already gone undercover for the mission before him.

As he rode, a phrase came to him from the tales he had been told since before he learned to walk(but not, he was a Mongol after all, before he learned to ride): "I have no friend but my shadow / And no whip but the tail of my horse."

And he compared himself as he rode to Genghis Khan, as all Mongol warriors did, as a way to measure his ability and his ultimate worth. This is what he thought: Genghis Khan, one man, had extended his will and focused his lifeforce upon the entire world — and the world had fallen into place accordingly. If I do the same — directed at just one man — then the result will also be the same. The same energy that created an empire, in my case, will level a kingdom — and shake the world.

That thought swept him along, and he felt as though he knew what it was like to be a typhoon, moving inexorably across the water, gaining speed and power with each mile, the devastation when he would at last strike the shore, inevitable.

⸙⸙⸙⸙⸙

Shark rowed himself and Pup across the waves of the Seto Inland Sea, towards a larger attack ship anchored just beyond the deadliest of the island currents.

The same bond was evident here as always between them – both close and distant: The man went nowhere without the child, but the inability to communicate was a gulf that he had never been able to bridge. As if they were islands apart from each other.

He had long ago stopped trying.

Shark and Pup clambered onto the deck, where Sea Lord Red was in the process of inspecting the vessel — as a dozen pirates under his command worked to get it battle-ready.

The Sea Lord saw Shark and motioned for him to approach. Shark complied, Pup following. There was no prologue with these hard sailors.

"I am attacking the Korean coast with the other Lords. You will pilot my flagship."

Shark gave a nod of acceptance. The Sea Lord placed over Shark's head a leather strap from which hung a large iron key. A match for an identical key strung from a thong around the Sea Lord's own neck. The only two keys to the tiller.

Shark turned and walked towards the stern, Pup again in tow. They reached the large tiller that was locked with a huge padlock and chain. Shark unlocked it with the key he had been given. The boy just stared.

৵৵৵৵৵

Choe Malli of the Confucian Academy moved across the dawn-lit grounds of the Palace with a singular intent. Towards the huge drum that stood just beyond the gate to the Assembly Hall. Christened the Petitioner's Drum by Sejong's father who had installed it, any Korean, no matter what rank or social position could amplify his — or even her — voice by booming it across the Palace grounds, in protest against any policy of the government: demanding to be heard in a public forum by the King himself.

Taking the big mallet from where it hung, Choe did exactly as prescribed, pounding loudly enough to wake the entire palace.

Sejong was seated on his throne in the rustic Mourning Hut, not asleep and not awake. At the sound of the BOOM BOOM BOOM his eyes opened and cleared. He knew exactly who had sounded the drum, and exactly why.

Moments later, Choe stood alone in the courtyard directly before the position always occupied by the King when he appeared at the Royal Assembly Hall. He shouted into the dawn, not even waiting for his intended audience.

"Your Majesty! Withdraw this promulgation! Your Majesty, hear your loyal subject!"

He went down to his knees in ritual supplication. Bowing and shouting. One voice that nonetheless spoke for all the aristocracy; all the bureaucracy: The voice of the Confucianists who dominated this government, this culture, even this century.

Scholars and officials arrived in no particular order, as soon as they could wake, pull on their garments and assemble themselves in the courtyard.

"Your Majesty! Withdraw these crude markings! Your Majesty!"

Then, horribly, Choe smashed his forehead down on the flagstones — the very steps upon which Sejong had written his alphabet for all the world to see. He cried out.

"Your Majesty! Please listen to your subject!"

Over and over, until his forehead split open and bled.

The King, still in his white mourning clothes, moved quickly through the corridors towards the Assembly Hall. He heard Choe's plea in the distance.

"Your Majesty!"

Sejong's expression was grim. He was exhausted and empty. Expected as this might be, it was still the last thing he needed right now.

By the time the King stepped into view, the courtyard was full, and Choe's face covered with blood.

"Your Majesty…."

"Stand up," commanded the King.

But Choe just bowed again, smashing his forehead once more. The action compelled the King to move to Choe's side and put a hand on his shoulder, helping him stand.

"Please."

Choe rose to his feet and the blood dripped off his chin. The King motioned to a nearby eunuch, who rushed over and wiped Choe's face with a cloth.

"Your Majesty," said Choe, as a kind of warning.

"Tell me," said Sejong, with no way to get out of this

confrontation.

"Your humble subject observes that the creation of a Korean script is a work of inspired invention, without equal in all of human history."

"And yet," said Sejong dryly.

Choe pulled out a petition on which he had written his demand. He consulted the page as he spoke.

"Our kingdom has always served the greatness that is Chinese civilization. Honored the Emperors one after the next, and followed the teachings of Master Confucius. Learned the Chinese language, and the ten thousand characters with which it is written. With those symbols we have kept the records of our history; maintained the business of government, composed poetry, written letters to our honored parents and our distant friends; have indeed, drafted memorials to counsel our Kings, just as I do now."

Choe indicated the letters of the new alphabet that still had not been entirely rubbed clean from the stones — letters that he had just bled upon.

"A vulgar writing system, based upon sounds heard in the streets and alleyways — such a thing is only found among nations of barbarians. What if word of this···. 'invention' reaches China? What will the Emperor think of us? We who seem willing to give up the fragrance of Imperial perfume for the emission of a local stinkbug?"

The King's face was like stone.

"His Majesty is said to be aggrieved by the inability of the common people to express themselves. But how will putting their complaints onto a page make any difference at all?"

He turned to indicate the big drum he just pounded to call attention to his petition.

"Let them pound on the Petitioner's Drum, just as I have done! If they wish to be heard!"

He turned again to the King.

"What does reading and writing have to do with it?"

The murmurs of assent from the assembled crowd indicated to all present that he was speaking for the majority. Choe now was bold enough to speak for them all.

"We your loyal subjects have looked at this thing from far and near, upside-down and inside-out. We still cannot see the value in any of it."

He tucked his notes away and again dropped to his knees to bow.

"Your Majesty! Withdraw the promulgation!"

One after another, officials and scholars joined him on the flagstones, dropping to their knees and shouting in unison.

"Withdraw the promulgation! Your Majesty!"

The King turned to them.

"Stand up. Please."

They stopped bowing and stood, believing the King had capitulated. But Choe stayed on the ground, knowing Sejong would not give in so easily. The King addressed him alone.

"You have gone much too far in your words."

And at this moment, after all that had occurred in the past several days, that is all the king had to say.

He motioned to the Security Officers standing in the sidelines. They moved in, grabbed Choe by the shoulders and hauled him to his feet.

Everybody was stunned. Choe most of all. Nobody expected the King to go this far. The King had always listened to Choe; always, eventually, taken his advice. Until now.

As Choe was dragged off by the Officers, under arrest, half-a-dozen supporters who had signed his petition threw themselves onto the stones, pleading, "Majesty, release him!", "Majesty, please!"

Sejong had them all arrested.

"Perhaps the rest of you should retire from government," he said to the crowd that remained. Then he turned around and headed back to his hut, and his mourning.

༺ஒஒஒஒஒ༻

In one corner of the Forbidden City in Beijing — one corner of these palace grounds being large enough to swallow up the capital city of a typical kingdom of this age, if not an entire kingdom — Emperor Yingzong of Ming sparred with a Captain of the Army, dueling with wooden practice swords.

No one in the Army, for obvious reasons, ever wanted to be the sparring partner of the Son of Heaven. One could do no right, as it were, in that position.

The young Emperor was dressed in extremely precious materials, far beyond what was appropriate for this potentially rough, daily exercise. He moved with great fluidity, however, having been training in the martial techniques since a child, reveling in the aesthetics of it, like a dancer.

Master Eunuch Wang Zhen watched with great delight, as he always did, seemingly smitten with his young ruler.

The sparring went back and forth, then the tip of the Captain's wooden weapon snagged on the Emperor's garment and as it twisted free, there was loud tearing sound.

The bout stopped instantly. Supreme displeasure crossed the eunuch's features, as if his favorite celadon vase had been sent shattering off the floor by the passage of a clumsy dog.

The Emperor scowled momentarily, inspecting the ripped material.

"I rather liked this thing."

The Captain fell to his knees, forehead on the ground. But the young ruler's natural good humor quickly bowled over the momentary shadow across his default sunniness.

"It is not as though I cannot get a replacement," he mused with a smile. "I'm the Son of Heaven after all! And Heaven wants me to be happy."

The Captain, still supine on the ground, cautiously raised his head at those words.

To see that the Emperor's face loomed inches away. The young ruler had crouched all the way down to the ground to tell him face-to-face with a playful smile, "You can get up now. All forgiven."

But to be on the safe side, the Captain kept himself

unnoticeable as possible until after the Emperor had departed the practice ground, at which point he motioned for a couple of his attendants to gather up his equipment, letting out a long breath of relief.

"The Son of Heaven is forgiving," said Eunuch Wang Zhen, taking him by surprise — he thought Zhen had already left. "I am not."

After being escorted to yet another corner of the Forbidden City, the Captain soon found himself tied facedown on a wooden board, screaming in pain as he was beaten across the back of his thighs by a pair of executioners wielding flat, cane-sized wooden rods. These were the so-called "light rods" — and Eunuch Wang had extrajudicially sentenced him to fifty strokes. The skin of his legs would burst open, he would bleed profusely and be unable to walk for several days. But he would not die. Especially at his relatively young age.

Had the eunuch ordered the oar-shaped "heavy rod," bones would have been broken. And the Captain would have been crippled for life. More than fifty strokes and he would have been dead. As the eunuch was unsure of the Emperor's level of affection for this somewhat handsome but otherwise undistinguished soldier, he held off on the death sentence. But only just.

Choe Malli, in white prison undergarments, hair loose and long, was hauled from his jail cell over the shouts and anguished cries of his imprisoned colleagues, and into the courtyard on the grounds of the Royal Palace in full view of the government officials who were required to witness the carrying out of this sentence.

"On what charge?" Choe pleaded to the man who held him tight under the shoulder. "What is my crime?" His voice was calm but his eyes told a different story.

As he was strapped down onto the same type of board the hapless Ming Captain faced at this very moment sixty days ride away in Beijing, his escort answered.

"Entering a falsehood into the public record."

"What falsehood?" Choe could not keep the creeping panic from his voice.

"The King is not a stinkbug."

Choe gave a bitter laugh. "This is unlawful."

"Seventy strokes."

Choe went pale. At his age, that was a death sentence. The executioner moved into view, wooden rod in hand.

"I must talk to the King," entreated Choe.

But nobody seemed to have heard him. The executioner raised the rod, then lowered it across his legs.

"One!" shouted the magistrate in charge. Tap.

"Two!" Tap.

Choe reacted, craning his head to look at the executioner — who had delivered literal taps. Light touches. No pain, no harm.

"What is the meaning of this?" asked Choe.

The magistrate moved close enough to be heard by Choe alone. "His Majesty's order," was his answer.

Another light tap. The officials assembled to witness this sentence looked away, embarrassed by the entire affair.

"Three," counted the magistrate.

Sejong had clearly commuted this sentence — and spared Choe's life. Choe felt a mix of emotions. Relief at not now having to die in excruciating pain. Fury at this public humiliation. But at least, he would live to fight another day. Another day and another night. As many as it took to turn the tables on the man who had done this to him. His Sovereign. His friend.

꧁꧂꧁꧂꧁

The Old Guard headed across the Palace Grounds in the light of the setting moon, making for the barracks

and a well-earned sleep, feeling his age in every limb —
even, he imagined, along the length of every hair he had
left on his head.

But he could not help but admire the quiet beauty of
the place. Taking comfort and thankfulness at this having been his lot in life.

In the barracks, the Sleepless Guard who had been
made that way, in his mind at least, by the older man's
frequent reminiscences, was still awake, mocking him
in his absence.

"'A hundred times over the years. I have saved the life
of the King,'" he bragged, in imitation of the Old Guard.
"'Face-to-face. Hand-to-hand. And once, when the His
Majesty was pissing behind a bush in the Royal Garden,
nose-to-ass'."

A couple of the other guards laughed. Most didn't pay
attention. The New Recruit to whom the Old Guard had
once — or twice or maybe three times — told his tale
just looked uncomfortable.

The Old Guard stood at the entrance, having entered
only moments before.

He had heard everything.

The man who did the mocking spotted him there —
and just looked away. Busied himself with getting his

pallet ready for sleep. The New Recruit felt too embarrassed for all involved to do anything but sit with his eyes cast down, waiting for the awkward moment to pass.

The Old Guard went to his pallet, took off his gear, then lay down to sleep.

But his eyes didn't close. He suddenly wished had kept his adoration of the King to himself. Closed up inside his own heart. And not exposed his precious memories to all who would listen — and those who did not want to. How easy it was for something that had seemed priceless and unique to appear common and silly. He wished for a moment he had never felt anything at all.

Because all he felt now was tired, old, and ashamed.

಄಄಄಄಄

The Mourning Hut in the morning light was wreathed in mist. A sight both lovely and saddening.

The two Princes, dressed in white, paused at the door, bowed, and then stepped inside.

They found their father seated on his throne; eyes closed. As if he had fallen asleep here, while ceaselessly mourning the loss of his wife — their mother.

The eyes of the young men glistened with tears they

barely held back.

"Your Majesty," said the Crown Prince in greeting, and in hopes of making their presence known.

"Father," said his younger brother. The Crown Prince shot him a look for being so familiar — though in this context, it was a minor and excusable breach of propriety.

But still Sejong was still. So the two young men just waited. On their feet, in the cramped surroundings, as if this was part of some penance, for all the times they did not show their mother the consideration that was her due — under both Confucian precept and natural human bonds. They waited until the sun rose high enough outside to angle through the rustic porous walls and strike the King directly in the face.

Sejong opened his eyes.

"My boys."

Both of them fell to their knees. They suddenly could not stop their tears.

Sejong stepped off the throne and moved to them, tu-gging on their sleeves to get them to their feet — and then embraced them both.

For a few moments, the three pooled their sadness, which seemed to spiral around them, carrying all the memories they had of her — or maybe it was Soheon herself who encircled them, to both say goodbye and reassure she would always be near.

It was a paradox of Korean belief — and by extension the Chinese traditions preceding it — that under the influence of both the deeply ancient practice of ancestor worship and a millennium of Buddhism, one could both hope for a better 'next life' for a loved-one who had passed — and simultaneously fully expect that same person to be within 'calling distance' as an ancestral spirit.

So it was for Sejong and his sons. They prayed for her and prayed to her. They hoped she would go somewhere happy and they would not let her go.

Sejong finally stepped back from the two Princes, and got to the task at hand. Nobody bothered to dry their tears as they spoke and listened. As though those tears belonged to Soheon, and they had no business wiping them away.

"To honor your mother, and her faith, I would ask you to translate the Life of the Buddha from Chinese into our language," Sejong said to the Crown Prince. "Using our own alphabet," he added, almost offhandedly.

The Elder Prince reacted. It was a startling command.

The King clearly wanted both to honor the dead Queen and to further the survival chances of the radical new alphabet. It was unclear which took precedent.

But the Crown Prince nodded his head in acceptance, "Yes, Your Majesty."

Sejong then turned to the Younger Prince.

"The 'Correct Sounds for the Instruction of the People' would not have come into existence without the Queen. Your hand has always been the best of the best. I would ask you to create a copy of my proclamation, in that hand, in her memory — to which I will add additional material in the coming days."

Again, the two goals at once.

"Yes, Your Majesty."

The two Princes emerged from the hut, and headed back towards their respective quarters.

Lady Hwang watched them do so, observing half-hidden from nearby, disguised in the daily working clothes of a eunuch. She had gone beyond the Inner Palace to be here, an offense that even one of her rank would be punished heavily for. An actual eunuch sympathetic to her cause hovered around, anxiously watching out for her, making continuously certain that she remained undiscovered by a passing official or member of the household staff.

She waited for the Princes to disappear from view, then she took a tentative step towards the mourning hut. She longed to go inside and comfort the King. But even as she found the courage to do so, she was blocked by the sudden arrival of the Academician Jeong Inji.

Lady Hwang stepped back out of sight as he entered the Mourning Hut with familiarity, as if this was already the latest of several visits. A look to the eunuch told him she was ready to go back to the Inner Palace. He moved to assist that return, seemingly empty-handed as it was.

The eunuch had grown up here, like the rest of his comrades — fellow victims of the process that had made him what he was. Enabling the whims of the denizens of the Inner Palace was second nature to him. That he would be punished even more heavily than his mistress should this latest small indiscretion become known was never far from his thoughts. And only spurred him to make sure that did not happen.

That night, the chamber of the Younger Prince was illuminated by the warm light of an oil lamp, which revealed page after page of single characters hangin from the walls and loosely covering every available surface

— multiple calligraphic depictions of the King's new alphabet. Some instances one letter was repeated, with minor variations, over and over; at others they occurred in sequence, just as Sejong had originally presented them; still others were almost surreal attempts to compose an image using the individual letters as building blocks — like the play of an artist.

All of them were beautiful, executed by an expert, sublimely talented hand. This is why Sejong had called the Younger Prince 'the best of the best' in that regard.

The Younger Prince himself was seated on the floor, with pen and ink and paper, drawing the first page of a new copy of the 'Correct Sounds' proclamation — referring at times as a guide to his own depictions of the new letters that stared back at him from every surface of the room.

The result that took form was as beautiful as a still-life painting by a master of the art.

ひひひひひ

As the son worked, so did the father. Sejong was seated on the floor of the Mourning Hut, writing with pen and ink. The slow and deliberate movements of his hand, the pauses and sudden bursts of speed indicated the composition of something new, not the rote copying more typical of a Confucian-trained scholar — which he was. As well as everything else that he was. He glanced at a stack of pages for reference as he worked: the result of his collaboration with Jeong In-ji, the next installment of 'The Correct Sounds for the Instruction of the People' Line after line written in Chinese, explaining the new alphabet — with a commentary that included multiple and easy to understand examples to aid the reader. He intended to finish composing these pages, and send them this very night to his sons.

Suddenly, he heard a scraping sound and glanced up at the source: A folded piece of paper had just been slid under the door.

The King reacted with surprise — this was totally unexpected — and moved to get it.

On inspection, it was clear that the folding had been done prettily, with good intent. He opened the paper to find a message, written with the letters of his new writing system.

The King was thrilled. This was the first 'note' he had seen created with the 'Correct Sounds' — possibly even the first under Heaven.

He read out loud. "'Lady Hwang can read and write now. Thanks to Your Majesty'."

The author herself, Lady Hwang, stood anxiously outside, in eunuch disguise, hoping a guard would not pass at this hour. Then a note slid back to her from inside.

She eagerly grabbed it, unfolding to reveal a response in the King's letters.

"'The gratitude is all mine'." she mouthed the King's reply.

Lady Hwang was excited and amazed. None of the women in the Inner Palace were allowed the years it would require to learn to read and write with Chinese characters, as all scholars and officials — the aristocratic class of men — were expected to do. This was not just something new and diverting. Until the King had announced the 'Correct Sounds' — this was literally inconceivable.

It felt like magic.

She plopped onto the ground and took out a tiny brush and a tiny inkpot and set the note on her legs and composed a response.

That response slid under the door and Sejong eagerly snatched it up. And smiled with delight at what he read. His deeply serious mood suddenly lightened, the weight upon him turned bearable.

He tried to vocalize the series of letters on the note, which recreated the natural sounds Lady Hwang had so imperfectly imitated for him in days and months and years past — and which was part of what he had boasted for the potential of the new writing system. That no sound was beyond the recording and recreating capacity of his alphabet.

He did his best to sound out what she had just written: The song of the songbird; the rush of the wing; the call of crane⋯.

Lady Hwang listened with her ear pressed at the door — but the King's attempt at a dog's bark made her laugh in spite of herself. Loudly enough to be heard from inside.

"You had better come in here," came the mock stern request.

The consort complied, sliding the door open and closed behind her, finding herself in a heartbeat alone with the King, who was now in good humor. Just what she had wanted to accomplish. Sejong indicated her note.

"I will leave the rooster to you."

She made a low, comic rooster call. He smiled. Then

she noticed the page after page of written words lying about the tiny room. Lady Hwang reached for one of them. Read it aloud.

"'In the last two dreams, he held the sun and then the moon in his hands'." She glanced up at the King. "It is strange. But pretty."

"I call it 'The Moon Reflected in a Thousand Rivers.' A poem to honor the memory of the Queen."

The small room was suddenly filled with that memory.

"What does it mean?" Lady Hwang asked quietly.

"That the Buddha is the original source of all wisdom, even if our understanding of that wisdom comes in multiple forms. As the moon is reflected in a thousand rivers."

Lady Hwang considered for a moment. And came to her own conclusion. "The Queen is the moon. You see her in every other woman's face. Mine, as well."

She looked again at the page. And glanced again at the rest of them. It looked as if the interior space was entirely filled with the King's letters. She suddenly had a realization.

"Is this in honor of her memory?" Lady Hwang's voice was even. "Or just another way for Your Highness to propagate the alphabet?"

It sounded like an accusation. Sejong quietly and carefully chose his words.

"Sometimes a thing can be two things."

At that moment, there was a shift in the cloud cover of the night outside, and the interior space around them was filled with moonlight, illuminating the words of the King's poem as if it were a prayer.

෨෩෪෫෬

The 'Correct Sounds' swept through the Inner Palace as quickly as the juiciest gossip. In a matter of weeks, the consorts and their attendants, the housemaids, even the kitchen staff — not to mention the eunuchs — all had taught each other the King's new alphabet, and notes were being shoved under doors, tucked into sleeves, transferred from palm to palm.

All of it right under the nose of the Head of Household. A situation that could hardly last, as she had a very good sense of smell.

CSCSCSCS

Choe Malli glanced up from his studies at the indominable woman in front of him. The Head of Household had just placed two handfuls of confiscated notes onto his writing desk.

He stared at them with revulsion. As if the scraps of paper had been retrieved from a latrine. Even that foul prospect, thought the academician, was more acceptable than the infernal symbols that covered every inch of paper. As if the women who had written them could not contain themselves. The King's invention, he thought, provided the means to vomit every trivial thought into potentially permanent existence. Onto the page. It had only been a matter of months since the announcement. And already, all of Choe's fears were coming to pass.

"This small-minded game cannot be encouraged," is all he said to the Head of Household.

CSCSCSCS

A laundry maid stood on a wooden box intended to elevate her several inches off the floor. Putting her calves in easy reach of the Head of Household who beat them over and over with a long switch of wood held in one hand. On the other hand was evidence of the crime: More of the crumpled notes written with the King's letters.

The maid had tears in her eyes, but tried not to cry out. Nearby stood half-a-dozen other working women of the palace, waiting for their turn to be punished — in accord with Choe's warning to their supervisor.

His counter-assault had begun.

A few nights later, he sat at his desk, reading a historical account written in Chinese characters by the light of a lone oil lamp. Taking comfort in the certainty that a few frantic scribbles of 'meet me in the kitchen' and 'did you hear about so-and-so?' scrawled on the equivalent of toilet paper in comparison with the immeasurable extent of knowledge and culture captured by the ideographs of the Chinese writing system was like a candle held up to the blazing sun. Its light, by comparison, so trivial as to be non-existent. So it surely would be for Sejong's alphabet. The plight of a tiny flame at noon. It did not have a chance.

"Master! Master!" Choe glanced up at the voice outside his door, bemusement instantly giving way to concern. It was far too late in the night for this to be anything but a problem.

"Enter."

The door slid open, a younger man — his assistant — lowered his head deferentially, but his voice was urgent.

"Please come."

༺༒༺༒༺

Woodblock printing had been in use in China since the Tang Dynasty — in the 7th century A.D. as reckoned by the Western Calendar — and moveable metal-type invented in Korea in the late 1300s. So the Government Printing Office a few streets away from Sejong's Palace had been printing documents with moveable metal type decades before Gutenberg and his Printing Press.

On this night, the Office again was humming along. A printer pulled a freshly inked page from a metal-type font tray — Chinese characters interspersed with the King's new alphabet: a printed version of the King's pronouncement with multiple pages of commentary and examples — the 'additional material' Sejong had mentioned to his sons, the Princes.

"Gentlemen," Choe Malli greeted them as he stepped in off the street. And stopped cold. Shocked at the sight of the King's secret publication. "What is this?"

"'The Correct Sounds for the Instruction of the People,

Explained',", came the off-handed reply. It was not their place to question or overthink a work-order from the Palace. But that very casual acceptance of the King's radical new writing method sent an avalanche of anxiety down Choe's spine.

He stared in a state of surprise bordering on shock at the metal letters on the printing tray. The fonts in front of him had just been used to weaponized the King's alphabet. To make it so commonplace as to be accepted by all and sundry without batting an eye. This was the worst thing he could have seen on this night, he thought, short of Yeomna, Judge of the Dead. As a proper Confucian gentleman, of course, infernal deities were not in his purview. They might or might not exist. Either way, it had no bearing — according to the Sage — on correct behavior in the world of the living. Especially, in the world of politics. So yes, these pages being methodically pressed and pulled from lines of ink-covered metal letters were most certainly the worst thing he could have experienced on this particular evening. Death itself notwithstanding.

A short time later, a short distance away, Chief Councilor Hwang Hui pulled on a night robe appropriate to greet the visitor who had come to call at his home while he turned and tossed on his bed, his dreams bespattered by slashes of blackness like the swaths of ink the King had painted across the Palace flagstones.

Choe met him in the courtyard. "Forgive the hour," apologized the Confucian.

"Forgiven."

Choe's voice was dark. "Persuasion, even at the end of a rod, is no longer enough. The Sage himself was willing to journey across China and join a rebellion when circumstances called him into action. Have we not ourselves been called? By the most intolerable of circumstances?"

The Chief Councilor just looked at him.

"And all we need do," Choe concluded, "Is journey across town."

By the time Choe had indeed crossed town, the Office of Publications was already in flames — and so was everything around it. The alarm bell of the Royal Palace had been tolling ominously, over and over, for the last hour, sending soldiers and volunteers to the site of the potential disaster.

For disaster it could become. The capital, Hanseong, was mostly built of wood — even the Palace itself — and it was not unheard of for entire cities in this era to burn down given dry conditions and an unlucky wind.

Choe watched as soldiers on the rooftops emptied buckets of water down onto the flames through the gaps burned open from below. As volunteers clambered up the outside walls hauling fresh buckets. And still more lined up carrying water from the nearby wells to the site.

Choe watched and told himself: Even if the entire city is left in ashes, this was the right thing to do. If the capital must die for the Korean people to live, then so be it. If an inferno the size of this entire valley is needed to turn the King's alphabet into smoke for all time — then let it all burn. Choe had heard it said already by the uneducated, by the poor, by women and slaves — even by more than a few of his own scholars — that the letters were divinely inspired. Fine. Then Heaven can have them back

Then he saw the King. Carrying water to the fire fighters. Or at least, the King's face. Wreathed in smoke and vapor, dreamlike — wearing the disguise he always wore when he left the palace to lose himself among the common people.

Their eyes met for a moment. Choe was responsible for this assault against the 'Correct Sounds'. Did the King suspect him?

Then the King smiled. And in Choe's mind, the smile was the same as that of the Haetae — the bulldog-shaped, lion-like creature of myth whose statues in stone guarded Palace and city from fire — the job folklore had assigned to them. Choe blinked hard, a rush of people brushed past in front of him — and then the King was gone.

Choe cleared his mind. Did he really see that? Had the King truly been there? Or was it a trick of the smoke and Choe's own feelings of guilt?

Suddenly, a security officer appeared and whispered into Choe's ear, "We have located the source." Choe glanced down at the man's open hand — which held a smoke-blackened metal type that had been forged into the letter 'ㅠ'. Choe nodded, assenting to what came next.

And what came next was the torching of the forge operated by the King's old friend — the Taoist Swordsmith — who had taken the figures of the new alphabet and given them form as metal. As the Tao manifests matter from the formless idea. It was he who had supplied the Printing Office with the new typeface.

The clay molds he had used lay broken and scattered across the workshop; the metal pieces were melting in the intense heat of the fire; and the waterwheel itself was burning — when it rotated through the water of the stream that ran through the building, steam shot up, creating a scene from one of the eight- to twelve-thousand hells of the Buddhists, depending on which Buddhist authority was being cited.

But the Swordsmith did not believe in those eight — to twelve-thousand hells or indeed, any type of afterlife at all. Though the thought momentarily crossed his dying mind, as both hope and fear. He lay broken on the dirt floor, skull cracked from the assault that had taken him down. His eyes had watched the masked intruders set the place on fire — using his own furnace as the source of the flames. Even as his consciousness faded, he thanked those flames for providing him with a livelihood for so many years, and saw no irony in being consumed by that which had so long been seemingly under his command. "Never a servant," was his last thought, "But my collaborator." And then he rejoined the source of the Tao that had brought him into being, as the matter that had given him form once again became formless.

Just like the tiny raised letters on the ends of each metal type rod that flattened out of existence as they became molten, vanishing into the color of the sun.

છબ્કુછબ્કુછબ્

The brother Princes dropped down from the walls surrounding the Royal Palace grounds, dressed in the clothing of laborers, hauling a large satchel between them, landing hard on the hard ground.

The Crown Prince glanced back up at the wall, "We have inherited the worst habits of our father."

His younger brother smiled, "If only we retain half of the best."

It was always debatable whether more problematic for a family to have genius off-spring and not-quite-that-way-parents — or the other way around. And this was most definitely, by all possible measures, the other way around. One might have expected that a son would be privy to the peccadillos and peculiar deficiencies of character that only day-to-day observation might reveal. But in this case, there was nothing in Sejong's personality or behavior to detract in any way from his brilliance. Even from ringside seats. The brothers could only watch in awe like the rest of the Kingdom if not history itself. And rather than envy, thank whatever sources of causality pertained in the cosmos to let that particularly burdensome cup pass them by.

And then the Princes vanished into the darkness of the capital.

൙൙൙൙൙

The Master Woodcutter was expecting them. He quickly slid aside the door to his shop, and invited the Princes inside. They opened their satchel and unrolled a scroll: Revealing a beautifully drawn calligraphic version of the first page of the King's expanded 'Correct Sounds' proclamation. This is what Sejong had assigned to the Younger Prince and what the young man had faithfully executed.

The Master sliced the first page from the scroll and handed it off to an Apprentice Woodcutter, who ran a roller of glue across the backside, then pasted it onto a woodblock.

Then Master himself grabbed a hand-tool and started gouging out the wood in the white spaces around the letters — beginning the difficult process of carving a woodblock for printing multiple copies of the King's proclamation.

This was intended all along to be the true fountain-head of the King's operation. The older, quieter method of woodblock printing was to be the actual source — 'hidden in plain sight' — as opposed to the Printing Shop with its large office and modern methods of moveable metal type.

The Printing Shop was the diversion — its highly public nature drawing the attention of the enemies of the alphabet and their arsonists. And the Swordsmith, the sacrifice. He had himself predicted that the King must lose all those whom he held dear in the furnace of Heaven's turning. And so it was coming to pass. With many more to go.

⋘⋙⋘⋙

The Captain of the Guard sat on the floor behind his desk, in his office at the Department of Corrections, studying a calendar.

The Old Guard appeared at the open door, still grimy with ash and dirt from fighting the fire of last night. Part of the massive effort to keep the capital from burning. It had succeeded. But the whole town seemed exhausted.

"Ah. Come in."

The Old Guard bowed and entered. His superior handed him a clean cloth. "That was a night to remember," said the Captain affably. "I'm glad you came through it with no more than some ash in what is left of your hair." He rubbed his own prematurely balding pate. "Granted, you've got more left than I do."

The Old Guard said nothing. The Captain indicated the calendar. "I am planning my escape."

"Sir?" The older man finally spoke.

"To the farm of the father-in-law. And my retirement." He indicated the floor in front of the desk, an invitation. The Old Guard reluctantly sat down. He was not used to 'socializing' with a superior.

"Already?" he inquired, awkwardly attempting small-talk.

The Captain poured a small cup of wine for the two of them. "I am older than I look," he said with irony. "And younger than I feel."

He handed the cup to the Old Guard. And as they drank, turned his head slightly — honoring age before rank.

"What are your plans?" he said offhandedly.

The man in front of him stiffened. "My duty."

"Yes. Well, one also has a duty to family."

"I have no family."

"Then to one's ancestors."

The Captain poured another cup for them, but the Guard didn't take it. Instead, he got to his feet.

"Sir, my shift is about to begin."

"It is time for you to retire." The Captain finally said what he had called the man here to say to him. And got the answer he expected.

"His Majesty needs me."

"His Majesty needs all his subjects. It is still time for you to retire."

"Is that an order?"

The Captain considered for a moment. "No."

The Old Guard instantly turned towards the door to go.

"Not yet an order."

But the threat was clear. The Old Guard continued out the door.

The Captain drank both cups of wine in quick succession. No point in wasting it. He vowed to himself that the next time he wouldn't be so easy on the oldest man in his company.

Another day. Another visit from the representative of the Suzerain. And another Confucian Rite with which to greet them.

The large diplomatic retinue from Ming China wound its way up the center of the city, towards the Royal Palace for an audience with the King.

As always, the Ming Envoy and Vice Envoy were seated on carried palanquins — Joseon soldiers guarded their movement; the locals came out to watch.

At the Royal Assembly Hall, the Ming Envoy raised up the scroll that had been placed on a stand in the position of honor where the King would otherwise be.

The Vice Envoy commanded in Mandarin,

"Prepare to hear the words of the Great Ming!"

Sejong was standing in a subordinate position before the scroll, as propriety — and power differential — dictated. This was the last thing he wanted to be doing now, but as always, he carried it off with the necessary — and by now expected — aplomb.

In accord with protocol, he swept his vestments back, and bowed down, awaiting the words composed by the young Emperor of China. Or at least, by the eunuch who had dictated over the shoulder of the young Emperor of

China.

The Ming Envoy unrolled the scroll, and he gave voice to the words of the Emperor and/or eunuch.

"Our thoughts have often turned to our small brother, Joseon King, with affection. Guiding with benevolence, a people whom we consider practically Our own."

As always, these words were borderline insulting — certainly patronizing. Choe snuck a glance at the King to see how he was handling it — but Sejong's face remained impassive.

"But now, those thoughts are colored with concern," read the Envoy. "The news of the death of the Queen has reached Our ears. As you have lost a wife, We have lost a daughter. Or so it feels to Us."

Nobody expected this. Sejong least of all. His eyes suddenly glistened. A reaction seen by everyone present. And in a cascade effect, they too, were struck with sadness and appreciation for this unanticipated acknowledgement of their sadness. No matter how warped or contorted by considerations of power, by whether or not this communication had come from Emperor or eunuch or a flock of cranes overhead — it was the words that mattered. And words became tears. For the Queen they had all lost.

Gyeonghoeru — the same faerie-like, seemingly float-ing pavilion that had always functioned as the setting for welcome banquets — did so again all this day. With dancers and musicians; elaborate dishes and 'bottom-less' drinking cups.

The event had been going on for hours and the glow from the wine was on everyone's faces.

The King and his ranking ministers and scholars were seated formally across from the Ming Envoy, Vice Envoy and their staff. But the atmosphere had gotten looser, as it always did by this point. The Envoy now used the local language.

To complain.

"The journey grows less and less tolerable every time I make it. Having a vassal kingdom is a sword with two edges. The tribute is good — but all these visits, I could do without."

Again, this was patronizing. And again, Choe eyed Se-jong for his reaction. But the King did not take the bait.

"The Emperor is indeed far away," he said evenly. Then he indicated a late afternoon sunbeam reflecting off the golden cup in front of him.

"But behold: A beam of light from the perfect sun,

strikes a cup of gold. And for a moment, it is as if the sun itself has reached out, and deigned to touch my hand."

He raised up the cup, and inclined his head to the Envoy.

"So I am honored by your light. And the sun behind you. For me, they are one and the same."

The Envoy was moved. This level of gracious dignity was not what he expected. He raised his own cup, in a toast.

"May Your Majesty live a thousand years."

"As a mountain is held in a grain of sand," replied Sejong, "So a thousand years of contentment is contained in this moment, here and now. It is enough."

"Hao! Hao!" An enthusiastic "Yes! Yes!" from the Envoy. Everyone smiled brightly, and drank a round together again.

But Choe downed his own cup with a kind of fierceness that revealed a growing desperation. Would the King never make a mistake that left him vulnerable?

Later that night, after the ceremony, Choe and Chief Councilor Hwang Hui paced along the shore of the artificial lake — the pavilion across the water was busy with the bustle of clean-up by eunuchs and Palace staff.

"The Rite of Diplomacy; the Royal Protocol for the Reception of the Envoy of Ming, perfectly executed," said Choe with unabashed awe.

"Confucius himself could not disagree," grudgingly admitted the Chief Councilor.

"His Majesty on one hand is faithful to our most essential values. But on the other, he betrays us without a second-thought."

"Academician Choe, you take His Majesty's actions too much to heart. He is not betraying you. He does not give you a 'second thought'."

Choe tried to hide it — but those words hit him hard.

"It is not necessary to hate or indeed be in awe of one's opponents," continued the Councilor. "Only to outmaneuver them."

He indicated the banner of Ming China, which was being furled up for storage and safekeeping until the next embassy.

"Do you intend to tell the Envoy of Ming?" he asked. "About the 'Correct Sounds' of His Majesty⋯?"

"Either that," answered Choe, "Or he finds out by some ⋯obscene method."

The Chief Councilor speculated with a nod. "A note written by a prostitute, slid under his door. Or from a seller of stolen goods, appearing alongside the wine in a local tavern."

Choe looked genuinely stricken with concern.

"Such possibilities should sicken all of us."

"Made possible by one man," underlined the Chief Councilor. "And one man alone."

Those words seemed to follow Choe home. He opened his gate and crossed his garden, and stepped into his office — where someone was seated in the shadows, waiting for him.

"What is your business here, at such an hour?" he said calmly as he could. Given that in such circumstances, a murderous bit of thievery or political assassin was the most likely business here, at such an hour.

The response came in the Mongolian language. "The same as yours." The speaker shifted position into enough light to reveal his identity: the Vice Envoy of Ming.

Choe was stunned. "Why are you speaking in Mongolian?"

"Is it difficult to guess?"

A long moment. Then Choe answered — in Mongolian. "It is not. The Ming overthrew the Yuan Dynasty not two generations ago. And sent your Mongolian forefathers back to the Steppe. For surely you are of Mongol ancestry."

"My great-grandmother."

"And that one-eighth share of your blood — female yet — is enough to betray your ruler?"

"It is."

Choe considered this for a very long time. He then continued in his own language.

"What makes you think that I will betray mine?"

The Vice Envoy took a thin document from his garment and handed it to Choe: 'The Correct Sounds for the Instruction of the People, Explained' — as a woodblock print. The King's 'How-to' book had somehow gotten out into the world. Despite arson and murder and all Choe's attempts at suppression.

His face lost all color, his legs went white. He did not know what to do.

"Is the enemy of my enemy my enemy?" said the Vice Envoy, now speaking in the Korean language, quoting the ancient martial proverb seemingly universal to all lands and all times. "Or my friend?"

Choe just looked at him. Pulled himself together. And asked, "What do you propose?"

Pyonghwa and Maedu — the long-suffering, far-traveling interpreters of the King — had stopped in mid-journey at the base of the famed Sakya Pagoda on Myohyang Mountain of Northern Korea. As they had done every time they had been sent to China.

But this time, they were spending the night under the bright moon, sleeping at the base of the structure.

As always, Maedu stared up at the slender, cylindrical stone pagoda, hung with dozens of tiny bronze bells.

And as always, the lack of a charming chiming sound annoyed him to no end.

"Of course, it was too much to ask for an evening breeze. And a little night music."

He picked up a small pebble and threw it at the nearest bell — missing.

"Take care what you say here," said Pyonghwa, sleepily. "Lest it be mistaken for a prayer. And you reincarnate as a local breeze."

"Confucius never even heard of reincarnation. Who are you to speak of it?"

But Pyonghwa kept his always pleasant demeanor. "Perhaps as death grows closer, even the most rigorous Confucian will consider a Buddhist notion or two. And thoughts of an afterlife."

"We are still young," objected Maedu. "Put such senti-mentalities off for another half-century at least."

Maedu pulled out a copy of the King's pronouncement describing the new alphabet. He leafed through it, reading aloud.

"'The sounds of our language are different from the sounds of the language of China···. Consequently, the un-complicated people of our Kingdom cannot express themselves···.' His Majesty means 'stupid', doesn't he? 'The stupid people of our Kingdom'···."

"His Majesty means exactly what he says," said Pyong-hwa. "No less and no more."

Maedu scowled, continued to scan over the page, quoting the most famous line of the document, "'This has made me sad'."

He glanced around at the beautiful surroundings — but his curmudgeonly nature did not seem to allow him to appreciate it.

"Well, I certainly know how that feels," said Maedu.

Pyonghwa just smiled good-naturedly and stretched out and closed his eyes. Maedu paged through the doc-ument for a bit longer, then closed it. "Try to see beyond your blind devotion to the King for a moment," he said.

Pyonghwa opened his eyes at that.

"And tell me what you really think about this⋯." Mae-du indicated the document, "Invention."

Many heartbeats came and went, replaced by the next and the next and the next. Stars sparkled overhead. The crescent moon was sharp as a set of horns. A nighthawk made the uncanny sound a nighthawk makes. Something in the grass nearby did what it always had done.

Pyonghwa's voice was quiet. "It is divine."

༺༻༺༻༺

The Hall of Eunuch Wang Zhen was a version in miniature of the Hall of his nominal superior — the Son of Heaven, Yingzong, Boy Emperor and Sitter Upon the Dragon Throne of Ming Dynasty China.

And as Emperor-like as he could muster — and he mustered quite well, truth be told — Wang had listened to the trip report of Envoy and Vice Envoy, just arrived from the Korean capital. And immediately upon hearing, had summoned Minister of War Yu Qian in order to relay and twist that intel for his own purposes.

"Rumors of an impending attempt on the Joseon King by Mongol agents have reached my ears three times over," he told Yu Qian. "As the Book of Changes says: 'When word goes round three times, believe it.' Indeed, tribesmen are reportedly even now gathering in the north-east, within striking distance of the Korean peninsula."

He stepped down from the dais upon which his own throne had been erected. He called it 'the Phoenix Throne' so as not to be accused of insurrection. But still. Throne it was.

"This is but a prelude to invasion," he continued.

"It must be stopped. Lest the Mongols destroy our strongest ally — and establish another locus from which to attack Great Ming."

"It is a ruse," said the Minister of War. "An assassination would sew chaos and eliminate our ally — they may attempt it. But a full assault with all their forces would be sent against Beijing. Not Hanseong."

The eunuch bristled. "Take a platoon and go have a look."

"And leave Beijing unguarded?"

Again, this angered the eunuch. "The Army remains here. Under command of the Emperor. And the wise counsel of myself. Are you saying that is not enough? Shall I convey your···opinion to the Great Ming?"

Yu Qian said nothing. But he was not happy about this. The eunuch suddenly glanced towards the Vice Envoy, remembering: the intense little man had mentioned something about a document⋯.

"And while you are out there, devote some resources to capturing these Joseon travelers," he commanded the Minister, as a young eunuch assistant handed Yu Qian a rolled-up page. The General unrolled and stared at the faces sketched upon it: barely representative line drawings of Pyonghwa and Maedu — Sejong's wide-ranging interpreters.

"They reportedly carry a potentially destabilizing document written by their King," explained the Wang Zhen.

The War Minister looked doubtful. "Is the Korean King an ally or not?"

"Yes. An ally. And not."

The General considered the undeniable political reality of that observation. While the Vice Envoy — the undercover Mongol operative who met in secret with Choe Malli against Sejong — just stared on. Confident in his own duplicity.

The Port of Geoje was the busiest of the islands off the southeastern edge of the Korean peninsula — having been in business, as it were, for millennia. It was strategically located as a kind of gateway into Korea, and historically had gone both ways: the place from which to launch an attack against Japan — or an invasion of Korea.

Only a couple of decades previously, the former had occurred: Sejong's father Taejong had stepped aside from the throne in support of his son and heir, but still maintained a deep interest — if not active pleasure — in matters military. Joseon had had a pirate problem; Taejong aimed to fix it. And so, a naval expedition was sent against the nearest Japanese pirate base. Both sides caused serious damage, and the result was a series of truces negotiated over the years that granted trading privileges to the defeated pirates as long as they promised to put a stop to all raids on the Korean coast — their own and those originating from the Seto Inland Sea.

The Sea Lords of Seto were not happy about this. As they had been left out of the negotiations and received nothing in return for putting an end to their raids. Despite also having suffered casualties at the hands of Sejong and his father.

But as Scholar Shin boarded a Japanese trading ship bound for Japan, a woodcut-print copy of the King's most recent proclamation of the 'Correct Sounds' tucked safely inside his garment and kept close to his heart, the last thing he imagined was that Koje was ripe for another invasion⋯.

He handed a small wooden chit of passage to the Second Mate checking him on board. And asked in Japanese,

"May I inquire as to our exact route?"

"Fukuoka, Yamaguchi, Hiroshima and Okayama," came the answer. "How far do you go?"

"Kyoto."

"You can find another ship at Okayama to Osaka. And overland from there."

"Yes, I will do so. Thank you."

But as the Second Mate waved Scholar Shin on deck, he seemed to study the Korean traveler for longer than was necessary for this trivial bit of private enterprise. Scholar Shin took no notice.

And that night, standing at the railing, staring up at stars he thought were never so bright as they were at sea, using a small but sophisticated astronomical instrument to determine the location that had been developed by his own King, he took no notice either of the padding sound of steps against the wooden deck, or the thwap against his skull when struck by the leather thong filled with sand — a less sophisticated device than that which fell from his hand, but still effective, given its narrow range of intended tasks.

The Second Mate helpfully caught Scholar Shin under one arm to ease him — now unconscious — to the deck, with the familiarity of an expert at this kind of thing.

When Scholar Shin regained his senses, it was in the bottom of a rowboat, seated with two other unlucky travelers, all with hands tied — neatly, even pleasingly so, as Japanese pirates were still Japanese, after all, with the all-pervading aesthetic appreciation intact. He admired the knot, and blinked against the bright sun, then took note of the pirate hovering above him, then the pilot — Shark, though he didn't know that name yet, and never would — and a small boy, Pup, whose name he would indeed learn, by a means most unexpected yet literally close to his heart.

The child without hearing and without speech stared at the prisoners, fixating for no reason in particular on Scholar Shin.

"Are we to be ransomed?" Shin asked aloud. Nobody answered. Not the pirate or the pilot or the little boy.

Shin took note of the child's blank expression, but did not think much about it, then took in his surroundings — which included the famously beautiful red wooden gate of the Itsukushima island shrine, floating in the middle of the water, just to the port side of their small craft. Shin could not help but admire it, despite his circumstances. The inevitable reaction of all who passed this way.

He had, in fact, passed this way twice before on 'errands' for the King — trading Buddhist scriptures and celadon vases with Japanese scholars and Daimyo for an assortment of documents that Shin now knew Sejong had been mining for inspiration while contemplating the invention of his new writing system.

Now in the hands of pirates, with an unknown future in front of him, Shin took a long look at the wooden pillars, letting the soft crimson quiet as a robin's breast imprint itself upon his memory. In case this was the last time.

Ironic it was then, he thought the next day, to stand in front of another crimson-bedecked creature — Sea Lord Red, leader of a sub-clan of the Murakami, seated on his beach-side throne — and explain what exactly Shin was doing so far from Hanseong and where he was going.

"I have been commanded by the Joseon King to present this document to the Ashikaga Shogun in Kyoto," he said in Japanese, as he raised into view the printed copy of 'The Correct Sounds' with examples and commentaries. "It is an explanation of the writing system that His Majesty has recently created."

The Scholar's attempt to explain this marvelous creation to a pirate king also had a built-in irony, thought Shin. But such were the yarrow stalks fate had thrown him.

The Sea Lord held out his hand. Scholar Shin hesitated. But did not have much choice. He gave the document to his captor, who opened it and seemed to read. Or at the very least, consider it in light of his own world of carefully crafted objects.

"The letters were designed for the Korean people," explained Shin helpfully. "But can represent the sounds of any language."

Suddenly the Scholar could not help but slip into the voice of the Evangelist for the King's alphabet that he had become.

"Indeed, any sound at all! That of a flying crane, a rooster announcing the dawn, a barking dog."

"It is not without interest," interrupted the Sea Lord.

He closed the booklet. Politely returned it. Then told Shin what was to become of him.

"You will accompany us into battle. After we conquer Geoje town, your King will pay the ransom for your return."

Shin was taken aback. This is the last thing he expected to hear. And his mission was clearly more than just a failure. He seemed to have stepped into a disaster in the making. And no conceivable way to even get a warning back to his King — let alone stop an invasion.

⊛⊛⊛⊛⊛

Pyonghwa and Maedu traveled along a road that wound through lush green hills, riding on their simple cart, drawn by a lone horse. This was the far northeast borderlands of the Ming Empire, neighboring the Jurchen tribes of territory that would eventually be known as Manchuria.

Semi-nomadic at most; mostly sedentary and agricultural in comparison with the nomadic Mongols with whom they were often compared due to a shared love of riding and killing things with arrows — the Jurchen had conquered China before (and would do so again —

rebranded as the Manchu, the last Dynasty to rule China). That being the case, their quiet cooperation — as had been the case for the past few decades — was never taken for granted. All the peoples around them — Chinese, Mongol, and Korean — pursued a dizzying amount of strategies involving trade and treaties; conferred titles and intermarriage — anything to keep them quiet.

The Jurchen were satisfied. For the time being.

In the distance, the Korean interpreters eyed a solitary roadside inn that constituted a tiny deviation along the winding road. They had been there before. This was to be the last time.

Their cart and horse secured outside, Pyonghwa and Maedu sat down at a small table — one of only three in this tiny place. Two of the other tables were occupied by rough-looking travelers.

The owner of the place casually moved to the newcomers and kept his voice low so as not to be overheard, speaking in the local dialect of the Jurchen tribes, a mash-up of Mandarin and Mongolian.

"You cannot stay here."

"We always stay here," responded Maedu in the same tongue, annoyed.

"Ming soldiers are looking for you."

That was different.

Half-the-day later, Pyonghwa and Maedu had put the inn as far behind them as a pair of Korean interpreters and a donkey hitched to a wooden cart could — and then some. The way had narrowed, as they had gotten deeper into Jurchen territory. Surely the Ming would not extend the search this far — and risk a political incident with the simmering tribes.

Then they came to a fork in the road.

Maedu didn't even pause, but continued to the right — where the path clearly headed upwards into the mountains. Pyonghwa stopped.

"Two ways forward and no discussion?" he said.

"What is there to talk about? We lose them in the mountains."

"More likely the path quickly narrows to that suitable only for deer and rabbits. And then voles and mice," his voice was pleasant as always. "A dead end for two Joseon interpreters."

"I respectfully disagree." Maedu kept walking, yanking on the donkey to follow.

His partner was taken aback. It was certainly in character for Maedu to be brusque and perpetually annoyed — but dictatorial, no.

"Please stop," said Pyonghwa.

Maedu didn't turn around.

"Maedu!" Pyonghwa remained at the fork. When it became apparent to Maedu that he was not being followed, he finally stopped.

"You are delaying our mission," he called down the hill.

"Our mission is best accomplished by the other path," Pyonghwa pointed. "Which descends into a valley. We have gotten ahead of our pursuers. We now have the opportunity to get beyond their reach. They will give up and return to Beijing."

"Where they would be beaten or executed for failure."

Pyonghwa was surprised by this sudden compassion in his typically self-centered companion. "Then that is their fate," he suggested.

"To avoid that 'fate', they will instead continue to search."

"But we will be safely on our way."

"It is not 'we' whose safety matters."

Pyonghwa just looked at him. Taken aback yet again. What was going on here? Or more to the point, what did Maedu know that Pyonghwa did not know?

The day before Pyonghwa and Maedu had left the capital, in the hour before dawn, at the water well that marked the border of the Inner Palace and the Outer Palace, Sejong had requested Maedu meet him here. 'Summoned' was never a good word with the King, as he tended to put his wishes in the form of invitations rather than demands — at least when it came to his loyal collaborators.

"There is a word of Mongols gathering for a strike against Ming's eastern border. Even against Joseon. Or at least against···the King of Joseon," said the King of Joseon.

"Your Majesty···." The deadly serious look of concern on Maedu's face at Sejong's statement would have been enough for his partner and anybody else who knew him to realize that Maedu's constant griping; his apparent doubts about the King and about the repeated missions abroad had all been a ruse: Maedu was more devoted to Sejong than any of them. His bad attitude was a cover story that allowed him to operate in secret collaboration with the King. As needed. And that need was now.

"I do not believe it," continued Sejong. "Or not entirely. As it was suggested millennia ago: 'Make a loud noise in the East, then strike in the West'."

"The rumors Your Majesty has heard⋯.?"

"Loud noises. I suspect. To distract Ming from the Mongols' true intentions. Regardless, in such a context — with the threat of war — I cannot send my alphabet anywhere near China. Or risk sending you."

Maedu considered for a moment.

"Your Majesty can and must. The 'Correct Sounds' must be sent to Ming — and even beyond. West, East, South, North, Down and Up, Inside and Out. There is no corner of this — or any world — that should be denied." The light in his eyes was that of yet another true believer — like Linguist Pak, like Scholar Shin, like Jeong Inji — who had embraced the King's creation as if was their very reason for taking breath. Again, nobody who knew him would have ever guessed.

"How?"

"'Make a loud noise in the East, then strike in the West'?" repeated Maedu. "We can play that game as well," he smiled. "Who makes more noise than me?"

CRCRCRCRCR

The fork in the road on which he held his ground suddenly seemed to Pyonghwa both literal and metaphorical. Not just two actual paths, but a division between his closest companion and himself. They had grown up together; together learned of the world of people and the world of language; the communion of speech and the bond of silence; they were more than siblings, more than friends.

And now, thought Pyonghwa, who was this?

"What are you talking about?" he said carefully. "Our mission is to deliver a copy of the 'Correct Sounds' to Liaodong"

"Our mission is to divert all Ming pursuit of His Majesty's alphabet to ourselves," revealed Maedu. "To consume whatever resources they have committed to that task. So that"

"So that other missions to China···or passing through China···might proceed unmolested," realized Pyonghwa, stunned.

"Correct."

"What are those other missions?"

"That was not ours to know. We are not military men. Under torture we would chatter like magpies."

Pyonghwa considered all of this. Saddened by it.

"I see."

And now he understood: Maedu was the King's man all along. And only pretended to be otherwise.

"I am sorry I deceived you," said the one who had been more than a sibling, more than a friend, and now seemed an absolute stranger. As if they had just now met.

"His Majesty did not trust me. As he trusted you," said Pyonghwa.

"That is also correct."

Pyonghwa looked deeply wounded.

"The King knew, that at a moment like this," Maedu indicated the crossroads, "I would give my life for His Majesty's creation."

"I would do the same!"

"And yours, too."

"I···." Pyonghwa could not finish the thought.

"You cannot say the same," continued Maedu.

"You would sacrifice yourself. But you would not sacrifice your friend. And for that, I love you."

Pyonghwa considered for a long moment. All was true.

"His Majesty knows us better than we know ourselves."

"Yes."

They stared at each other for a long time. Then Pyonghwa indicated the left dividing path that led to safety and escape. His voice quiet but insistent. "This way, please."

"No."

"Then I will carry you."

Suddenly, they were fighting. These were middle-men not martial artists; friends not enemies. And so, the action was crude and violent and bloody and desperate. Punches and tackles and crashing across the hard ground.

By the time the Chinese Captain and his squad came upon the same fork in the road, the two translators were barely recognizable: Bloody and begrimed; exhausted and unmoving, they held each other up, no longer capable of throwing ano-ther punch.

The Captain reined his horse, dug into his satchel and unrolled the drawing he had been given in Beijing: the match between the charcoal-sketched faces on paper and the men in front of him would barely hold up even in a court predisposed to summary justice.

But his soldiers were tired; the further they roamed out here, the more likelihood of encountering a band of Jurchen on a hunt — and if the hunters hadn't already bagged a buck, they might just decide on some impromptu target practice against the Empire.

With a nod, the Captain ordered his men to proceed.

Pyonghwa and Maedu observed their own arrest as if from behind a glass or from within a fever-dream; too exhausted to put up even verbal resistance let alone attempt to flee. It was all they could do to speak to each other through bloody and swollen lips.

"Forgive me?" asked Maedu.

"Yes," answered Pyonghwa.

ๆๆๆๆๆ

The Exile Huang Zan spent this morning contemplating the Scholar's Stone on his writing desk — an accoutrement any man of letters of the time was loathe to be without. His was an asymmetric shape, two-hands high, of Lake Tai limestone, and therefore featured the porousness that typified such an origin, a characteristic much-prized in this sort of thing.

The stone did not resemble any famous actual peaks or known natural formations, but he imagined it to have originated in a never-before-seen-by-mortal-eyes cliffside on the immortal mountain island of Penglai — as noted in 'The Classic of Mountain and Seas' — a fifteen-hundred year old copy of which was kept in the library of Imperial Palace behind the walls of the Forbidden City — which he had only intended to borrow for the night, and would have successfully done so, were it not for the librarian's assistant, a eunuch who seemed to have had eyes in the back of his head.

Enough of that, he thought. Exile is exile, and pining about it all day and all night never got him anywhere. Except to the next day and the next night.

The sudden creak of a large wooden wheel that could be heard even from inside his study dispelled that reverie.

When he stepped into his garden, his servant already had sent the unseen cart creaking on its way. And handed over to Exile Huang what he himself had just been given. A small package wrapped in unassuming cloth, which upon unwrapping revealed itself to be a thin, woodcut printed pamphlet.

"The Correct Sounds for the Instruction of the People, Explained." announced the title in written Chinese. He opened it to reveal the continuing Chinese description interspersed with letters that the wide-reading scholar had never seen before. Some few of the forms he instantly observed, were recognizable as pieces perhaps — fragments — of the consonants created by the Monk

'Phags-pa — a line here a vertical stroke there; others resembled symbols from further west — but what was this? The actual anatomical configuration of the human organs of speech? As the primary inspiration and guide for the shapes of the letters?

That had never been done anywhere, at any time.

He closed the pamphlet and closed his eyes. To be an Exile was a lonely business. This was like finding a new friend. Or rather, finding out that an old friend was secretly a King. A cause for great celebration. No, that wasn't it. A King had created this, after all. King Sejong. So it was like realizing that the King was in fact an Immortal from Penglai! For who else could do something like this?

But that wasn't it either. Banishment had gotten to him. To be an Exile was to have one's thoughts chase each other like tigers and wolves and foxes and rabbits and carrots. He did his best to stop it. For just a moment, as he opened the booklet once again and absorbed what was inside.

Not an Immortal. Not even a King. Above all, this was the work of a human being. Just like himself. Divinity and inherited rank were irrelevant. This was what a person was capable of. And that optimistic and even joyous conclusion was enough to stop the chasing of his thoughts, and make him happy.

At least for the rest of the day.

ﾟ｡ﾟ｡ﾟ｡ﾟ｡ﾟ

When that day turned to night, Sejong paid another visit to the room-filling Water Clock a few steps from his bed chamber, to talk again to the Clock's inventor, his dead friend Yeong Sil.

"Yeong Sil, have you eaten?" He set up a small bowl of rice on one of the thick horizontal supporting beams of the time-keeping apparatus. "Have you anything to drink?" He poured two small cups of rice wine.

Then the King watched silently as the water reached the top of its two-hourly cycle, and set the Rube Goldberg-type mechanical sequence in motion. The water flowed, the pistons rose, bronze spheres fell, levers clacked, the doll-like figures banged drum, cymbal, chimes⋯. Sejong took comfort in its every motion; every sound.

"Ah, yes," he laughed. As if those sounds were the voice of his dead friend, and had actually responded with some small joke between them. "So you say."

Until finally, the King-like figure emerged to mark the

time. Then the mechanism shut everything down again as it reset itself for the next cycle. The chamber was silent.

"Dear Friend," he said, almost whispering.

"I think I will see you again, very soon."

He had never felt so vulnerable. As if he stood alone in this world. With nothing and no one awaiting him in the next.

გიგიგიგიგი

Midway across the Korean strait separating the Japanese islands from the peninsula of the Koreans, the Wokou armada continued with the help of the wind. A kamikaze, in fact — 'divine-wind' — as everything including a breeze was dubbed in wartime if it was even remotely favorable. And this strong Easterly — along a stretch of water that typically saw the opposite — was encouraging indeed.

Sea Lord Red's throne-like chair had been relocated from its sandy perch on the beach of his island-stronghold to the middle of the deck of the lead ship — running to the far left of the line of attack boats, and slightly ahead, positioned to attack first anything that tried to stop them. Sailors busied themselves around him, with sails and lines and tackle. Shark — designated pilot for this invasion — was at the tiller, guiding the ship — which meant a constant negotiation with the wind, prevailing and in their favor as it might have been. And so he did not mind that Pup was apparently amusing himself in another part of the ship. He took his son's inability to speak or hear as an indication of insurmountable impairment — but the child could swim like a tarpon, and so the father had no concern for the son's safety anywhere near water — including the middle of the sea.

The boy at this moment was in the cramped hold below deck, where he had been keeping an eye, more or less, on Scholar Shin — who was roped to a post.

Pup was crouched on the planks of the bilge, drawing with his finger a line in some water that had been sloshed against the flat planed horizontal timbers.

Scholar Shin took notice of this instinctual urge towards 'writing' — or at least, so he assumed — and as a 'true believer' in his King's new alphabet, could not help but see the child as a potential convert.

"Boy," he called out in Japanese.

There was no response.

When he was very young, Pup knew that each day was so profoundly different from the yesterday that had preceded it; so very other than the tomorrow that would follow; that the division of time by the rising and setting of the sun seemed arbitrary and even wrong; that instead, time had a shape and sometimes even a fragrance that shifted and changed like something living: time was perceivable, not just measurable.

In that context, he once stepped out into a morning and saw that the day was gold. And inside of him, without the mediation of language, formed instead of pure revelation, was this: 'How wonderful.'

He had run back into the house to tell them — his parents, his uncle and his aunts — but his tongue did not move no matter how much he willed it to do so, and his face, which surely must have expressed the same thought — 'how wonderful' — went unseen. The adults did not even look at him. They had already given up; marked him as without ears that could hear, absent a voice that could be heard. And so he had become all but invisible to them. Was always there but not there.

At that moment, he felt his wonder fold in on itself, collapse and disappear. He would never know a day to be golden again. And that it ever was had been instantly forgotten.

In one of the many stories told about a god, it was said that the biggest of gods — the God — was aware of every sparrow that fell. And so by extension in both directions, every star that exploded, and every subatomic particle that decayed.

All that has ever been forgotten is remembered.

❦❦❦❦❦

"Boy." Again, Scholar Shin called out.

Still nothing. He considered the silent child. Then, on a directed whim, suddenly stamped the flooring below him hard with one boot. The child reacted to the vibrations transmitted across the surface of the wood and glanced up, staring for a long moment.

Then, as the boy started to turn back to his own business, Scholar Shin stamped twice in a row. The boy suddenly banged back with his fist on the floor — two times.

Shin considered the results of his little experiment and thought, "There are many ways to find a voice in this world."

Deep into Lesson #1, Scholar Shin, still bound, took the boy's hands in hand as though he was holding writing brush and paper, and 'drew' the King's new characters with the boy's own index finger on the palm of the boy's other hand, spelling out the word in phonetic Japanese.

"Hand," he said in Japanese, knowing Pup could not hear the word.

He gently shook the boy's hand for emphasis. Then he directed the boy's hand to a nearby puddle in a warping of the boards, and filled his palm with: "Water." He said the word aloud. Then used the boy's index finger to spell the Japanese word for 'water' into the boy's palm.

Scholar Shin then took Pup's hand and moved it to the top of the child's head, closing the boy's fingers on the boy's own: "Hair."

But as Shin spelled out the word in the same method he had been using, the Boy suddenly pulled away, his thoughts and emotions overwhelmed. He had exceeded his tolerance level for something so radically new as communication.

Pup moved off, and sat again the other side of the bilge. The 'lesson' was over⋯.

The pirates had paused their attack ships in the middle of the strait for a meeting to narrow down the parameters of the impending raid. Three launches met in the water, equidistant from their respective flagships. The prows faced inward like a tri-part pinwheel — Shark and his two counterpart pilots on the other launches skillfully kept them inches apart without bumping — close enough for the Sea Lords to shout at each other and be heard over wave and wind.

"Land at night, they will have no warning," shouted Sea Lord Green.

"We will kill them in their sleep," agreed Sea Lord Blue loudly. "Loot the town. And be back at sea before dawn."

Sea Lord Red considered all this for several silent moments.

"You sound like pirates." He did not have to shout for the insult to be heard. The others bristled at this. As obvious and accurate as the term was, pronounced with a certain inflection it sounded like an insult. Red continued. "We are Lords of the Sea. Shoguns with ships. This is no mere raid, but the vanguard of an invasion."

"The Imperial army is with the Ashikaga Shogun!" shouted Sea Lord Blue.

"To conquer the port is to demonstrate the vulnerability of Joseon," continued Sea Lord Red, cutting him off.

"And the weakness of their king. The Ashikaga Shogun will smell the blood in the water even as far as Kyoto."

"You drew us away from our islands and onto the waves and into this raid," said Sea Lord Green with a hard look on his face, "Knowing all along your intention was to start a war?"

"Start and finish," came the answer.

The other two just looked at him. Then Sea Lord Blue laughed out loud, nodding "Yes." Sea Lord Green nodded gravely in agreement.

The plan had gone from a mere raid to an actual invasion. From a nuisance plundering to an existential threat to Sejong himself.

Shark considered all this without any change of expression. He would do whatever was required of him by his master. That's what he had always done. The world may have called him and his Lord Wokou — but to be a pirate was not to jettison the Bushido ethos of the Samurai. There were times, perhaps to over-compensate for the(lack of)expectations mainland Japanese society had of him and his kind, that Shark felt he must be more thoroughly Samurai than any warrior who stood ready at the right hand of the Shogun in Kyoto — or indeed, the

Japanese Emperor himself.

And so, in Shark's mind, Sea Lord Red could do no wrong — no matter how wrong whatever his Lord wanted to do might be. Someday, Shark knew, he would follow his master to a watery grave, his only hesitation was Pup. What could a boy like that possibly do on his own? How long would he survive a life that would offer nothing but torment? The only option, Shark had decided — when that grave opened up upon whatever wave he was sailing at the time — was his own blade across his son's throat. Shark did not like to think about that. But what else could he do? — he must spare the child from much worse at the hands of the uncaring world.

⊚⊚⊚⊚⊚

Mid-day slump at the western gate to the Royal Palace of Joseon. A handful of laborers and wagon-driving suppliers were still trickling in after the morning rush; exiting traffic heading back the other way had not yet started.

The Old Guard was on duty. As he and his two colleagues screened those coming through, a rustic cart came into view, pulled by an uncooperative old nag pulled by a hooded provisioner.

A scene that might be replayed tens of times a day at this working gate. But the Old Guard ignored all that for what he had trained himself to look for without even thinking: the small piece of yellow fabric tied to cart or horse or laborer himself that would indicate to anyone 'in the know' standing watch that this was the King in disguise.

And there it was: a tiny wisp of amber-hued muslin wrapped around the back panel of the cart — exactly where it should be.

The Old Guard instantly waved the cart through, lowering his eyes so as not to stare at what he assumed from decades of practice was the King.

But he could not help but respectfully watch as the apparent provisioner continued into the Palace grounds — and take note of the same type of boots Sejong had always worn. As a final confirmation of identity — just to be on the safe side.

The man with the cart continued along, yanking again on the recalcitrant worn-out horse; the Old Guard turned towards a pair of workmen carrying tools. He checked their wooden entry passes, and let them proceed.

Business as usual. Or so it seemed.

A short time later those same boots were striding across the common grounds, heading for the supply depot that was a typical stop for providers of the sundries of mundane life in the Palace — the same conveniently sequestered location that provided Sejong the cover he needed to change back into his requisite effects and rejoin the Royals.

But the Old Guard had gotten it wrong, the only time in his long career.

This was not the King at all.

༺༻༺༻༺

Below deck on the Wokou flagship, Scholar Shin rested at the base of the pillar to which he was still tied, watching as Pup watched him. What was going through the boy's mind? wondered the Korean. Had this sudden introduction of what must have seemed like pure magic — to hear without hearing, to speak without speaking, a way to revision the entire world — was it too much for the child?

Then Pup suddenly moved across the wet planks, grabbed Scholar Shin's hand, and with his finger wrote 'water' onto the palm of the man's hand, using the new

Korean alphabet to represent the sounds of the Japanese word — just as Shin had tried to teach him. Then the boy stared him in the face, as if looking for confirmation.

Shin was elated.

"Yes! 'Water.' That is how you spell 'water'!"

The Boy seemed unsatisfied with that response. He wrote it again — more insistently.

"I think you are asking if I want water," Shin considered aloud. Then, "The answer is 'yes'."

He grabbed the boy's hand, spelled out 'yes' in his palm. Then mimed splashing water in his own mouth.

Pup instantly moved off, filled a metal cup with water from an open barrel and brought it back to the Scholar Shin. Who drank it between his tied hands.

He was absolutely thrilled that the boy had learned this. As if it was some kind of proof of the legitimacy of Shin's own dedication to his King's dream.

"Thank you," he said to the child.

He wrote with his index finger into the palm of the boy's hand. Then, as if not wanting his student to get the mistaken idea that 'finger-on-palm' was a necessary part of this process, he dipped his fingertips into the water cup and drew on the wood next to his face — the same letters he had just written in the boy's hand.

The boy stared at it. As if yet another light had gone off in his head.

He moved across the floor, found a piece of charcoal from a pile of cooking fuel, grabbed a rag off a rag pile, and carried the two objects back to the Scholar Shin.

He dropped to the floor, spread out the rag and wrote on it with the charcoal — spelling out the other words Shin had tried to teach him.

"'Hand'····.", "'Water'····.", "'Hair'····." Shin pronounced aloud the phonetic Japanese.

Then the boy wrote once more.

"'Thank you'." read Shin.

Shin's eyes grew wet with emotion. He spoke quietly in his own language, "Thank you, young man."

⊹⊱⊰⊱⊰

The bilge was lit by one of the ballast weights — a heavy stone lamp that had been boosted from a Buddhist temple somewhere, at some time or another during the working life of this pirate ship.

Korean Scholar Shin and Japanese pirate boy Pup were pulling an 'all-nighter,' as it were. So energized by the results of their first couple of lessons, they couldn't stop. The floor planks were covered with the contents of several now-opened wooden chests. Functional items: Tools and provisions, water and weapons, armor and wine; and stolen goods: Multi-colored fabrics, flags, painted scrolls, dining ware, assorted ornamentals — anything that could serve as an object to think with.

"'Bird'···.", "'Deer'···.", "'Tanuki'···." said Shin aloud in Japanese.

The Boy was seated on the floor with a stack of paper onto which he wrote with a sharpened piece of charcoal. Spelling out the name of each creature that Shin indicate on an embroidered piece of cloth.

"'Boar'···.", "'Horse'···.", "'Kitsune'···."

This was 'review' of creatures learned a couple of hours before — and so the boy was rapidly moving along.

Scholar Shin pulled a painted scroll into view and pointed to three objects one after another: sea wave, sky, a painted Samurai's bright costume.

The boy looked stumped.

And watching the boy look stumped from the ladder from the deck was his father, who had taken a break from piloting the ship and come down to check on the prisoner. He silently dropped to the floor. Face even. Uncomprehending.

Teacher and student did not even notice.

Scholar Shin took the charcoal and wrote, "'Blue'" in phonetic Japanese, saying the word aloud as he did so, indicating them again for emphasis. "All these things are blue."

It was a next-level concept, and the Boy stared for a long time, struggling with the idea. Then he looked again at the image of the horse they had studied earlier — which sported bright blue battle harness. He drew right on the cloth the same word.

"'Blue'!" read Shin. "That's right! That's blue, too!"

The Scholar transliterated the Japanese affirmative with Sejong's new letters on the paper. "Yes," he pronounced the word in Japanese.

And Shark was suddenly right on top of them. He grabbed Pup by the arm and yanked him away, sending him sprawling across the floor.

Then he grabbed Scholar Shin by the throat and shoved him hard up against the pillar he was tied to. The man's head smashed into the wood and the skin split open.

Shark stared down at the now-scattered scrolls, cloths, and almost magical-seeming words written on the paper.

"Are you Tengu?" he demanded, without fear.

Shin was dizzy from the blow. "'Tengu'?" he answered in Japanese. "A goblin? I am a scholar…of the King…of Korea…."

"What are you doing to my son?"

"I have taught him to read and write."

SMASH! Shark struck him hard in the face. It made no sense to him. The Korean was lying. Or worse, the Korean was a madman.

"With the letters of my King."

SMASH! Another blow. Blood flew from the Scholar's mouth.

"In Japanese! Phonetic Japanese!" He sounded proud — even in the midst of blows that might at any moment end his life.

SMASH! SMASH! SMASH! Now Shin slipped in and out of his native tongue and his rote pitch for the new alphabet. As his sensibility scattered with each slam.

"The letters…were designed…for the Korean people! But can represent…sounds…of any language!"

Death moved closer and closer, as the blows continued over and over.

"Any sound at all! A crane! A rooster!" He was delirious now, as he slumped against the ropes that secured him.

"A barking dog⋯." His head hit the floor. And from there, the kicks to his torso registered as distant impressions — echoes and rumors.

But still he could see. And he saw that the boy had shoved a piece of paper in front of his face, carrying words he had just written. Dazed, barely conscious, Shin sounded out the phonetic Japanese.

"'Mother'⋯, 'Pink'⋯, 'Snow'⋯."

Shark went numb. It was as if, with three words, the blows he had just struck rebounded back to him an order of magnitude more in killing force.

He could barely speak. "What. Did. You. Say?"

Scholar Shin could barely speak for the blood that filled his mouth; as his consciousness narrowed into a funneled vision that saw only the words in front of him.

"The child wrote," he mumbled in Japanese,

"'Mother'⋯, 'Pink'⋯, 'Snow'⋯."

Shark turned to his son, as the memory of the funeral of his wife took over his mind. Springtime. Cherry Blossoms. And snow.

The late fall had surprised everyone. It was rare. All the more so as a parting gesture of the world to Shark's wife, even as her parting took his world away from him.

The funeral. The blossoms. The snowfall.

Mother. Pink. Snow.

Pup had not even been two years old at the time. But what did that matter? Two or twenty? His son was barely human. Wasn't he?

"You remember," Shark said quietly.

'To show no sign of joy or anger' had been inscribed by the code of Bushido on Shark's deepest layers of being. That is what had turned pirate into Samurai. He felt those years of self-control vanish so completely in this sudden moment of heretofore unfathomable closeness with his son — my son! — that it was as if there had ne-ver been such a thing in all of history. Samurai? What was that?

The boy's eyes answered him, "Yes." Eyes that Shark seemed to see for the very first time. Pup remembered. And not just that. He knew. He had known all along. Everything.

Shark took the paper from the boy's hands. Stared at the letters. He could not read them, of course, but that didn't matter at all. He knew what these symbols had done. All that the Korean had claimed.

Shin watched this through a haze of blood. Watched as Shark abruptly crumpled the page in his hand, turned away and climbed back up the latter to the deck. He saw the boy just sitting there.

And then he saw nothing at all⋯.

Shark returned to the tiller and his place on the flagship as the pilot of this invasion; with the key that hung around his neck he unlocked the chain that secured it even in his brief absence. No one took notice of him. All slept or were otherwise involved in their own business.

He straightened out the crumpled page still in his hand and stared at it.

Lines drawn across paper. Three Japanese words written in Korean lettering. Like a Nue — the creature of legend with the body of a tanuki, the legs of a tiger, the face of a monkey, a snake for a tail. A monstrous combination that could not exist in real life. And yet here it was.

A shared memory. A communication. The first such moment he had ever experienced with his only child. He never knew it was possible. Never believed otherwise. But here it was.

He doubled over and sobbed. The page fell from his hand, was caught up by a breeze and sent over the railing. Where it vanished into the blackness of the night sea.

The boots that the Mongol Agent wore to disguise himself as the King disguising himself as a commoner now slammed into the spine of an actual commoner — the last still alive of the half-dozen others who had the misfortune to find themselves trapped in the supply depot when all disguises were cast aside.

Moments later, an agitated scholar strode with great purpose across the other side of the palace grounds. He now said aloud — though still under his breath — the words he had repeated silently like a mantra all the previous night long — "Mandate of Heaven, Mandate of Heaven⋯." — to convince himself that King Sejong had lost that divine imprimatur and therefore he was justified in doing what he was about to do.

The King had just entered and taken his seat in the Royal Council Hall, to start the day hosting the 'Classics Matt' — a lesson in the teachings of Confucius — as he had done three times a week for the past thirty years, for the edification of a sampling of Hall of Worthy scholars who had assembled to participate. For some, this was a chore, and the empty chairs represented those few, for the majority it was duty and they did not question it, but for a handful — the young scholars Sejong had taken under his wing — this was the highlight of their day.

The King opened a book with ritualistic care, but he had no need to see on the page what he had long since committed to memory. "The subject today is 'Analects' of Confucius, Chapter 7, line 27."

He paused as five different scholars chimed in with the relevant quote: "The Master went fishing, but did not use a net; The master shot a crossbow, but not at a sparrow."

But between the group of them, the overlapping and discordant recitation came out a garbled mess. The entire room broke out in good-humored laughter.

"I wonder then," smiled the King, "What was the Master seeking?"

The agitated scholar reached the Petitioner's Drum — "Mandate of Heaven, Mandate of Heaven" — and grabbed the huge mallet next to it. The Official of the Drum stood nearby, ready to consult with any person of the realm who might approach about whether or not disturbing the peace and tranquility of the Royal Palace and everybody therein was such a good idea or if other means of redress might be possible. But as this highly public mode of disagreeable expression was only rarely used, he was caught off-guard by the speed of the agitated scholar's approach.

The latter had told family and friends of his *han* since he was arrested along with Choe when Choe had memorialized the throne against Sejong's alphabet. Indeed, if scholars Shin, Pak, and Jeong had felt invigorated and even give new life by the 'Correct Sounds', this man had felt plagued and even attacked — by knives of thought and stinging wasps of emotions that gave him no peace, disturbed his sleep, turned daydreams to nightmares; made night and day intolerable. And so he was here, reaching for the mallet, about to give voice to his *han*. And to take his revenge.

But this was not *han*. This was not the heart/mind soul/sickness of the Korean people. Han by definition is that which cannot be avenged. This was anger. Nothing more. And at some deeper level of his psyche that he would never be able to touch or acknowledge, it was envy. Not at the accomplishment, the alphabet itself — but at the passion of those who loved it. And if he could not love, only hatred was left.

BOOM! The drum sounded. "Mandate of Heaven!" shouted the man with the mallet — voice drowned out by the thundering instrument.

Across the yard, in the Royal Council Hall, the lesson

in Confucius came to an abrupt halt. Sejong took a long breath. As if in anticipation. It could only be the alphabet.

"Your Majesty, please ignore this complaint!" shouted one of the scholars.

BOOM!

"We have not had the pleasure of your instruction for too long!" added another.

BOOM!

"The drum disagrees," said the King, as he rose to go and listen to whomever the instrument's voice now represented. The scholars quickly got up to accompany him.

CRCRCRCR

In the supply depot across the grounds, the Agent had swapped the provisioner's garb he was wearing for his Mongol battle gear.

He then reached along the inside of one of the wheels of his cart to find his war bow fixed to the felloe — the curvature of the wheel matching perfectly the curve of the bow — a perfect way to smuggle the weapon past any checkpoint.

Bow freed, the man reached below the cart where he

had fixed dozens of arrows to the underside. He pulled them loose and jammed them into the pair of quivers belted low around his waist.

Then he moved to his pack animal, threw off the old blankets and knocked away the dust from its mane: beneath the "old nag" disguise was his warhorse.

It snorted in anticipation of battle.

The light saddle, stirrups and reins were freed from inside the cart where they lay hidden in plain view among a jumble of tackle.

The Agent quickly fixed them to his horse.

Finally, he roughly chopped with a knife the hair from the sides and back of his head — leaving only the distinctive forelock of the Mongol warrior.

He leapt onto the back of the horse. It reared, barely able to contain its excitement at finally being allowed to become again what it was by nature and by nurture: a bringer of death.

꽃꽃꽃꽃꽃

A five-year-old Prince, royally-dressed — Sejong as a child — ran in slow motion, then fell — the Old Guard reached out to catch the boy — in accord with the man's recounting of this event. But his movements seemed frozen — he could not reach the falling child — who suddenly became the twelve-year-old Prince falling backwards off a wall, again in agonizing slow motion. And again, the Old Guard tried reach him, but could not seem to move.

And then the scenes of the boy who would be King dissolved away, replaced by that of the provisioner's cart passing through the gate only a short time ago, heading into the Palace grounds. The Old Guard stared down at the boots as they passed. And passed again. And again. As if in a continuous, maddening loop.

࿐࿐࿐࿐

With a startled gasp, the reverie ended. The Old Guard reacted to where his drifting thought process had just taken him.

"The boots were turned-in," he said aloud.

"What?" One of the other sentries glanced over.

"Like a horseman," continued the Old Guard. "Not like a king. Not like our King."

With an expression of terror on his face, he rushed through the gate and into the Palace grounds.

As the doors of the supply depot crashed open and in full battle mode the Mongol Agent atop his war horse burst into view.

He charged his horse across the common grounds — everybody scrambled in uncomprehending shock at the sight — as he ran down two bureaucrats who did not get out of the way in time.

BOOM!

The King and his handful of scholars had just reached the open courtyard to see what the petitioner pounding the drum wanted to say.

The angry young man spotted them heading his direction. But rather than shout his complaint in public as was the accepted next step, he just hit the drum again.

BOOM!

Sejong and his company were puzzled. What was this scholar up to?

Then suddenly: BOOM! BOOM! BOOM! Another drum from another part of the palace. Sharper and more strident.

A warning signal.

The King was taken aback. What was going on? His typical ability to observe a set of conditions and arrive at a likely extrapolation of probable events was at least momentarily arrested.

This was exactly the effect his assassin had intended.

Across the grounds where the sentries pounded the alarms, the Chief of Security shouted at the company of guards he was rushing into action. "Go, Go, Go!"

As the men ran in the direction he pointed — towards the reports of an armed intruder — the Old Guard instead ran as fast as he was able towards where he knew the King would be at this hour, and in these circumstances: somewhere between the daily Confucius lesson and the Petitioner's Drum.

Somewhere out in the open and defenseless.

CRICRICR

The Mongol Agent atop his battle-crazed horse rode at full gallop along a corridor — suddenly half-a-dozen guards appeared in front of him, cutting off his way forward.

He jerked the reins of the horse and continued without break in speed up a narrow staircase — an officer caught midway on the stairs leapt off the side to avoid being crushed. As the warrior went up and up — the only way that was not blocked.

As Sejong and his scholars crossed the courtyard of the Royal Assembly Hall, approaching the still-booming Drum, the young man who pounded on it saw them and instantly threw the mallet to the ground — as if panicked by the sudden reality of the presence of his King. He bolted, a frightened look on his face.

In the sudden silence of the instrument that summoned them here, the strident alarm drums and distant shouting across the Palace grounds — until a moment ago overwhelmed by the Petitioner's Drum — was all that could be heard.

Linguist Pak was suddenly concerned.

"Your Majesty. Let us go back inside."

The other scholars protectively surrounded the King and they all began to move as one back towards the cover of the Hall.

"Secure His Majesty!" shouted the Chief of Security, grim-faced, hurrying his men along, as they rushed across the grounds — taking no notice of the Old Guard rushing along a side-route to the same location. He knew these grounds like the back of his hands, surely he would get to the King in time — as he had done before. He felt his purpose narrow to that end, like the tunnel vision that occurs when one races towards eternity at the moment of death.

ⓖⓖⓖⓖⓖ

Surrounded from all sides, the Mongol Agent drove his horse off the side of a small stairway he had half-ascended, hitting the ground hard — then galloped across a small courtyard and up another set of stairs, climbing it in three bounds, and then leapt his horse up and onto the Palace rooftops — to the astonishment of his pursuers left below.

Incredibly, the horse kept its footing, shattering and scattering tiles as the Mongol maintained his balance and goaded the horse across the length of the narrow roofing and into an amazing leap across space to yet another rooftop — that which covered the corridors surrounding the Royal Assembly Courtyard.

Just as Sejong and his scholars rushed up the stone steps towards cover, tiles started crashing all around them. They could not help but look up.

As the Mongol Agent slid his horse down the side of the rooftop adjoining the open space they had just fled — stripping tiles all the way — plummeting down through space and landing hard on the ground within striking distance of the King.

His goal all along.

Sejong and Company were so astonished that it took a moment to register the danger.

Three security guards rushed into the courtyard — the first to arrive.

The Mongol rushed his horse towards them — raising his bow. He shot two arrows so fast in succession that it seemed he loosed them at the same time.

Two guards dropped with arrows in their chests.

The Mongol wheeled his horse around — turned 180 degrees in his saddle and shot one more arrow behind him, dropping the third guard. Then he raised his bow, fixed another arrow — and charged straight towards the King, who had nowhere to go.

To all those in witness, time seemed to slow, events proceeded like the turning over of a succession of cards, each image only slightly different from the last.

The arrow was released. It flew towards the King.

The Old Guard came seemingly out of nowhere, from

the paths and passageways he knew like the back of his hands — hands that now grabbed hold of the King and spun him away, replacing his own body in the path of the arrow.

Which buried itself right in the middle of his back.

The Mongol warrior was astonished at this missed attempt. He wheeled his horse around for another try as the young scholars grabbed the King and pulled him away from the Old Guard, trying to rush him to safety.

The Old Guard — dying — swayed on his feet and then dropped to his knees.

Sejong could not bear to leave him. The man who just saved his life. Even if it meant he would lose it now.

The King broke away from his scholars and rushed back to the Old Guard, going down to the ground to catch and hold him — to stop him from falling.

But this spontaneous action left the King open to a second attempt on his life.

The Mongol Agent could not believe his luck — and this sudden turn of events. He thought he had failed. Battle-hardened as the creature was, the horse under him went wild in the action, but the Mongol — like all of his tribe — could shoot from any position.

He notched an arrow and took aim.

The tip of the missile saw its target — the exposed front of the King's neck — and just as it was released.

WHOOSH! WHOOSH! WHOOSH! WHOOSH!

Dozens of arrows hit the would-be assassin simultaneously — throwing off his aim at the last possible instant — his arrow flew past the King's head and shattered off the stones behind him.

The company of archers who were now on the rooftops surrounding the courtyard fired yet another round. All striking their target. The war horse finally settled down and went quiet, as its master and companion died, pin-cushioned to the saddle.

৩৩৩৩৩

The King had the Old Guard cradled in his arms. The man's eyes were glassy as he met the gaze of the Sovereign he had all but worshipped for four decades.

Sejong's voice was quiet. Meant only for the man who had just given his life in the King's service.

"The first time, I was five years old," he said. "Chasing something. I don't remember what. I stumbled, falling — and there you were. I said: 'Thank you, Sir.' Do you remember?"

The man remembered. He had thought of it every day since.

"The second time, I was twelve," continued the King softly. "Trying to go over the western wall. I lost my balance, falling — and there you were. I said"

The Old Guard silently mouthed the next words as Sejong spoke them aloud. "'Ten thousand pardons, Sir'."

"Do you remember?" asked the King.

The man's eyes glistened.

"And now, this very day. Again, I fall. And again, there you are," whispered the King as the man in his arms died.

"To catch me."

The King gently closed the Old Guard's eyes with his hand. He could barely get the words out.

"Thank you, Sir. Ten thousand times. Thank you."

His own eyes were wet.

෨෨෨෨෨

The official courier of Ming strode southwards out of the Hall of Supreme Harmony, passed through the Gate of Supreme Harmony, then paused at the Gate of Uprightness where he mounted a horse being held for him, then rode out the Great Meridian Gate at the southern end of the Forbidden City; passed security checkpoints at two more walled portals within Beijing itself, continued along the wide street between the Altar of the Agriculture God and the Temple of Heaven; finally exited the city through the last gate leading into the countryside, and only then was free to goad the horse to a full gallop.

He carried a time-sensitive document — a sealed letter from the Ming Emperor of China to the King of Joseon Korea — and as time is the enemy of all messengers, this one knew he had a battle ahead of him.

༺ஒஒஒஒ༻

The drum-pounding God of Storms and the wave-churning Dragon of the Sea were assigned just as much causality to the most famous examples of kamikaze in Japanese military history as was the God of Wind himself. In this case, the three deities may have worked in concert, as the wind that filled the sails of the pirate fleet bearing down on the Korean coast indeed seemed divinely driven, so constant, strong and true was its impelling force.

The ships flew like arrows across the water.

Sea Lord Red's flagship still sailed at the far left of the flotilla, slightly ahead, as if leading his brothers-in-arms into battle.

A vassal helped the pirate-Lord pull over his head a wickedly frightening helmet in the shape of a red-faced water demon, and handed him his two swords — even as he remained seated on his throne at the prow of the ship, gazing at the sea — and land ahead — that he wanted more than anything in life to rule. Or barring that, to devastate and ruin.

His crew yanked over their limbs whatever rough armor they might possess, readied weapons, and painted garish swaths of crimson across their faces intended to terrify any local opposition once they landed.

Shark was at the tiller. His expression blank. There was no indication of what he might have thought or done after the heart-breaking moment of 'first contact' he had with his son. It was if he kept his mind clear and empty on the chance his lord — with an almost preternatural instinct for sensing betrayal — might read his thoughts. And undo what he had planned.

A solitary watchman walked the stone wall above the shore of Geoje. The moon was bright over the sea beyond it, idyllic and peaceful as it always seemed to be, especially over these past years of truce.

The watchman and the port he watched were completely unprepared for a surprise attack.

Smoothly cutting along, the invading ships — full wind behind them, armed and deadly — adjusted course slightly, so as to race head-on towards the distant twinkling lights of Geoje.

Sea Lord Red, now fully armored, weapons in hand, stared off the prow, eyes front, gripping his swords in anticipation. Even through the fright-mask of his demonic helmet, his eyes shone with confidence.

Aft, at the stern of the ship, Shark's willfully blank mind suddenly became flooded with purpose. He shoved the tiller hard as he could to port side — the ship lurched as the rudder responded, turning the vessel suddenly and unexpectedly hard to starboard.

Sea Lord Red gripped his throne to keep himself upright against the sudden jarring movement — several of his men were thrown off their feet.

The flagship that had lurched so hard to starboard with Shark's inexplicable action now headed straigh for the vessel to its immediate right. Impact in a matter of seconds.

Shark wrapped the tiller with its heavy chain, fixing its position so it could not be changed, then locked it with the key entrusted to him by his Sea Lord.

He threw the key overboard. And grimly waited for the consequences of his actions. His mind now allowing him a momentary glimpse in memory of what had oc-curred below deck a few hours before.

꧁꧂꧁꧂꧁꧂

Scholar Shin, still bound, was conscious and on his feet, the blood on his face cleaned off. Shark and Pup were there.

Shark indicated his son, and the lines of the 'Correct Sounds' the boy had drawn on surfaces all around them.

"Your King's letters have given him his voice. It is gift I cannot equal. My son will now become all that life has intended for him."

He had a hard time saying the words.

"In exchange for your freedom, you are to be his guardian, for the rest of your life. As if he were your blood and your flesh. Do you agree to these terms?"

"In the middle of an invasion?" replied Scholar Shin.

"I cannot guarantee his safety."

"This invasion is over," said Shark with absolute certainty.

Shin had no idea how Shark would stop it. But he believed. "I will watch over him even beyond my grave," he promised.

Shark cut the ropes that bound the man. Then gently guided his son to his new guardian. Even though he knew the boy could not hear him, he said it anyway:

"Go. And remember me."

But the boy seemed to understand what this was all about. He took Shark's hand, then traced into the palm with his finger a new word he had learned, with the shapes created by the King of the Koreans.

Shark and Shin watched him complete the word. The scholar's voice was quiet: "I think I do not have to tell you what that says."

Shark could barely get the word out: "'Father'."

Shark pushed the memory from his mind, stood with his back to the tiller, and readied his sword.

As the flagship sped straight towards the exposed side of the next vessel to starboard, sailors began shouting alarm. But it was far too late to stop it.

The Red Sea Lord leapt off his throne with a roar, and turned towards the stern where he saw Shark waiting for him.

The Lord's own personal key to the tiller still swung from its cord around his neck — he knew he must take back control of the tiller or the invasion was over before it could begin.

He launched himself with another roar into a crouching run, down the length of his ship toward the traitor who had betrayed him.

As the narrow prow of the flagship smashed into the front left side of the next ship in line.

The Sea Lord was thrown to the deck just short of lunging distance from his target.

Shark held onto the tiller to keep his feet. As the grinding and buckling of impact violently rippled through every timber of the vessel.

The flagship cut all the way through the prow of the

adjoining vessel — sending it spinning and reeling and lurching — and then headed for the next ship in line, picking up speed, as if willed by the increasingly fierce wind behind it.

The sailors on board shouted in alarm at what they had just witnessed. One of them grabbed a mallet and started pounding a battle drum — trying to alert the other vessels in time for evasion action.

The lone watchman of Kobe Port was suddenly curious. Was that a drum he heard off-shore, beyond the crashing surf? He squinted in the distance, perceived a shadowy outline of something that perhaps shouldn't be there. But he was uncertain. Should he take action that potentially might wake the entire town over a trick of the moonlight and waves and risk a beating by doing so?

As the watchman debated internally, Sea Lord Red lunged with both swords at Shark, who defended the tiller with all the skill he possessed. They parried back and forth with great violence and ability, even as the ship continued on its cutting course across the line of vessels.

A rocket suddenly launched from the shore. Like a lone firework. It soared higher and higher, then exploded in a sun-like burst that for one moment lit the sea.

And revealed the line of Japanese invaders and the lone flagship cutting through them; the chaos and the confusion of it all.

The watchman was stunned by what he saw: Kobe Port was under attack. He rushed to a huge drum and beat on it.

As the flagship continued to careen across the waves, Sea Lord Red shouted at his crew to get back on their feet, pointing to the billowing cloth above them.

"Cut sail!"

Two of the men scrambled up the mast to comply. As the Lord resumed his attack on Shark over control of the tiller.

The fight was violent and hard and had become personal: A vassal had betrayed his master. The Sea Lord tore his own helmet off, so that his fury could be unmasked, so that Shark could look into that face at the moment of death.

Suddenly: WHOOSH. Hundreds of fire arrows launched from shore. With incredible velocity and distance — these were the same long-range missiles Sejong had experimented with on the testing ground. Here, for the first time, deployed in actual battle.

In the blackness before dawn, it looked spectacular:

like tracers heading for the moon.

Then they reached their apogee and began to fall.

In the sudden illumination of the death raining down, the two swordsmen continued their duel — burning arrows struck all around them, penetrating the wooden deck, the mast, the railings, then a moment later exploded. But it was only the prelude to a sudden crashing impact, as the flagship tore through the second vessel in line.

It was chaos.

Both swordsmen were thrown off their feet.

A second volley of fire arrows was loaded onto the line of *hwacha* launchers — and sent aloft again with a searing WHOOSH.

Shark scrambled to his feet. And in the sudden glow of illumination provided by the second volley high in the air, he inexplicably stared out to sea. His gaze swept the waters, as if searching for something. Until it found a dim outline, hard to perceive at this distance, in this unearthly light.

Was it a small rowboat?

SLASH! The Sea Lord had regained his footing and attacked while Shark had lowered his defenses to stare out to sea.

The pilot was spun about by the blow, which cut deeply down his back. Another lunge, through his mid-section. He was done for. Shark dropped to his knees. Then grabbed onto the railing to prop himself up, and again stared into the distance — fixating on the tiny dot that he hoped would be the last thing he saw in this life.

He got his wish.

Sea Lord Red roared, moved in for the killing stroke.

Then the deck around them was lit up as if by the noonday sun. The Lord looked up to see hundreds of fire arrows plummeting straight toward him. And that was the last thing he saw, in this life.

Across the water, a small rowboat carried Scholar Shin and Pup out of reach of the disaster. They both stared off at the distant fires, the Japanese pirate ships in disarray and destruction. Shark had put the two of them on the tiny skiff and sent them to safety right before he sabotaged the invasion.

The sun started to rise in the east. The east where lay Japan — land of the rising sun.

For Scholar Shin still had his mission. And now, an adopted son.

He thought back to when King Sejong had given him this assignment, under the cover of the mourning hut for Queen Soheon. The King had handed him a wood-block print copy of his declaration.

"As a pine sends its seeds into the air to find a more distant ground in which to grow, so I send the 'Correct Sounds' with you," he had said. "Even if, on occasion, you might find yourself going against the wind."

Scholar Shin checked the air — it was still blowing to the west. The opposite from where he would go. He took his King's words to heart. And rowed against the wind towards the dawn.

༺༺༺༺༺

The mutilated man who was the virtual power behind the Dragon Throne held sway in his office that was like the Emperor's Audience Hall in miniature. He was seated on his throne-like chair; the two captured Korean interpreters had been forced to their knees in front of him.

They wore the white undergarments of criminals, their top-knots had been cut loose and their hair was long and straggly. A double cangue — a heavy wooden yoke like a mobile pillory — hung from both of their necks, binding them together, side-by-side.

The pair were caked with dried blood from their own

fight against each other and a more recent layer from rough treatment in jail. A kind of archeology of beatings.

Eunuch Wang Zhen studied a copy of the Korean King's alphabet — confiscated from the travelers when they were arrested.

"I was told to expect the worst. Evidence of Joseon's slide into barbarism," spoke the eunuch in Mandarin, as he considered the booklet and its deceptively simple letters interwoven with the explanation in Chinese.

"I see instead, a parlor game," he glanced up at his prisoners. "Something surely intended to accompany singing girls, cheap wine and spicy food. A night of vomiting in the gutter. Regrets. Prayers to Buddha or one of those mountain spirits you people prefer — begging relief from your headache. With a vow never to indulge again."

He considered again the pages in his hand; shook his head in disbelief. "Either that, or your King has gone mad."

Pyonghwa quietly quoted one of the most famous lines of the document. "It is a gift of Heaven."

Wang Zhen scanned the document. "Yes. I read that right here." He looked back up at them. "Heaven gifts the Son of Heaven only — the Emperor of Ming. How dare a vassal King make that claim?"

"Not a claim," said Maedu calmly. "A point of fact."

"The boast of a pretender," countered the eunuch, anger rising. "An insult to the Emperor himself. If not a direct challenge to His Imperial Majesty's authority."

He closed the document. And rose up to his full height as if pronouncing sentence. "How can this go unpunished?"

჻჻჻჻჻

The Ming courier had reached the man his message was intended for: He stood before King Sejong, in the Royal Council Hall. They were alone in the chamber, at the courier's request. An unusual, even unprecedented occurrence. This was a private message from the Emperor of the Suzerain state of Ming, the overlord of Joseon, Korean, and technically the ruler above Sejong.

Sejong had cracked open the Dragon Seal of hard wax, and studied the letter he had just been handed. He could not help but consider the circumstances of its composition, given the personalities involved.

As the young Emperor of Ming tried on an assortment of beautifully crafted military uniforms to see what most flattered him for the upcoming war with the Mongols, Eunuch Wang Zhen wrote the letter to Sejong, saying the words aloud for the Emperor's benefit.

"One-hundred thousand of your finest soldiers."

"One-hundred thousand?" reacted the Emperor.

"Is it too much?"

"For the defense of the Empire even too much is not enough," came the answer.

"Well then, why not grant him some kind of⋯favor in return?"

"My thought exactly, Lord of Ten Thousand Years."

Sejong's announcement of the 'Correct Sounds' sat on the desk next to where the eunuch was writing — the same copy taken from the captured Korean interpreters.

"'We have been made aware of your Majesty's newly concocted writing system'," Wang Zhen spoke aloud as he wrote. "And are inclined not to interfere with your plans for its promulgation among your population. Why should such a quaint novelty ever come between us?"

The Emperor smiled in agreement with this strategy, then struggled with a sleeve for a moment, as the letter vanished from his mind. The eunuch continued to write silently for a moment, finished with the standard closing of this format, then folded and secured the letter himself with the heavy jade seal of the Emperor.

CENTRAL

Sejong finished reading the letter, and maintained his composure, expression of benevolence never leaving his face.

"Thank you," he said to the courier. "You must be tired. Please stay a day or two and rest. Before you return to the Emperor."

The courier nodded his thanks and backed out of the Hall. When he was gone, Sejong slumped suddenly, grabbing a wall hanging to keep from collapsing entirely. He felt utter despair.

That night, alone in his bed chambers, the despair had only deepened. He did not sleep, and was filled with foreboding.

With little ceremony, the two Koreans were moved from their jail cell to the adjoining courtyard and the chopping blocks that awaited them. A minor magistrate oversaw the process. The eunuch who had pronounced this sentence had better things to do with his time than to watch it being carried out.

Two executioners stepped into view, each carrying a huge, heavy sword forged specifically for this task.

Pyonghwa and Maedu were terrified. The cangue was removed from their necks, and they were shoved towards the blocks. They glanced at each other for support of some kind, anything to assuage the terror of the final moment.

"'The sounds of our language are different from the sounds of China, and so cannot be expressed in the writing of China'," recited Maedu haltingly.

His partner picked it up from there — continuing to quote the King's pronouncement, finding courage in the words. "'Consequently, the uncomplicated people of our Kingdom are not able to make their concerns understood by those of us who have been educated'."

"'This makes me sad'!" said Maedu in a louder voice.

Together they shouted, "And so I have made twenty

-eight letters!"

The executioners took up position behind them. Pyonghwa and Maedu locked eyes — holding onto each other's image to the last.

"Carry out the sentence," ordered the magistrate.

"A thousand years of health to Our King!" shouted Maedu. Then amended the declaration with a blessing reserved by law only for the Emperor himself. "Ten thousand!"

And Pyonghwa joined in the chorus.

"Ten thousand years! Ten thousand years!"

SLASH! The blades descended.

෬෬෬෬෬

At the Sakya Pagoda in the mountains of Myohyang, the slender, cylindrical stone tower hung with tiny bells, beneath which the two interpreters had always rested on their trips back and forth to China — the air was still. The bells Maedu complained they would never get to hear were silent as always.

Then a gentle breeze swept through the trees, along the ground, and around the pagoda, setting the chimes in motion.

The gentle ringing was like a prayer.

Ten small bronze bells that dangled from the back of an oxcart that crossed the Chinese countryside seemed to jangle and chime in resonant sympathy with those of the pagoda in Korea.

The cart was driven by the Nestorian Priest of Joseon, who made his way along the lonely road, all his belongings packed for a long journey ahead, accompanied only by the jingling of bells — and his own great faith in a God that no one else for thousands of miles in any direction had ever heard of.

Sejong stood in the candlelit chamber of the Water Clock, the letter from Ming in hand. He was exhausted and heart-sick. As if he felt in his heart/mind — and across his own neck — the sacrifice of his two interpreters. And dreaded what he now faced.

"Yang Sil," he said aloud to the memory of his old friend. "I am lost."

He stared up at the complex mechanism that filled the room.

"'To know time is to command time' — is what you said. What you promised. When you built this⋯thing. Then why does it seem precisely the opposite? Time has harried and commanded — and broken — me."

He went quiet for a moment. Then spoke again.

"If even Ming is under Heaven, I asked myself, then should I not serve the higher power? In this way, I thought to protect my nation. My people."

Then the truth of it: "And the 'Correct Sounds'."

He held up the letter in his hand.

"This is Heaven's answer? A letter from the Emperor — or the eunuch who runs him, it is the same. Demanding one-hundred thousand of my people. For a war against the Mongols. To send such a population is to guarantee Ming's tolerance for a Korean alphabet. Perhaps even their active support."

This was all he could have wished for. And yet: one-hundred thousand!

"What if they are killed in battle? All hundred thousand? Is it worth the cost? One hundred thousand of my people must die, so that twenty-eight letters might live?"

He thought silently, all along knowing the answer.

"If that is what Heaven is asking of me, then I no longer have time for Heaven."

He held the Emperor's letter over the open flame of the nearest lamp. It caught instantly, vanishing in a wisp of smoke.

The great clock marked the moment as it struck the hour: the first falling metal sphere passed a ratchet that suddenly broke asunder — and this caused a cascade effect, sending spheres plummeting all at once, wheels and ratchets snapping and breaking, until the whole apparatus came apart.

Sejong watched in stunned silence. The final effect was the mock-up of the King himself, carved in wood, as it emerged with a shutter from its internal space, then fell to the floor and shattered.

As if Heaven had given its reaction to his decision.

જ્જાજ્જાજ્જ

Yu Qian, Minister of War of Ming, stood on top of the Great Wall at its furthest point east, staring into the distance. Where a mini-horde of Mongols raced their horses back and forth. As if taunting him.

His next-in-command indicated a series of hills in the

distance near the riders. "Behind those hills, the Mongol army surely lies hidden in its entirety. Waiting for us to take the bait. It is a trap."

An cue, a great shouting went up from the Mongols. As if an invitation to the Chinese to engage the battle.

The Minister of War considered everything: what he saw in front of him, what he knew of the current dynamic between Empire and Periphery, what he had learned from history.

But as the proof has always been the purview of the pudding, Yu Qian had no choice but to take his army into the field, marching towards the Mongol riders, who stayed ahead of them, not engaging, leading them instead around a bluff.

And nothing. Nobody was there.

The Mister of War had only proven what he already knew. "'Make a sound in the East, strike in the West'."

෯෯෯෯෯

To the west across the Empire and north of Beijing, was the bastion of Datong and the most heavily fortified section of the Great Wall. Beyond the always relative safety of that mountain of brick and earth, Eunuch

Hwang Zhen had convinced the young Emperor of Ming to answer the challenge of the full Mongol horde.

And as the two vast armies faced each other on either side of this great battlefield, the Nestorian Priest of Korea and his oxcart continued blithely along — right between them, ambling across the 'no-man's land' in the middle of the field. The tinkling of the bells on the back of his cart was the only sound.

The Emperor and the eunuch just stared, astonished by the oxcart's unexpected — even surreal — appearance.

The Mongols also could not believe what they were seeing. Esen Taishi, commander of this army, brought out his powerful bow, notched an arrow, and raised it to take aim.

On the Ming side, the best archer in the Empire, on the horse next to the Emperor, had already done the same. The two loosed their respective arrows simultaneously.

The arrow from the Ming side and the arrow from the Mongol side both soared through the air, describing long, high parabolas…and both fell short, striking the ground shy of the ox cart.

Which continued to calmly move along without pause. The bells still tinkling.

Eunuch Wang Zhen turned to the archer. "This is insulting." Then he ordered a Captain to ride out and strike the Nestorian down.

But the Emperor laughed brightly. "Let him go." Explaining, "The first ox was a gift to humanity from the Emperor of Heaven. How can this not be a sign of good luck?"

Upon seeing that the passing oxcart was out of range from both sides, a Mongol warrior rode up to Esen and indicated his sword — also volunteering to ride out and end this odd provocation.

But the Chieftain shook his head no. "This is a sign of good luck. It is said that an ox predicted the rise of Genghis Khan, in a shaman's dream," he explained. "Let him go."

The oxcart continued on its way. The Priest seemed not to realize how close he had come to death from both of the massive armies he had passed between. Or his faith gave him the courage not to care either way.

And still the only sound on the field of battle was the creaking of the wooden wheels and the bright jangling of the small bronze bells on the back of the cart.

The Priest thought back to the last time he saw the man who sent him on this curious path.

King Sejong had surprised the Nestorian with a night visit, in disguise as was his habit, handing him a heavy string of silver coins and explaining, "For your return to the West. Until the times change in the East. For you. And for your god."

The Priest accepted it with a nod of his head. "In the Sutra of the Buddha Jesus, it is said: 'Every valley shall be filled, and every mountain brought low, and the rough ways made smooth, and the twisted path made straight'."

As the oxcart continued towards the distant West and safety, the small bells on the back jangled with an almost joyous sound. That music receded as a mounted officer galloped up to the eunuch in command of the Emperor who commanded the Empire. Wang Zhen moved out of earshot of his sovereign for the report. "There is no answer from His Majesty Sejong. And no sign of the requested Korean troops."

The eunuch was livid. "I will burn Joseon to the ground. And see that little king die choking on his own alphabet." But first, the Mongols. Even without the Korean troops he had demanded, Ming's army outnumbered the Mongols five to one. This should take but the afternoon, thought the eunuch.

And so, with the pounding of drums, the blasting of horns, and the roaring of soldiers and warriors — the Army of Ming and the Horde of the Mongols finally rushed towards each other.

৵৵৵৵৵

The agitated scholar who banged the Petitioner's Drum and then fled the scene right before the Mongol attempt on the King's life was tied to a chair, hair loosened, two long staffs of wood scissoring his legs in an "X" shape. The default stress position in this place and time for interrogation under torture.

Two men pulled hard on the wood — applying pressure strong enough to shatter the man's femurs if they did not let up in a matter of seconds.

He screamed. The torturers held it for another moment, then paused, relaxing their grip.

"Who told you to strike the Petitioner's Drum?" asked the Chief of Security. "At the hour of the snake?"

The scholar just looked at him, terrified. The chief

motioned to his guards to start again. The man started screaming even before the pressure was applied.

⊚⊛⊚⊛⊚

Choe Malli was dressed in his official robes, seated on the floor at a small table, in the study of his home. A small cup of liquid was on the table before him. Tea or liquor? No. Given the circumstances, something much stronger was called for.

He steeled himself and drank it. Then settled in for the inevitable.

Suddenly, a servant appeared at the door.

"My Lord. The Chief of Security is here."

"Of course. Please show him in."

The servant vanished, a moment later, the Security Chief stepped inside, with a polite bow of his head.

"His Majesty requests a meeting."

Choe was taken aback. He expected to be arrested. And he just drank⋯.

"Where?" he asked.

"Where are we to meet⋯at this hour?"

When Choe reached the water well that divided the Inner and Outer Palaces, the King was already waiting for him.

"Good evening," Sejong greeted him. "Have you eaten?"

"Yes, Your Majesty. And more. Thank you for asking."

There was an awkward moment of silence between them. Then Choe confessed everything.

"The Taishi of the Taisun Khan, of the Mongols of the West, was behind the plot against Your Majesty's life. But my role was instrumental."

"You gave away the key to the palace. As it were. And drew me into the open."

Choe nodded.

"The Mongols sought my death," Sejong concluded, "To send Joseon into chaos and prevent us from sending troops to support Ming. You would risk the Emperor himself···to stop my alphabet?"

"Emperors come and Emperors go," answered Choe. "The Mongols have ruled China before — they may do so again. But China endures. And so must Korea. Once your letters take root in the world, there is no going back. Our bond with China and its culture will be broken. For all time. What then, the fate of this land and its people?"

"We will become our essential and authentic selves," declared Sejong.

"Without China?" countered Choe. "Without Confucius or the Classics? What will that look like?"

Sejong indicated the creatures real and mythological carved into the stone walls around them.

"White Tigers and Blue Dragons? Flying Phoenix and Fire-eating Haetae?" His voice became quiet. "It is not for us to know."

Choe's voice was even. "Though Your Majesty is still alive. I have won."

Sejong just looked at him.

"All Ministries, all Departments of Government, all scholars save the youths you corrupted," continued Choe. "Everyone is against your alphabet. All are watching you, now. You will never print another copy of the 'Correct Sounds for the Instruction of the People'. And more: No one in any official capacity will ever use it. It will die of neglect. Like an infant left exposed on a hilltop, at the mercy of the elements and the wolves."

Sejong was silent.

"Let the maids write their love notes," mused Choe. "Let the monks copy their prayers. When the novelty wears off, even that will end. And Those twenty-eight letters will join you in the grave."

"Then I will have good company," smiled Sejong.

"How can you still⋯believe?"

"I have nothing else left."

Choe smiled. His eyes, too, were filled with sadness and nostalgia. "You have me. For a few moments more. At least."

Sejong was puzzled. "Malli⋯."

Choe suddenly slumped.

"What have you done?" asked Sejong, alarmed.

Choe's eyes were dazed as the poison — for that indeed is what he drank in his study — took effect.

"It is good," Choe said, with genuine relief. "That you are alive." He gripped the ancient stone of the well. "That we are here."

"Someone come!" shouted Sejong.

Choe's eyes were distant. As if staring off at something in deepest time. His thoughts scattered, under the influence of the poison now reaching his brain.

"I won the battle," he said haltingly as if undergoing some revelation. "But I did not win the war. I understand that⋯now⋯."

"The war, too!" Sejong tried to comfort him. "I cocede defeat⋯."

"Your Majesty was right⋯. Heaven is on your side."

"I was wrong," insisted Sejong. "Heaven is on everyone's side. Everyone and no one. How can it be otherwise?"

"You have always been too kind. And you have always been⋯. my King."

"Please don't go. I am sorry. Don't go. I command you." Sejong again shouted into the darkness. "Someone come!"

He put his hand on Choe's unbeating heart.

"Don't go."

꧁꧂꧁꧂꧁꧂

The King called an Assembly of the government — minsters and scholars — to the Royal Assembly Hall. He stood before them with a small scroll in hand, and read from it aloud.

"Let the family of Choe Malli be supported by the government for one thousand years. Let the record state that Choe Malli maintained his integrity in the service of that government for his entire career."

Sejong set the scroll aside and poured a libation in Choe's honor.

"His counsel was essential to the good rule of this

kingdom, and so···." For once in a public ceremony, the King's voice momentarily failed him. "And so was his friendship."

Thousands of dead Chinese soldiers were scattered across the battlefield of Datong. Victorious Mongol horsemen methodically moved among them, spearing any who still exhibited signs of life.

Yu Qian, Minister of War of Ming had reached Datong too late. He stared at the devastation from the top of the gate at this section of the Great Wall — a disaster he had predicted. The Ming Army was destroyed, the Mongols had captured the young Emperor but decided not to breech the Wall and invade. They too had suffered losses on the field and preferred to regroup and negotiate from a position of newly acquired strength.

Eunuch Wang Zhen suddenly rushed into view, fresh from the mess down below, accompanied by a handful of bloodied and defeated captains. He tried his best to keep his composure and therefore his authority over the situation.

"The Emperor is unharmed. But the Taishi will be

demanding a ransom."

"This is my answer," answered Yu Qian, as he closed the distance between them instantly, grabbed the eunuch by his neck and belt, hauled him across the stones to the edge of the Great Wall — and hurled him over the side.

As the latest 'Power-Behind-the-Dragon-Throne' plummeted to his death, he took with him the threat he made against Sejong and the alphabet.

ⓇⓈⒼⒼⒼ

Many days ride to the west, along the Old Silk Road, at Dunhuang, the last official outpost of the Empire before entering the great desert of Taklamakan, the Nestorian Priest continued to roll along with his patient ox and simple cart. He passed by a massive hillside dotted with caves containing literally a thousand tiny temples to the Buddha.

The Christian would never have stopped to make an offering, as he took seriously the 'No Gods Before Me' dictate of his own religion. But he could not help but give a slight nod of respect in passing — one believer to another, or rather, to the evidence of faith left by tens of thousands of others.

And as he went, continuing westward on a trail that might potentially put him as far away as Rome, the small bells on the back of his cart continued making their pleasant jangling sound with each bump of the cart.

Forged into the surface of the bronze of the bells, like filigree tracings in the metal itself, were the letters of the alphabet of the King of Joseon.

And so it seemed that the letters sang, as they went.

രോരോരോ

The Harvest Ceremony took place in Autumn, on the same field where King Sejong and his full court had performed the Planting Ceremony in Spring.

The Palace people and government officials were arranged as before; and again the musicians played, and the local farmers stood by to accomplish the real work when the officiants had executed their choreography for the benefit of Confucian propriety and the ancient gods.

But this time, the Queen was not here. And neither was Choe.

Sejong stood in the middle of a field of grain, under a bright sky, and swung a scythe, cutting the stalks. His royal yellow garments were a perfect match for the color of the grasses — all was golden. As if he was harvesting the sun.

But he felt profoundly alone.

Suddenly, there was a murmur of voices from those gathered for the ritual. Sejong looked up, puzzled. The Eunuch Dong Woo who had been by his side for as long as he had a side to be by rushed into view, and conveyed the news that was so important as to interrupt these sacred proceedings.

"The Ming army is defeated by the Mongols! The Emperor hostage! Eunuch Wang executed!"

Sejong was stunned and nearly staggered with relief. There would be no Chinese army to punish him for his refusal to send his soldiers. No Chinese agents coming after his alphabet.

"We are spared," was all he could say.

꧁꧂꧁꧂꧁

The King, wearing his royal garments, had left his bed chambers and strode directly for the main gate of the Royal Palace — intending to 'go among the people' as he had always done, but not bothering himself with a disguise.

Eunuchs and staff scuttled after, and did their best to dissuade him: "Your Majesty, please!", "Your Majesty reconsider!", "Your Majesty!"

The King exited the gate and the palace denizens followed close behind. The common people outside were astonished to see what appeared to be their king in a flurry of movement and excitement.

The first place he went to was the first place he always went to — the stand of the Granny with the roasted meat sticks just outside the gate.

But this time — without his disguise — she was terrified at the sight of him.

"I will have the usual," he said with a smile.

But the woman seemed frozen in place. Dong Woo nodded to her to comply. And she did so, going through the motions as if an automaton, until Sejong had his prize in hand.

The King walked deeper into the city, munching on the stick of charred meat, as his Royal vestments billowed in the breeze.

All around him, people were startled: either they bowed or were too afraid to move.

The Palace staff continued to follow, and security officers had joined them, making sure the King was protected on all sides.

As they moved, an officer spotted a paper flyer of some kind glued to a wall. And covered with the letters of the King's alphabet. The man rushed to it and ripped the offensive item down off the wall. But Sejong was curious — and thrilled to see the 'Correct Sounds' in use by the general population.

"What does it say?"

The officer handed it over, and Sejong read aloud.

"'Taxes are as high as a wild goose can fly'."

He smiled, charmed as could be. "Not wrong!" he agreed. "Not wrong at all! We must lower them again!"

Sejong continued along the street, checking the walls for more and more of these spontaneous expressions of discontent, completely enjoying himself among the people he loved.

For one last time.

෬ඁ෬ඁ෬ඁ෬ඁ෬

The King had to be helped into bed. He looked stricken. As if this last adventure into the city had pushed his health over the edge. He closed his eyes.

When they opened it was hours later. His vitality had faded precipitously during the night. His eyes now opened and closed in a rhythm measured not by moments but by excruciatingly long minutes; now clouded with blindness, then clear with the return of vision.

His childhood companion Dong Woo knelt close to the bed mat, near tears; the Royal Physician stood by — but could do nothing to slow the King's decline.

"Is the Queen here?" asked Sejong after his dead wife.

"Your Majesty," answered the eunuch, hating to speak the truth to the dying man. "She is not."

In the corridor just outside the door, Lady Hwang and the other consorts hovered near, listening, distraught at this exchange. The voices continued from the other side of the door.

"Fetch her please," they heard the King say.

"Your Majesty⋯." came the halting voice of Dong Woo.

"If her schedule⋯allows⋯." continued Sejong.

This was too painful for them all to hear. Tears started to flow. But Lady Hwang suddenly turned and rushed off — it was as if she could not bear to hear his dying loneliness any longer.

But moments later she burst into the Royal Wardrobe Department. In the middle of everything hung one of the

Queen's Royal Dresses — as if waiting for the return of the dead monarch. Lady Hwang indicated the garment and commanded the mystified sewing staff.

"Bring it down."

The staffers glanced at each other — though Lady Hwang far outranked them, surely they could not do what she had commanded. But they had never seen Lady Hwang use her authority before. Nobody had. It was terrifying.

"Now."

Moments later, Lady Hwang, now wearing the dead Queen's dress and hairpiece, was moving quickly along the halls, back towards the chamber of the King.

Various eunuchs and maids followed after, appalled and frightened, but with no authority to stop her. Their voices dogged her all the way: "Please Lady!", "We beg you!", "Reconsider!", "Please stop!"

As she reached the entry to the chamber, the other consorts still listening outside the King's door took one look and could not believe their eyes. "Lady Hwang!", "Take that off!", "How dare you."

But she paused just outside the door, putting her ear up to the wall to listen.

"Have you sent for her⋯.?" Came the King's voice from

within. Weaker even than before.

"Your Majesty," struggled Dong Woo with the truth.

"The Queen⋯. The Queen⋯."

Lady Hwang turned to her fellow wives — all of whom outranked her.

"Say it," she ordered.

Again, the surprising imperative of command was in her voice.

"Say it."

"The Queen enters!" shouted the two of the consorts in unison, unable to keep themselves from speaking.

Inside the chamber, Sejong glanced up at the announcement, and smiled with expectation.

"Prepare for the Queen!" continued a voice from outside the door.

Which then slid open, as Lady Hwang stepped inside. Her movements were regal and lovely. Just like those of the dead Queen.

Sejong stared. His vision, informed by the reverie of his death, and the perfect masquerade of the consort, showed him what he most had wanted to see:

Queen Soheon.

He saw her standing before him. Lady Hwang had done what she intended: give the dying King a last look at the love of his life. Even if only by way of failing vision and memory.

"Ah. There you are," he smiled.

She boldly took a step towards him, risking that further proximity would burst the delicate illusion. Then she took another.

"Shall we look at the moon?" said Sejong. And Lady Hwang realized she had taken this too far. And there was no way out but further in.

Thinking quickly, she glanced around — saw a silver bowl of water among other items the Royal Physician had brought.

"Yes," she answered, in another's voice.

She sounded exactly like the Queen.

For once her attempted mimicry was flawless. As if all previous failures had been necessary for this one perfect honoring echo to happen.

"Let us do that," she continued, as she glanced at Dong Woo with meaning, and indicated the bowl. He had some inkling of what she intended to do, grabbed and handed it to her.

Lady Hwang placed it next to the King, took his hand, and traced both of their combined fingertips across the surface of the water.

In Sejong's mind he saw the Moon Garden — a small reflecting pool constructed for viewing the moon, where he and Soheon had spent many nights many years ago, until the responsibilities of Inner and Outer Court took them away from the moon, and sometimes from each other.

Now, in the reverie of his death, choreographed by the masquerade of his most recent consort, he saw his fingers intertwined with that of the Queen, as they skimmed together the surface of the water. And then brought their hands together to form a single 'cup' — raising it full of water, which trembled with the movement. And a hundred little reflections of the moon in its surface trembled along with it. Like floating pearls.

Or the Reflection of the Moon in a Thousand Rivers.

"I think, my dear wife," said Sejong quietly, as they looked into each other's eyes. "That I will sleep now."

"I will be here⋯." said Queen Soheon/Lady Hwang, her face shining with love, as their hands parted, and the water — and the tiny moons — fell away.

And the King again knew himself to be on his deathbed, staring up at Lady Hwang, dressed as the Queen.

"When you wake."

Everyone around them was in tears. But she kept her

face dry for the King's benefit. He stared at her. As the Queen's face vanished; and became Lady Hwang.

"Ah. It is you," said Sejong.

She knew he saw her true face again.

"I am glad," he smiled gently. His words cradled her heart — the words she most wanted to hear. Now her tears started to fall.

And Sejong again entered his death, and for the last time.

The tears of Lady Hwang seemed to dissolve into emerald, became the falling green leaves he had always seen, falling around him, filling and displacing the chamber and the palace; the kingdom and this world.

He closed his eyes, and a memory came up from below: A Buddhist depository of sacred scriptures, lined with row after row of woodcut printing blocks, neatly inserted like books into wooden shelves. Sejong had come here with a gift for the Abbot, a neatly tied stack of freshly cut woodblocks. The Abbot had untied the silk wrappings, revealing the top block to be the first page of the King's proclamation of the new writing system. The Abbot indicated the long rows.

"We will find a comfortable place for them," he had said.

"Thank you," the King had responded, and the Abbot had detected the hesitation and doubt in his voice — and his fears for the future.

"All beings must suffer, die, and be reborn," the Buddhist had said, as he indicated the woodblocks the King was leaving in care of the monastery. "Perhaps this is true for ideas as well."

"Or perhaps my letters are only going to sleep," said Sejong. "For a while."

He considered them one last time. "I wonder what they will dream of."

And now the green leaves fell through this memory as well — around the Abbot, the woodblocks, the King and his creation. Until there was nothing but the leaves. Until they began to blur.

Finally coming back into focus as:

The twenty-eight letters of the King's alphabet. Cascading in monochromatic green down a computer screen.

The King smiled. Had he seen this image? This vision of the future? The place where his creation would awaken, after a sleep of centuries?

If he had, it was the last thing he saw.

A eunuch held the garment worn by the King when he died. Shook it hard in the air according to the rite for the death of a monarch.

"Your Majesty please come back! Your Majesty please come back!"

He threw the robe down from the roof to those waiting below.

As it fell, the garment was caught by a sudden wind, which billowed out the sleeves and carried it upwards — as if to Heaven.

Your Majesty please come back.

Post Script

"King Sejong's creation was suppressed from general use by the Joseon aristocracy and Confucian government, but never completely eradicated. It was preserved in the centuries that followed by women, poets and Buddhist monks functioning outside of the traditional halls of power. Until the 'Correct Sounds for the Instruction of the People' was reclaimed in the 20th century, renamed 'Hangeul' and declared the official Korean alphabet. It is currently in use by more than 70 million people worldwide."

"In 1914, a copy of 'Songs of the Moon's Reflection on a Thousand Rivers' — the verses King Sejong wrote in memory of his wife the Queen, using his own alphabet — was found hidden inside a centuries-old Buddhist statue."

"Copies of the King's original block-printed pronouncement have been found in China, in Japan, and in South Korea — as recently as 2008."

한국의 역사에 친숙하지 못한 영어권 독자에게는, 이 책이 한글에 대한 이야기를 소개하고 심오한 인간의 위대한 업적 뒤에 숨겨진 특유의 마음가짐과 인간성을 알려 줄 수 있으면 좋겠습니다. 그리고 한글의 창제 과정에 대해 알게 되었을 때 제가 느낀 흥분까지도 전달 할 수 있기를 바랍니다.

한국 독자에게는, 한국 문화에서 가장 위대한 이야기 중 하나를 재해석하여 창작한 저의 과욕에 대해 넓은 아량과 용서를 구합니다. 제 동기만은 세종대왕과 한글에 대해 경외하는 마음에서 우러났음을 알아주시기 바랍니다.

Epilogue

To English-speaking readers unfamiliar with Korean history, I hope this book can be an introduction to the story of Hangeul, but that it can also convey at least something of my original excitment upon learning of that creation — and of the unique mind and personality behind such a profound human accomplishment.

To Korean readers, I can only ask forbearance and forgiveness for my presumption in attempting to retell one of the great stories of Korean culture. Please know that my motivation was always awe.